ACCOLADES for *C*

"*Cayman Cross* is simply *the* classic for adventure, murder and mystery on the high seas... with the incredible added beauty and history of the Cayman Islands thrown in for a bonus..."

Jim Mast, Author
Bloody Sunset in St. Augustine

"*Cayman Cross* is a fascinating, poignant tale of treachery and justice, perseverance and friendship, faith and family."

Cindy Vallar, Editor & Reviewer
Pirates and Privateers.com

"Though it is a work of fiction, this tale is based on the true story of piracy, mutiny and the official investigation into the mysterious circumstances surrounding the appearance of a Cuban schooner in the Cayman Islands in 1922... The combination of fast-moving action, colourful seafaring characters and a surprise twist at the end makes this book a delightful beach read."

Shurna Robbins, Reviewer & Journalist
Cayman Airways Skies Magazine

"*Cayman Cross* is a great read for anyone who loves adventure, especially sailing or adventure on the sea."

Jane Connors, Editor & Reviewer
Hidden Coastlines Magazine

"The only documented account of true piracy in the Cayman Islands was in 1922 on the Juana Mercedes, where the Captain was murdered and two boys went overboard and were left for dead... The historical aspects of *Cayman Cross,* combined with mystery, murder and revenge, make this a very compelling read by first time novelist Jack Scott. It's a real page turner with a surprise ending."

Highly Recommended Reading Section
Cedar Key Guide Magazine

"This book is a classic... not just a good read, but a *great* read!"

Goodreads.com

"This story has just about everything I look for in a good novel: swashbuckling adventure, murder on the high seas, and... PIRATES! I highly recommend you pick up a copy of this book."

Kent Holloway, Author
"ENIGMA Directive" Series

"I loved the book! I read it cover-to-cover in one sitting. It makes me want to go find the cathedral and see if the Spaniard is still there."

Ken Callahan, Author
Suwannee's Crucible

CAYMAN CROSS

A Novel By

Allen Jack Scott

Cover Art: Allen Jack Scott

 For information, address Vigilant Publishing, 99 Orange Street, St. Augustine, Florida 32084.

ISBN: 978-0-615-50697-5
ISBN-13: 9780615506975

This book, including additional information regarding the author and subject matter, purchase information and additional historical content, may be found at:

www.caymancross.com

Cayman Cross is also available at:

www.amazon.com; and

www.kindle.com

To my love—my life and my inspiration—my wife JJ; and to my Cayman forebears, who gave me my birthright and the pride and the salt to remember my roots.

Prologue

Mama was on her deathbed when she first told me about my father's old World War II steamer trunk. In those last days of her life she insisted that my father wanted her to make sure that I got the trunk before she died.

Daddy had passed away several years earlier and of course left all his earthly possessions to the love of his life, my mother. But he had apparently told Mama that he wanted me—their oldest son—to have his personal memorabilia when she died. Mama, being always loving and loyal to a fault, decided to make me drag Daddy's trunk out of her closet while she was watching, and from her bed she dutifully instructed me to take it to my car. She knew she was dying, and she wanted the comfort of knowing that even in the end she had fulfilled my father's wishes.

I protested, of course, assuring Mama that she would be well soon and there was no need for any of us to start taking anything from the house. But she insisted. She explained to me that the trunk contained a lot of Daddy's family history and that "there are some old skeletons hidden in there."

The scuffed and chipped trunk in and of itself was not spectacular by any measure. I had seen it from time to time while I was growing up, but it was always locked and I never paid it much attention as a boy. After I left home to seek my fortunes as a young man, I never gave it another thought. That is, until Mama demanded that I take it home with me that afternoon.

"Your Daddy loved you, Jack," Mama said, "and he specially wanted you to have his trunk. Now go on and get it and no more talk about it." So I did as I was told. That was the last time Mama scolded me. A week later I gave the eulogy at her funeral.

It was months after Mama's death before I could bring myself to open the trunk. It reminded me too much of the parents I had lost, and it simply took me a while to deal with that loss.

Finally, one rainy and overcast Sunday afternoon, I pulled the trunk out of my own closet and just looked at it for a while, thinking gloomy thoughts about my own mortality and the parents that I had so much loved and lost. But somehow, Daddy's trunk particularly piqued my curiosity that dreary afternoon. I even imagined that I heard Daddy's quiet but forceful voice whispering to me, "Go on son, open the trunk. I saved these memories for you to share—open the trunk…"

The trunk itself was nothing more than an old military-style footlocker, dull olive drab in colour, faded and scuffed with age and miles. It had apparently rested undisturbed for almost half a century in Mama's closet. Stenciled on the top and front in faded white letters it read:

Scott, Jos.
Capt. USMS
Army Transportation Corps

This time when I tried to open the trunk I found it unlocked, no doubt just another kind forethought from Mama.

The top hinged up easily and, at first glance, the contents seemed pretty unremarkable as well. There were stacks and stacks of World War II era love letters between my parents and some from after the war while Daddy was at sea in some foreign place or another. After reading just a few letters, I felt uncomfortable. I felt like an eavesdropper or voyeur, spying on my parents in their youth. So I gave it up for a while. I closed the trunk and stored it back in my bedroom closet where it laid in repose for another year or so.

But it is said that time heals, and so it was for me. The next time I opened Daddy's trunk I was intent on putting together a family history that I could pass along to my own children. Then it came to me: There it was before me—a whole trunk full of family history to start with.

Of course I knew from my youth that Daddy was from the Cayman Islands, a Caymanian citizen who won his United States citizenship and ultimately his veteran status by his service to America in World War II. And I also knew (believed) from the tales told to me by that great old sailor, my Granddaddy Tenny Scott, that the

Caymanian Scott family, like most of the few other original settlers in the Cayman Islands, were retiring pirates, British Navy deserters, wreckers, or just plain shipwrecked refugees without a way home.

In my case, my father was always my only real hero. That may have been partly because he was gone most of the time—at sea—when I was a little boy. And he always brought my sister and me presents from strange foreign places when he came home. But he was also tall and handsome with piercing blue eyes, mostly dressed in starched khaki uniform with gold braid on his black epaulets and silver insignia on his gold braided, white captain's hat with shining black bill.

So these many years later, I immediately dug around for and found his medals, maritime and military insignia (including epaulets and captains hat) which I put on display in my glass trophy cabinet. Daddy was a World War II veteran, U.S. Army Transportation Corps (Merchant Marine) Captain, and I treasure his military "dog tags" as I do my own.

But those are other stories.

One day, several years ago, finally rummaging to the bottom of Daddy's trunk I found—at the very bottom—a cigar box. I mean a real Cuban cigar box, colourful and gaudy, printed in Spanish, still slightly scented with the sweet smell of the Cuban Macanudas that had once rested there. It brought a smile to my face to remember that Daddy, even to the end of his life, loved to smoke a good Cuban Macanuda once in a while. But when I opened the box, it was not filled with cigars, but an array of old papers and newspaper articles and photographs, most fading or brown with age.

The very first document at the top of the box was a brown and faded front-page newspaper article from the Kingston, Jamaica ***Daily Gleaner***, December 2, 1922, edition. That article became the cornerstone of the personal quest that has become this book. The article reads as follows:

A MURDER IS ALLEGED ON BOARD SCHOONER

Vessel Detained at Grand Cayman and Persons Placed Under Arrest.

THE STORY RELATED

Well-off Gentleman from Isle of Palms who Wanted to Purchase Vessel.

SEVERAL ARE SLAIN?

The story as told to a representative of the Gleaner yesterday runs thus: A well-off gentleman who resides in the Isle of

Palms recently decided to proceed to Cienfuegos, Cuba, to purchase a schooner. He was accompanied on board by certain people, and it is known that he had with him fully twenty-five thousand dollars. They set sail on a schooner and whilst the vessel was at sea a plot was hatched to murder the gentleman. It is said that two or three men of Spanish descent who were on board endeavoured to get men of the crew to join them in this plot, but failing to get accomplices, they not only murdered the Captain (so it is alleged), but also the money man. There seemed to have been a pitched battle on the high seas and in all four or five persons lost their lives. With the death of the Captain and other members of the crew the boat drifted in the direction of Grand Cayman, eventually entering the harbour of the Dependency. When the Cayman authorities boarded the vessel they were given particulars of what transpired, although the story was incomplete in many respects. The matter was reported to the Commissioner and certain parties on board the schooner were placed under arrest.

It is understood that investi-gations are now being carried out, and the Cuban authorities have been communicated with.

Part One

September 21, 1922

Chapter 1

Havana, Cuba
September 21, 1922

Jose Martinez was only nine years old when he was paroled from the orphanage in Havana to become an apprentice cabin boy aboard the Cuban cargo schooner *Juana Mercedes*. He was a quiet boy whose blue eyes and fair skin suggested Castilian lineage, but who knew nothing of his true parents or family. From his earliest memories it was Sister Elena who had given him special love and attention, and who had seen to his education—so much as it was at nine years old when he left the orphanage. In any event, it was agreed between Sister Elena and Father Tomas that an opportunity to apprentice at sea would provide Jose the chance of a practical education and an honourable profession.

So it was that on September 21, 1922, young Jose Martinez was escorted by Sister Elena to the train station in Havana to embark upon his future.

Sister Elena had taken the best of his clothing and personal possessions and packed them in a small canvas bag that morning, together with a cardboard packet of bread, dried meat and fruit to last him until he reached his destination. She had also found—he knew not where—a new pair of black leather shoes with heavy soles and leather laces for his long journey. The shoes were too big, as were his tan canvas trousers, but his new linen shirt was dyed to the color of India ink, fresh washed and dried in the sunshine. The smell of his new shirt and shoes gave Jose a feeling of excitement and adventure that morning that he had rarely experienced in the strict and protected environs of the orphanage.

So at eleven that morning, Jose shook Fr. Tomas' hand and walked together with Sister Elena out of the ancient iron gates of the orphanage and into his new life.

Even though the train to *Batabano* would not leave until noon, Sister Elena demanded punctuality, and this day would be no exception. The morning was bright and already steaming with humidity when they departed, walking at a leisurely pace side by side down the dusty avenue toward the *Terminal Central* of the English-owned United Railways of Havana, which was located by the steamboat terminals on the bay south of central Havana. Although taxis and trams were busily traversing local residents and *touristas Americanos* through the avenidas of the city, payment of a small fare was beyond the station of Sister Elena and her small ward.

As they walked south toward the railway terminal, Jose said simply, "Sister, I am frightened." Without speaking, Sister Elena reached out and took his hand in her own and they continued to walk quietly toward the station. They passed many shops and street vendors along the cobbled streets until Sister Elena stopped at the window of a small storefront emporium.

She gazed for a long moment through the window at the Spanish and French tradewares displayed in the storefront—beautiful handmade Spanish laces, shawls, silk and linen lingerie, and fine gold and silver jewelry. Finally, she went to one knee beside Jose and looked into his face. He could see tears welling in the eyes of her pale, kind face, even behind her wire rimmed glasses. He had never seen her except in the habit of a nun, and the love that she expressed from time to time could only be read through the expressions on her face and the words that she said.

"Jose, my child," she said, "I am frightened also. I have spent my life in the service of our Lord and He has kept me safe as a child, the same as you. But you must now go into the world on your own and become a man. I know you as a mother would know you, and I love you as a mother would love you, and I know in my heart that you will be a good man. You must only believe these things and have the strength to love your Lord and to love and protect those who love you in order to endure in this world. Do not be afraid. I have a special gift for you from a friend, and if you have faith, it will protect you always." She put her hands behind the habit at her neck and in a moment, she had a heavy silver chain and silver crucifix in her hands. She put the chain around his neck and arranged it, along with its suspended crucifix, beneath his indigo shirt. Then she sobbed quietly, holding him close to her breast.

The *Terminal Central* of the United Railway of Cuba faced upon a paved plazuela in the southeast quarter of the city near the Ward Line and P & O Steamship Co.'s docks, within an easy walk from the orphanage through the hotel district and the residential quarter. Its twin towers and red tiled roof stood out above the neighborhood long before they passed through the entrance. It had taken only half an hour, even at their leisurely pace, for Sister Elena and Jose Martinez to make the walk. There, at 11:30 Sister Elena and Jose stood at the ticket window and asked the *agente de boletine* for a one-way child's pass for *Batabano.* The ticket agent responded briefly and Sister Elena paid the half-price fare, second class, for Jose's transportation to *Batabano* on the southwestern coast. Jose could hear her hushed whispers to the Ticketmaster, but did not understand the words that were said. Then they walked across the grand Italian marble lobby of the *estacion* and sat quietly among the passenger benches awaiting his call to board.

"Sister," he said, with his hands clenched before him, "I know nothing of the sea."

After a pause, she responded, "The sea is not to fear, Jose. She is created by God to provide for us and to give us her bounty. You will learn to love and respect her, and she will teach you her lessons. She will provide for you and if it be God's will, she may take you for her own. But above all, you must believe that God has a special plan for you, and if it be to go down in the sea, it will be only a small part of God's plan. Do not fear, Jose, be brave, because fear will make you weak and will not gain you a minute beyond the life that God has planned for you."

When the boarding call came, Sister Elena walked Jose to the platform and handed him his small canvas bag. This time, when he stepped up the stairs into the passenger car, she did not embrace him, but clasped her hands together in front of her face as if in a prayer. He saw her head bowed, but did not look back. He found a cane seat in the far side of the coach and looked out the window in the opposite direction, for he knew that if he saw her again he would cry.

As the train moved from the *Terminal Central*, Jose began to feel excitement and elation. For the first time in his life, he was on his own. Although his body was yet small, Sister Elena's words had given him strength, and he knew that he could, and that he would make her proud. The train slowly gathered speed and the rhythmic clack of the wheels on the tracks gave him comfort. He began to think about all the things that Fr. Tomas had told him: That he would be met in *Batabano* by a great sea captain who would take him aboard a fair sailing ship and teach him the skills of seamanship and all the secret lessons of the great oceans of the world; that he would grow into manhood with pride in himself and the future that he would make for himself upon the sea; that his family and his life would be that which he makes for himself with the help of God and those that he loves…

These were the thoughts that occupied Jose Martinez as the train followed the contour of the bay and traversed the sprawling Havana suburb of *Jesus del Monte* and passed into the open Cuban countryside running southward over the *Pinar del Rio* Province toward *Rincon* Junction. There, the track turned southeast and he watched toiling field workers in deep, rich red soil, tending their crops. He watched, for the first time, as broad canefields, meadowlands and orchards of mangoes and siebas passed in the afternoon sun. He began to see and understand that the known world ranged far beyond the orphanage in Havana where he was raised.

Jose was aroused from his daze of thoughts and daydreams with the jerking and squeaking of the cars as the train began to slow for the *Estacion San Felipe*. There was a buzz of activity as the train slowed to a noisy stop in the small station. Conversation was loud and boisterous and mostly unintelligible as the *touristas Americanos* doused cigars and scrambled to exit. Street vendors had already run their carts alongside the cars, hawking food and drink for those exiting and boarding the train. Most of the *Americanos* were scrambling across the dusty street skirting the tracks toward the several cantinas lining the opposite side. The stop was scheduled to be just long enough for a shot of hard liquor and a quick local lunch for the *touristas*.

Jose sat quietly with his canvas bag clenched in his hands on his lap. With the train standing still on the tracks, the heat became stifling and he wondered if he should dare moving into the station until departure. He was startled from his reverie by the voice of a stranger who had boarded the train and found the seat next to him.

"*Hola, Chico!* You must be Jose Martinez, the new sailor I have come to find. My name is Angel Perez, and I am your shipmate!" Jose could not find words to speak to the short, jovial, brown skinned man addressing him. "*El Capitan* told me to meet you here Jose, since I live in *San Felipe*. Do not be afraid, I will travel with you to *Batabano*." Angel Perez held out his hand and Jose instinctively responded with a tentative handshake. "*Bueno, muchacho!*" Angel said as he stowed his seabag and sat down beside Jose. "We will be sailing together aboard the *Juana Mercedes*, Jose, and I will be your friend. I will teach you the ways of the sea! *El Capitan* is a great man, and he says we will teach you the ways of the sea!" Then, without a word from Jose, Angel Perez began to tell Jose his life story, and all about his family and forebears since the Spanish fled from Jamaica to Cuba in 1655 in the wake of the British armies of Cromwell. As Angel's monologue started, Jose heard the engineer's several whistle blasts and saw the dusty *Americanos* scurry from the cantinas and reboard as the train slowly pulled from the station.

The drone of Angel's friendly voice and his happy stories quickly put Jose at ease. He was relieved that he was no longer alone, and that he had a new *amigo* to accompany him. Angel's brown eyes sparkled in his chubby face as he told his stories. His voice was animated, rising and falling with the importance of each phrase, his small chubby hands emphasizing every point with a gesture. Within minutes, Jose Martinez was enthralled with the stories of Angel Perez, and was again comforted by the rhythmic clack of the wheels on the rails.

From *San Felipe*, the rail line ran due South to *Batabano*. An explosion of beautiful flowering trees and a myriad of palms passed outside the windows of the train until it moved into the agricultural flatlands crisscrossed with cane and tobacco fields. Jose listened to the comical stories of Angel Perez, sometimes even laughing out loud, as he watched the passing of the innumerable cabins of field workers, their yards alive with chickens and guinea hens, goats, pigs, dogs and cattle, all amongst a riot of tropical flowers and trees growing wild in the fields. Flying insects and birds rose in hordes above the stone fenced fields where shirtless workers, skin slick with sweat, toiled in the thick cane and tobacco.

"You see, Jose, my family has worked this land for the centuries," said Angel Perez. "But I had a calling to the sea. And now my wife and children always happily await my return, for I bring money and the things of the world that we cannot have living in the old farm cabins of slaves, where freedom is a word but not a reality." Jose began finally to feel a real liking for this chubby, talkative man whose constant smiles crinkled his brown eyes into narrow bowed slits with his toothy smile pushing everything else off his face.

Then Jose began to respond—to talk—and to tell Angel of his life and Sister Elena and Father Tomas and his friends at the orphanage. Angel urged him on, smiling and asking questions, until the words and thoughts so long stored in Jose's heart spilled in a steady flow as the train sped on its way across the flatlands and past the cultivated fields, plodding ox and donkey carts, cane-elevators, sugar mills, jungle and chaparral toward the southwest coast and *Batabano.*

The countryside shimmered under the afternoon sun and the twin line of rails before them ran straight toward a level southern horizon, there fading in the distorted mirror of rising heat waves.

Chapter 2

Batabano, Cuba
September 22, 1922

The *Juana Mercedes* was a Cuban motor-schooner built in 1917 in *Cienfuegos* on the southern coast of Cuba. Like her sisters built in Cayman, she was fashioned after the lead of Canadian schooners of the time, designed for the cod fisheries of the Newfoundland Banks and adapted for the salt fish trade of the West Indies. Like her Canadian forebears, she had a cut away bow to her short, straight keel for increased maneuverability. Her minimum drag underwater was accented by her sudden rise in body to her wineglass transom, and her wide beam allowed her to carry huge sails on her masts in a fair wind for speed. Under sail, her grace and beauty were unsurpassed on the south coast of Cuba.

She was owned by Barbiete & Cia Shippers of *Batabano*, and sailed under the command of Capt. Juan Bautista y Silviera who, at age 41, was a Master of all Oceans under Sail. Although he had not been born of a seafaring family, he had built his fortunes on the sea as a young man, living out a life under sail broken only by short visits with his wife and children between the voyages of the *Juana Mercedes*. On September 22, 1922, Capt. Bautista-S. was enjoying a short time with his family at his home in *Batabano* before the next scheduled departure of the *Juana Mercedes*.

On that day, the sun broke the horizon with Jose Martinez sleeping peacefully on one of the several bunks in the fo'c'sle of the *Juana Mercedes,* the most forward compartment of the vessel. He woke to the musty, wet-wood, sour odour of the schooner, opened his eyes briefly and rolled under his blanket toward the hull, seeking to escape the bright light falling diagonally through the open hatch above. After a while, the scent of tobacco smoke, onions, fresh fish and other food cooking brought him to consciousness. The unfamiliar cabin startled him and he swung out of the bunk and stood up briefly in his rumpled clothes. Then he sat back down on the bunk, his face in his open hands, momentarily trying to remember where he was.

Eventually, the clank of pots and pans and the bright singing voice of Angel Perez brought him to reality, and he stood, tucked in his shirt and walked barefoot up the companionway toward Angel's song. There in the galley—cooking, talking and singing to himself—was Angel Perez. Angel turned to see Jose and a bright smile captured his face.

"*Buenos dias muchacho*!" Angel said, "Are you hungry?"

"*Si, por favor.*" Jose responded, realizing that he had not eaten anything the night before. He sat down at the small table adjacent to the gimbaled oil stove where Angel was working.

"Alberto has already eaten," Angel said, "and he is finding our dinner as we speak."

After a moment, Angel spooned a large portion of battered brown fried fish and corn hominy grits on a pewter plate and placed it before Jose with a fork on the side. Before Angel could sit down across the small galley table, Jose was eating ravenously.

"Jose, my son," said Angel, "we must make meat on your bones! How can you haul anchors and haul sails as skinny as you are?"

"I am ready to learn," Jose responded briefly, and went back to his meal.

"We must teach you as we did Alberto," Angel said absently, "he knew nothing and is now almost a man, as you will soon be also."

After Jose hungrily cleaned his plate, Angel said, "Come, you must now meet Alberto, who will be your new friend and teacher."

Jose followed Angel up the companionway stairs and on to the deck of *Juana Mercedes*. She was lying still alongside the wharf in *Batabano* as the sun cast it's bright morning rays on the bay. Over the rail, the water of the bay was crystal clear to the bottom below the *Juana Mercedes*. On the deck by the taffrail of the stern were a half dozen fresh wet conchs scattered at random. "There he is!" shouted Angel, gesturing toward a black spot in the open bay beyond. As Jose watched, Alberto's head disappeared below the surface of the bay for what seemed long minutes at a time, surfacing only occasionally with a white smile in a dark face.

Eventually, Alberto swam easily back to the *Juana Mercedes* and tossed another fresh conch on the deck. Then he swam to a line hanging overboard amidships and scaled the side of the schooner to the deck in a moment, as if he had simply walked up the side of the ship. He stood momentarily at the rail, his thirteen year old dark body tall and strong, shining with dripping salt water in the morning sun.

Alberto Monson had grown up on the streets of *Batabano* under the tutelage of an older brother now long since gone to make his living upon the sea. One of eleven children of a widowed mother, Alberto necessarily grew quickly and escaped the hovel of his birth with one of his older brothers at an early time in his life that he could not even now remember. They survived the streets carrying the bags and luggage of tourists for pocket change to and from the railway station and the ships in the harbor. They had fished, and they had learned to swim and dive for the bounties of the Bay, and from time to time they panhandled for their meals. Alberto was proud to be a *batabanero*. He had learned to fight in the tough streets, and he carried a bone handled switch blade knife in his pocket everywhere he went.

Alberto's life changed again at the age of nine years when he first met Captain *Juan Bautista y Silviera*, Master of the schooner *Juana Mercedes*. Alberto had by then grown tall and strong enough to work cargo on the fishing and freight wharfs of *Batabano*, and his brother had found him a place on the docks offloading fresh fish, lobsters, crabs, shrimp, and other shellfish for shipment to the Havana markets. On the day that he met Capt. Bautista-S., Alberto was offloading and sorting a load of sponges at dockside, making them ready for shipment to the United States, then a major consumer for *Batabano* sponges.

As he worked on the wharf that day, Alberto watched the approach of a beautiful schooner across the Bay. Plying the Bay amongst the small sails of the fishing fleet, her tall masts and huge white sails, her *velas* were full of wind and the water of the blue Bay broke in a frothing white stream at her bow.

He knew at that very moment in his young heart that she, this beautiful creature of the oceans, was to be his home. He walked absently from his work at the sponge dock and across the waterfront to the freight dock. As she approached, the *Juana Mercedes* doused her main sails and came to dock under a single trysail, as gently as if she were lying down after a long day. Alberto caught a stern line thrown by one of the crew and dropped it over a bollard on the wharf, and then stepped aboard as she touched alongside to rest.

Captain Juan Bautista-Silviera had left the helm and was giving orders for securing the vessel at dock. Then in his late thirties, he was weathered but handsome in a rough cut way, his hair silver flecked in black and his skin as brown and thick as leather. But when his eyes set on Alberto, they were kind eyes, not the eyes of a stranger. In less than a moment, Alberto stood before him and said, "*Capitan*, I am ready for the sea."

So it was that on September 22, 1922, Alberto Monson was a seasoned sailor at thirteen years of age. He crossed the deck of the *Juana Mercedes* and held out his hand to Jose Martinez and said, "I will be your friend, little one, for *El Capitan* has brought you from the church to be my little brother." Jose shook his hand and dropped his eyes, feeling small in the presence of the man-boy before him. Angel Perez broke the brief silence with a laugh and said, "We will see who is the little brother when Jose has your years!"

Chapter 3

Batabano, Cuba

The next days were the beginning of a new life for Jose Martinez. *El Capitan* and the rest of the crew of the *Juana Mercedes* were ashore on leave, and Jose was free to work and wander with Alberto Monson as they chose. Alberto told Jose all the stories of the sea that he knew, and they explored every corner and crevasse of the schooner, and they climbed her masts to look down with a heady joy at the ship and small town below them.

They swam in the Bay, and Alberto taught Jose his first fledgling strokes, Alberto swimming beside Jose and holding him above the water. Alberto opened his knife and cut Jose's canvas trousers into ragged shorts, and they shed shirts to explore *Batabano* in the bright October sun. Days later, Alberto lowered one of the ship's dories into the Bay and rowed out into the open crystal waters.

While Jose tended the dory, Alberto dove for lobsters with a small net on a handle, occasionally surfacing with a spiny giant to throw in the boat. Jose huddled in the stern of the small dory, boldly shouting encouragement to Alberto while carefully avoiding contact with the alien creatures rattling about in the bottom of the small boat. The day was sunny and calm, and the flashing sails of the fishing fleet were all around them. Later, Angel Perez prepared a lobster feast for the brave young princes that they believed themselves to be.

Angel set the plank table on the stern of the *Juana Mercedes* with pewter implements under the light of two oil lamps and the full moon. There the three of them gorged themselves with lobster, Angel and Alberto singing familiar tunes until they could remember no more. Finally, full and content, Alberto and Jose retired to the fo'c'sle for the night. Close quarters in the bow of the ship, the fo'c'sle had six bunks, three on each side, stacked one upon the other. The boys had chosen middle bunks on each side so they could lie facing each other and talk until they faded into sleep.

This night, they stripped to their shorts and Alberto said:

"The crew will return tomorrow."

"Does this mean we will sail tomorrow?" Jose responded.

"No, but we will have to work. *El Capitan* will arrive on Friday and the ship must be clean and ready to sail."

"What will he do with me? I know nothing of the sea."

"Do not fear, little brother, for *El Capitan* is a kind man and he will teach you as he did me." Alberto rolled into his bunk and was quiet for a long moment. The light of the moon cast a glow through the hatch in the small cabin, and Jose could see his face clearly. Alberto's green eyes glowed like embers in his dark face, and he said simply, "You will not like the Spaniard."

"Who is the Spaniard?" Jose inquired.

"He is the Mate, and he is an evil man. I have known evil men since I can remember, and I know the Spaniard is an evil man."

Jose was puzzled and a little frightened. "What will he do to me?" Jose said.

"Do not worry little brother, he will not harm you so long as *El Capitan* is with us. The Spaniard is a coward. He would not cut your throat unless it was a dark night in a strange place when no one could see. So long as we are on this ship with him, we will be safe."

Jose thought long about Alberto's words, and finally fell into a restless sleep.

The next morning broke to the sound of heavy chain rattling on dcck above. Jose sal up and cleared his eyes, then stood and pulled on his shirt. Alberto was gone already, as always out of his bunk with the break of day. Jose found Angel Perez tinkering in the galley, where he ate quickly and then made his way on deck. Alberto was chipping and painting rusty anchor chain laid out on a tarp on the foredeck. Jose wordlessly picked up a brush and began to work alongside him.

By mid-morning they were dripping with sweat and splattered with thick black paint when Alberto paused to glance up the wharf to the cobbled street beyond. Jose followed his gaze toward a swarthy white man making his way through crowds of fishermen, nets, cargo crates and longshoremen toward the *Juana Mercedes*. At a distance, he looked somewhat a handsome dandy in a crème linen coat and bright white pith helmet resembling those worn by colonial soldiers and policemen. As he came closer, though, the hard lines of his unshaven face, high cheekbones and deep set coal black eyes caused Jose to shift his glance back to the work before him.

"It is the Spaniard. Pay him no attention, Jose," Alberto said under his breath and continued his work.

"*Hola, Negrito*!" the Spaniard said to Alberto as he walked up alongside the moored schooner, "The sun has made you more black than I remembered. Who is this dirty white boy you have found?" Then he tossed his canvas seabag on the deck by Jose, causing him to jump to his feet. "Take my bag to the Captain's cabin, *chico*, if you have yet figured out where that is."

Jose heard Alberto mutter "*Cabron*—he-goat!" a common epithet making reference to the Spaniard's ancestry and lack of morality. Jose had heard this word many times before in the orphanage, but never spoken by a boy to a man. The Spaniard laughed aloud and said to Alberto, "That is what I like about you *Negrito*, you try to be a man even when you know I can cut out your heart and have it with rice and beans for my dinner!" Then he laughed again, apparently pleased with the thought he called to mind. Jose scrambled toward the Captain's cabin with the Spaniard's bag as he heard the Spaniard tell Alberto, "I will be found in the *Dos Hermanos Hotel* on the bayfront. You will come and fetch me when *el jefe* arrives tonight. You understand?"

"*Si, patron epanol!*" Alberto responded sarcastically, "How could I ignore the words of an important *hombre* such as yourself? I am only a *negrito pobre*, always at your command!" Jose winced at the venom and insolence in Alberto's voice, and he scurried below deck with the Spaniard's bag to avoid any more of the confrontation.

Jose did not go back on deck for half an hour. He went to the galley and listened to the happy rattle of Angel's voice, telling the same stories, but from time to time, changing the ending to make whatever moral point he had in mind at the moment. Finally, Angel paused long enough to look at Jose and said, "*Por Dios*, you have more paint on yourself than we have on the anchor chain! Go and get Alberto so that I can clean you both."

Jose scrambled up the companionway to deck and found Alberto still working in the same spot, deliberately chipping rust from each link of the heavy chain before applying the thick, tarlike paint. "Come Alberto! Angel says we may stop work and he will clean the black paint from us." Alberto continued his work without speaking. Finally, Jose sat back down and made a trivial effort to continue painting the anchor chain. "Alberto, what is wrong?" Jose said after a long moment.

"When I am a man I will kill the Spaniard." Alberto responded quietly. "His heart is cruel and darker than my skin."

The boys continued to work without another word until mid-afternoon, when they finished the entire length of the anchor chain. Then they went to Angel, who led them to the small engine room in the stern hold of the *Juana Mercedes*, adjoining the Captain's cabin. The only means of entering it was through one small door, where Angel took them, wetted rags with fuel oil and rubbed the paint from them one at a time. "Now go and swim and have fun *muchachos*, you have worked well and I will be sure to tell *El Capitan* when he arrives!"

After soaping and scrubbing on deck from buckets of brine pulled from the Bay, the boys took a short swim to rinse themselves and dressed again in their shorts, donned cotton shirts and sandals and disembarked *Juana Mercedes*. Angel Perez had stuffed them with Cuban bread, cheeses and fruit, and they felt like young soldiers on leave, marching up the cluttered wharf and bustle of workers in the waning afternoon sun. The local *pescadores* were unloading their catch of fish for the day, and the sponge docks were busy with cleaning and packing. Pelicans and seagulls were squawking, chatting and making quick work of any scraps, pieces and throwaways along the waterfront. The boys strolled up the main street of *Batabano, Calle Independencia*, and passed the railway station. Further along the bay, they walked past the *Dos Hermanos Hotel*, reminding Jose momentarily of the swarthy Spaniard. Eventually they left the inhabited part of the bayfront and continued to walk along the rocky shore of a shallow lagoon, finally stopping to rest on the trunk of a fallen palm tree.

The sun was low in the western sky and its waning rays had spread a bright orange-red cast over the western horizon. "My brother and I spent much time here when I was a boy," said Alberto, "I like it here. We fished and we dove and we cooked on the beach, and we broke coconuts and ate wild fruit, and on many, many nights we slept here on sandy spots in huts we made from the fronds of the palms."

To Jose, who had no memories except his disciplined and cloistered life in the orphanage, the thought of a life growing up free in this tropical cove seemed nothing less than Heaven. In only a few weeks, he had grown to admire and respect Alberto, as would any little brother looking up to his mentor and protector.

"Sometimes," Alberto continued, "we caught *caimans* in the lagoons and swamps along this stretch and skinned them, and ate them and sold their skins in *Batabano* to a leather cutter to make shoes and boots and purses. The *touristas* especially like the skins of the *caimans* and will pay much money for the things made from their hides."

"What is a *caiman*, Alberto? How do you catch one?" said Jose.

"He is a huge crocodile, Jose, like a giant water lizard with jaws full of teeth and the strength of a lion!" Alberto responded, more for effect on his young friend than for meticulous description. "They lay in the sun on the banks of these lagoons and marshes in the hundreds, maybe thousands, and when we would catch one my brother lassoed him with a rope and held him while I would kill him with a machete or a spike pole. Sometimes the *gringos* would hunt them with guns, and we would make money showing them where to find the biggest. They would pay us much money for finding the big ones to shoot, and after, I would skin them with my knife. They would keep the skin and the head, but we kept the meat and sold it, or kept it and ate it until it went bad. We spent many good times here together, but now he is gone to the sea and so am I. But now I am never hungry, and I am learning the ways of the sea and *El Capitan* has promised that I will be his apprentice until I become his Mate, and that one day I will have a great sailing ship of my own…"

Jose was mesmerized, at once both frightened and enthralled with Alberto's stories of giant crocodiles and the sea, Alberto's bravado capturing the imagination of his younger ward completely. "Alberto, where will we sail when *El Capitan* returns?"

"We will sail all of the South Coast of Cuba and the Caribbean Sea, and perhaps we will even sail to Honduras and Nicaragua, or Mexico. And we may pass the islands of the *Caimanes* along the way, or maybe even stop there."

"Why will we stop in the islands of the crocodiles, Alberto? Must we hunt them there?" Jose said with some hesitation in his voice.

"No little brother, we stopped there last year and we saw no crocodiles, only *tortugas*—giant turtles—many of them in the waters. But nothing else. We go there sometimes for water and turtle, and we unload supplies for the *ingles* that live there, but don't worry. It is at the end of the world, and it has no crocodiles, only turtles."

The sun was below the horizon when Jose and Alberto started to make their way back to the *Juana Mercedes*. The glow of the receding sun still left enough light to travel by foot even before the moon rose. Eventually, the boys made their way back to the outskirts and into the perimeter of *Batabano*, walking quietly along narrow streets in the direction of the bayfront wharfs.

When they approached the *Dos Hermanos Hotel* Jose said, "Alberto, must we tell the Spaniard when *El Capitan* arrives?"

"The Spaniard is a dog, Jose. I tell him nothing unless *El Capitan* tells me to find him."

"But what will he do Alberto, if you defy him?"

"Little brother, the Spaniard is a coward as I have told you. He will only hurt me if he catches me alone, and he has a gun, and he has friends to help him. Otherwise, I will cut him to pieces if he comes close enough to touch my knife."

The conviction in Alberto's voice assured Jose that this was not youthful bravado, but a stated intention that his older mentor could fulfill.

When they stood in the street before the *Dos Hermanos Hotel*, Alberto said, "Come little brother, and we will see what the dog is doing." Then he moved Jose into the side shadows of the large white frame building and up some outside stairs to a wide, columned, covered porch that surrounded the first floor. Only occasional gas lamps cast circles of weak light on the porch, and the boys kept to the shadows as they moved around the side of the hotel to the grand, wide covered porch fronting on the bay. Only the interior light streaming through the tall plantation windows lining the bayside cast light on the white cane chairs and tables scattered around the porch.

Alberto pulled Jose down to his knees at the corner of the porch and motioned silence. There, through the window, they could see the grand dining room of the hotel, finished in various precious Cuban woods, lit by occasional gas lamps on the walls and candles on the tables, with linen, silver and china place settings arranged impeccably on the polished tabletops. Only a half dozen of the tables were occupied, and seated at a dark back corner table the Spaniard was engaged in conversation with a stranger.

The Spaniard, Pablo Konig, as he now called himself, sat at the candlelit table in the *Dos Hermanos* dining room looking Antonio Rivas intensely in the eyes as they spoke. Pablo Konig, born *Galician* in the northern provinces of Spain, was twenty-five years old but was weathered to thirty-five. His hair was black and greased back, and his swarthy face was covered with a three day stubble of black whiskers. His eyes were black as well and set deep in the sockets above high cheekbones. Although he was medium height, his shoulders were broad and his trunk thick and powerful.

To his companion across the table, Pablo Konig looked formidable in the candlelight, almost frightening.

"And that is the story, my friend," said Konig, "on Sunday we depart for *Cienfuegos* where we load provisions and cargo for *Tunas de Zaza*, only a short day's sail. But we will need help, one more man—the right man, you understand?"

Antonio Rivas thought for a long moment and then said, "I have a cousin, Giddy Ebanks, a Caymanian, who will arrive in *Cienfuegos* shortly. I believe he will be the one we need if we can find him there."

"Does this mean we have a deal?" The Spaniard took the bottle of brown rum before him and poured their two shot glasses full.

"It is a deal, Pablo, we will do it together," responded Antonio Rivas, his ruddy complexion even more flushed from the whiskey they had been drinking through the afternoon and into the evening. Even so, he shuddered as he met Pablo's toast and took down the jigger of rum in a gulp. Then he put the small glass down and rubbed his eyes and face with his hands as if to reassure himself that it was really him in this place and in this skin on this night.

Across the dining room, outside the plantation windows in the shadows, Alberto motioned Jose to depart with him. They had watched the conversation for a few minutes, but could not understand the words spoken by Pablo Konig and the stranger in the dim light of the dining room.

When Alberto and Jose arrived at wharfside, the *Juana Mercedes* was lying peacefully at rest. The waterfront was quiet, and the only sound was the lapping of swells against the hull of the sleeping schooner. There was no light aboard ship, so the boys shed their sandals, jumped the rail and crept up the deck to the fo'c'sle hatch, which was propped open to circulate fresh air below decks. Alberto sat down on the deck, dropped his legs through the hatch, turned himself and swung down through the dark hole, clinging to the hatch combing with his hands and then silently dropping to the cabin floor below. Jose followed, trying to emulate the lead of his older mentor.

When Jose swung down, Alberto caught his legs and lowered him silently to the cabin floor. Then they shed their shirts and climbed into their bunks. Breathless and quiet, the boys rolled over to face each other in their bunks, only scarce moonlight dropping through the hatch to light their faces. After a moment of silence in his bunk, Jose heard the rhythmic sound of snoring below him and looked quickly at Alberto.

"It is only Christobal, Jose, he is our shipmate. Do not worry, he sleeps always like a stone."

The boys had drifted to sleep for only a few minutes when they were awakened by the murmur of voices on the wharf beside them. A moment later the schooner listed slightly as Pablo Konig and Antonio Rivas stepped aboard from the wharf, their footfalls clearly audible on the deck above. They moved to the galley where the boys could hear their muted voices and the rattle of an oil lantern as they lifted the globe and lit the wick. They came back on deck and walked forward to the fo'c'sle companionway.

The light from the lantern bounced in the stairwell of the companionway as Rivas and Konig descended.

"I sleep in the Captain's cabin," said Konig, "you will sleep here in the fo'c'sle Antonio…" Pablo Konig, standing behind Antonio Rivas, raised the lantern above Rivas to throw light into the close fo'c'sle, causing both the boys to wince in the glare.

"So Antonio," said the Spaniard, "I see that your bunkmates, *Negrito* and his little albino brother have been awaiting your arrival. Take the bunk that suits you."

Antonio's face was obscured by the light behind him as he studied the cramped quarters of the fo'c'sle. "The high bunk is too high, and the low bunk is too low," said Rivas, "I will take the bunk of the little brother. Get out of my bunk little one."

Jose could hear nothing but the pounding of his heart, and his eyes were wide in the glow of the lantern, fixed on the men before him. It seemed an eternity before he heard a metallic click and looked to the floor beside his bunk. Without a sound, Alberto had moved from his bunk to the cabin sole, standing bare chested in the flicker of the lantern. The bone handled switchblade knife was open in his hand; it's grey steel blade reflected clearly in the dull light.

The green eyes in Alberto's dark face had taken an eerie yellowish hue in the light of the lantern, and his white teeth were bared.

"You will not take my little brother's bunk, *hombre*." Alberto said in a slow, deliberate voice.

Antonio Rivas took a half step back and the Spaniard raised the lantern above his face to cast a clear light on Alberto. When the Spaniard raised the light above his face, its glow set on his forehead and cheeks, leaving his eyes and stubbled chin in shadow. Jose pushed back in his bunk as he looked into the skeletal visage of the Spaniard, only pinpoints of reflected light in Konig's liquid black eyes giving a hint of movement in the face.

The silence seemed deafening to Jose, and he squirmed further back in the shadows against the bulkhead. Slowly, the Spaniard lowered the lantern slightly to cast the full light on his face again, and his mouth broke into a wide grin. For the first time, Jose saw the silver cap sparkling on the Spaniard's left front tooth. Then the Spaniard laughed out loud.

"Antonio," he said, "I forgot to tell you about *el tigre*. He fancies himself to be a man. I think *El Capitan* keeps him aboard to entertain me." Then he chuckled again. "But still be aware, this boy is garbage from the streets of *Batabano* and you must be careful not to dirty your hands with him."

Alberto stood motionless, his eyes fixed on the men before him.

A long moment later Antonio Rivas grumbled, "Look, *muchacho*, I mean you no harm. I will take the bunk below you. Put down the knife."

Alberto took a slow step back and Antonio Rivas came in and sunk down on the lower bunk, kicked off his shoes, laid back and closed his eyes. The Spaniard was still grinning behind the glow of the lantern in the companionway. He looked into the eyes of Jose and said, with a smile still on his face, "You must be careful of the friends you keep, *chico*, they may get you killed one day." Then he turned and climbed the companionway stairs leaving the fo'c'sle in dark silence.

When Jose's eyes finally adjusted to the darkness, he could see Alberto lying quietly in his bunk above Rivas. Alberto was awake, looking at Jose in the darkness. His green eyes still seemed to glow. For a while, they did not sleep. Eventually, they could hear the discord of both Cristobal and Antonio Rivas snoring, the sound resonating in the small cabin. Jose realized that Cristobal had slept through the entire confrontation.

"I told you he sleeps always like a stone." said Alberto, as if he were reading Jose's thoughts. "Go to sleep, little brother." Then Alberto rolled over in his bunk and was silent.

Jose fell asleep later in a confusion of dark thoughts.

Chapter 4

Cienfuegos, Cuba
October 16, 1922

Gideon Ebanks was twenty-five years old and a seasoned seaman when he was discharged from the American schooner *Lady Marian* at *Cienfuegos* on the Southern coast of Cuba. He was born into a respected family in Grand Cayman, and like almost all the young men of his generation from the Cayman Islands, he had been raised to live on and support himself from the sea. From his earliest remembrance, he had fished with his father to help support the family. Later he learned the turtle trade, first locally in the Caymans and later, on the more remote Honduran and Nicaraguan banks.

As he grew into his early twenties, he found a market for his skills on foreign sailing vessels plying the Caribbean and the east coasts of Central and South America. There he found work sailing schooners on the cargo trade routes to the more remote regions that the modern motor ship carriers passed by. He had even made a few trips to America, mostly Tampa and Mobile, and his ultimate goal was to someday live in that land of dreams and perceived plenty.

Unfortunately, during the course of his wanderings, Gideon Ebanks, or “Giddy” as he was called by his friends, had taken on the burden of alcoholism. And it was not just an affinity to drink, but a full-fledged addiction that cost him loss of his senses for days on end while in port. He also suffered a growing inability to function normally at sea without smuggling rum in quantity for secret consumption aboard the vessels that he sailed. Inevitably, on each of his recent passages, he had fallen out of favour with his officers and was regularly discharged from further service at the next port of call. It had become increasingly difficult for him to find a berth on a ship where his reputation was not known.

It was not surprising, therefore, that Gideon Ebanks was discharged by the Captain of the *Lady Marian* on October 16, 1922, the day she reached *Cienfuegos* on a return trip from Tampa. By the time he walked down the gangway that bright autumn afternoon, Giddy had already knocked down a pint of straight rum from a pocket flask. His plan was to make straightaway to his favorite bay front cantina to continue the celebration of his own arrival. In fact, he was so happy to be back on familiar ground that he didn't think to resent the Captain for his untimely discharge from the *Lady Marian..*

Although *Cienfuegos* was a major commercial port city, Ebanks had rarely wandered beyond the immediate port environs during his many visitations. Along the bay front, he knew all the cheap hotels and bars and he could invariably find an old shipmate to drink and carouse with. Hell, even if he couldn't find an old shipmate, he thought, he could find a new friend or acquaintance to pass the time with.

Ebanks was dressed in faded khaki trousers and a long-sleeved, white cotton shirt when he disembarked the

Lady Marian. The light shirt and white fedora hat that he wore made his tanned leather skin look darker than it was, and his ambling pace made him appear to be much older than his twenty-five years. His sea bag, with everything he owned inside, was thrown over his left shoulder.

He ambled up the wharf almost gaily and set a direct course for his favorite watering hole, the *Cantina del Mar*.

On the morning of that same day, Alberto Monson shook Jose out of a sound sleep and whispered, "Jose, you must get up, *El Capitan* is here!" The sky was still mostly dark with a dim orange haze just breaking the eastern horizon when Jose scurried up the fo'c'sle companionway and met Alberto on deck. The other crewmen were still snoring below decks, and the early morning was cool and still. Light shining from the ports of the Captain's cabin was the only sign of life aboard the *Juana Mercedes*.

Jose was still tucking in his shirt and his shoelaces were untied when Alberto took him by the shoulders and stood him at attention.

"Jose, *El Capitan* has asked to meet you and I must take you to him. Finish tucking in your shirt and I will tie your shoes."

When they were finished, Alberto stood up and inspected his young friend in the dim light. He licked both hands several times and ran them over Jose's disheveled hair to arrange it into reasonable order. Then he led Jose to the door of *El Capitan's* cabin and whispered, "Jose, you must stand still, listen, and say nothing until you are told to speak." Then Alberto pushed the cabin door open and urged Jose through with a hand on his shoulder.

The Captain's cabin was sparse, with two over and under bunks on either side and a wide chart table at the back. Several gimbaled kerosene lanterns lit the room, and *El Capitan* sat studying papers on the chart table. Jose, with Alberto standing a head taller behind him, moved quietly up to face the master of the *Juana Mercedes*.

Capt. Juan Bautista y Silviera had a strong, rough but handsome face. As he looked up at the boys before him, a clean white smile broke the smooth tanned skin of his face, and his black eyes crinkled at the corners with his smile. At forty-one years old, only the salt and pepper gray in his wavy black hair told his age.

"Alberto, who is this young sailor?"

"*Capitan*, his name is Jose Martinez and he is my charge, as you have ordered, Sir!"

"Thank you, Alberto, you may be excused."

Alberto turned quickly and silently left the cabin, closing the polished wooden door behind him.

After a moment the Captain said, "Jose, I have been looking forward to meeting you. Sister Elena has told me much about you. She says you are quiet but very bright and willing to learn. She believes that you will be an able apprentice for me on the *Juana Mercedes*, and a fine seaman as you grow older. How do you feel about that?"

Jose felt the heat rise in his face as he tried to form an answer. "I am honored sir, but I know nothing of the sea and I do not wish to be a burden to you."

El Capitan studied the boy before him for a long moment and then said, "Let me tell you a story, Jose, that I want you to remember. Long before you were born, my father was killed in the Spanish-American War. Cuba was in disarray and I was left homeless and penniless to wander the streets of *Havana*. Sister Elena and Father Tomas found me and took me in and fed me and got me my first job as an ordinary seaman. I was young then, but still much older than you are now, and I knew nothing of the sea. But I was quiet and I listened and I learned and I worked hard, and it was not long before I was a mate and then a captain. And as you see, the sea has been kind to me. Sister Elena believes that you can do the same. Do you understand?"

"*Si Capitan.*" Jose murmured, lowering his eyes to the polished planks of the cabin floor.

"Jose, do not be afraid, I have promised Sister Elena that I will protect you…" Then, after a pause, he continued, "Did she give you a silver cross?"

Jose shook his head and reached up to feel the heavy crucifix suspended on its chain below his shirt, as if for reassurance that it was still there.

The Captain smiled again and said, "Jose, that is the cross that Sister Elena gave me when I departed for the sea those many years ago. It protected me and gave me solace, and now it will protect you. Will you make me proud that I have now given it to you?"

Jose was still clutching the silver crucifix beneath his shirt, and he smiled back as he looked up into the face of Capt. Juan Bautista y Silviera.

"*Si Capitan!*"

By six o'clock that afternoon Gideon Ebanks was drunk. He sat on a high stool at the bar of the *Cantina del Mar* and stared vacantly through the open restaurant and out across the patio to the bay. Rum, served neat in a clear glass, stood on the bar before him.

The *Cantina del Mar* was built on the commercial waterfront of *Cienfuegos* overlooking the harbor. The wind was blowing freshly from the east through the open restaurant and the bar, and the light was still bright outside. The air was fresh and cool that October afternoon and Ebanks seemed mesmerized, lost in reverie. He stared out over the many wooden-hulled merchant ships laid up against the creosoted pilings of the commercial docks. The harbour was bright blue and rough, and the bay was frothed in whitecaps. The entrance to the bay from the Caribbean was hidden from his view by a fold in the hills, but miles of its brilliant surface ran to the south. A lush range of mountains ran close down to the bay on the northeast, and in the lee of the hills numbers of fishing smacks were anchored along with several gray gunboats of the Cuban Navy. The verdant mountains stretched to a blue horizon, and there were a sprinkling of yellow, green, azure and pink houses in the foothills running along the bay. So Gideon Ebanks, lost in the fog of drink, looked out across the open terrace of the bar at the bay, watching the small fishing boats crisscrossing it under sail, trolling for dolphin.

There were four or five other seamen at the bar and two tables of fishermen sitting on the terrace. The fishermen must have done well the day before, Ebanks thought, to be drinking here on a workday. Some of the fishermen wore old straw hats and others were bareheaded. They all wore a myriad of mismatched old clothes and some were barefooted and others wore shoes or rope soled sandals. But they were cheerful and self-confident, sharing stories in a language Gideon Ebanks did not understand, for he spoke only Cayman English. Even so, he knew them, and he knew they were fishermen, because they reminded him to a man of his father and uncles and cousins in Grand Cayman. They drew their lives from the sea, and he knew them by their hands. The hands of the old men were gnarled and brown. Their palms and fingers were cut and scarred by handline fishing, and their exposed skin was a patchwork of sun blotches. The young mens' hands were sun brown and strong, but still bore the scars and open cuts of the fishing trade, and the calluses of handling rough hemp rope. The hair on the hands and sinewy arms of all but the darkest seamen had been bleached by the sun and salt.

Suddenly, Gideon Ebanks was terribly lonely. He was lonely for his family and friends back home on Grand Cayman. He was lonely for the simple, austere, but honest life on his family's obscure island at the end of the civilized world. He remembered his endless boyhood days on white beaches and in crystal waters—fishing, diving for conch and lobster, swimming and family picnics. He felt a growing sense of desperation and despair. Here I am, he thought, drinking away my wage from the last trip with no idea where I will be tomorrow. I must think. *I must think.......*

Immersed in his foggy reverie, Ebanks had not noticed the three Chinese men that had taken a remote table at the back of the bar. They watched him intently for some time, occasionally exchanging muted comments in Cantonese. Finally, one of them rose and deliberately approached him. He tapped Ebanks gently on the shoulder and said:

"You sailah, yes?"

Taken by surprise, Ebanks could only shake his head in affirmation.

"You wan' work?" the Chinaman said, "then come wi' me an' I buy you drink." Then he turned and made his way back toward his table and his friends. *What the hell*, Ebanks thought, *this may be my answer*. Then he stumbled off the barstool and followed the Chinaman.

Chapter 5

Batabano, Cuba

The next four days for Jose and Alberto were spent making ready for sail at the quay in *Batabano*. The *Juana Mercedes* had come alive with the arrival of *El Capitan*, and the days that followed were little more than work, dawn to dusk. The *Juana Mercedes* had been laid up for much of the hurricane season, and now it was time to get back to work in earnest. And so they did.

El Capitan was kind but stern and relentless. He knew what must be done to put his ship in good order, and none of the crew was spared the rigours of his orders. The first two days, Jose and Alberto spent in the hold of the *Juana Mercedes* and in her dark, dank bilges. Armed with caulking irons and hammers, they recaulked every seam below the waterline with tarred hemp and manila fibers picked from old, worn out ships' lines.

Angel Perez sat on deck above the main hold with a marlinspike, first separating the strands of old rope and then stripping it to fiber for caulking. The oakum, as the stripped fiber was called, was lowered into the hold where the boys soaked it in a pitch tar mixture and stubbornly recaulked every seam, stem to stern. The heat and the stench of the bilge and hot tar was almost unbearable, but the boys did not stop until called from below decks for an occasional meal or break. On the topsides, the crew were checking and patching each sail, chipping and painting the hardware against salt and rust, and generally making the *Juana Mercedes* ready for sail.

The Spaniard, Pablo Konig, directed the crew when the Captain was in *Batabano* arranging for a new load of cargo, and when the Captain was below decks working business papers and charts for their voyage. But the boys never saw him, emerging only briefly from their work below decks. At night, they were exhausted and fell immediately asleep after washing and eating the evening meal that Angel had prepared for them.

On the third day of preparations, Jose and Alberto were finally back on deck, this time with buckets and brushes, on hands and knees, scrubbing the deck of the *Juana Mercedes*, and everything else above the waterline. Nonetheless, it was a blessing to be back on the open deck, where a soft breeze and gentle autumn sun brought them alive again. They talked, and laughed, and the caress of the breeze and the tingle of the sun on their backs made them feel strong again and heady, anxious to embark on the great adventure still before them. Mostly, Alberto talked while they worked and Jose listened, and remembered, all the simple secrets and stories of seamanship that Alberto told him.

On the fourth day came the cargo. *El Capitan* had decided to take on a load of dry goods for shipment to *Isla del Pinos* before his trip to *Cienfuegos* for general cargo. The day was spent moving crate after crate of goods into the hold, lifting freight from the wharf with the main boom and topping lift rigged with the main sheet block and tackle as a cargo hoist and swinging it around to lower into the hold. Again, Jose and Alberto were below deck helping to move and arrange the crates in the hold. Despite the work, their level of expectation for the upcoming voyage began to grow. Although he had sailed many times before, Alberto was full of excitement and pride at the prospect of taking his young friend to sea for the first time.

That night, Alberto and Jose lay sleepless, facing each other on their middle bunks in the fo'c'sle. The rest of the crew had gone ashore and all was quiet except for the lapping of the bay against the hull.

"Are you ready little brother?" Alberto whispered.

"With you I am, big brother."

The boys were sleeping soundly when the rest of the crew returned that night.

On October 21, 1922, there was a gentle onshore wind from the northeast pushing over *Batabano* to the southwest. The morning broke clear and quiet, and the crew of the *Juana Mercedes* had gathered at daybreak around the crew table on the fantail. Angel Perez had prepared a breakfast of *huevos rancheros y tortillas*, and his dark coffee was freshly ground and steaming in the pot that he passed around. The crew ate heartily and the conversation was disjointed, each crewman pushing anecdotes about his own life and family while the others competed for a better story. Alberto and Jose ate quietly, listening to the tales of their shipmates, but too young to compete in the conversation.

At exactly seven o'clock that morning, Capt. Juan Bautista y Silviera stepped on deck and addressed his crew, still at the crew table on the stern of the *Juana Mercedes*.

"*Senores*," he said, "we will now sail to *Isla del Pinos* and take up cargo for *Cienfuegos*. From *Nuevo Gerona*, we will deliver provisions to *Cienfuegos*, and from there we have a special delivery of cargo to *Tunas de Zaza*. Are there any questions?"

Hearing nothing in response, the Captain said, "Mr. Konig, call your crew to stations."

All jumped from the crew table as if it had been a synchronized drill, and took their appointed stations. Several of the crewmen took up rope fenders from alongside the wharf and stowed them, and Alberto jumped to the pier to await Captain's orders.

"Take in the after bow spring line and the forward quarter spring line Alberto," the Captain said, as he walked the crew through the disembarkation.

Alberto scurried from line to line responding to *El Capitan's* orders, removing each as he was instructed and tossing it back aboard the schooner. The onshore breeze and ebbing tide began to move the *Juana Mercedes* back and out from the pier, and the crewmen fended her off as she slid back toward the open bay. After clearing all the lines, Alberto leaped back aboard and stood awaiting further orders from *El Capitan*.

As the bow of the *Juana Mercedes* slipped back past the end of the wharf, the Captain shouted, "Lift the top jib!" Both of the headsail jibs had been shackled to the forestay, so with the breeze steady on the starboard forequarter, two of the crew hauled the halyard tackle to lift the upper jib. As it rose the land breeze popped it open with a snap and a flutter, and the bow of the *Juana Mercedes* began to swing to port with a lurch. As her nose came around with the wind, the crew reset the jibsheet on the starboard and without any order raised the lower jib to fly below.

El Capitan spun the wheel, letting her come back around gently toward the wind in a semi-circle and then ordered the crew to set the mizzen and the main sails. The crew worked wordlessly until all the sails were set and the Captain nosed his vessel back to the south on a broad reach toward *Isla del Pinos*. The main and mizzen booms were let far out to starboard and their sails filled with the light breeze from shore. Responding to the wind, the *Juana Mercedes* healed slightly to starboard and struggled to catch up with the wind passing from behind her.

Jose sat in awe on the main hatch, staying out of the way of the crew as they worked and set the ship's gear and rigging. As the sails all deployed and the *Juana Mercedes* picked up speed, Jose could hear the creaking of the ship's planking and bulkheads as she stretched herself out again in preparation for her flight with the wind. He was elated with the breeze on his face and the quiet gurgle and hiss of the sea passing beneath their hull and the seabirds in flight above in the pale clear sky. He smiled and thought about Sister Elena and her plan for his life.

In a fair breeze and good weather, the *Juana Mercedes* made her crossing of the *Golfo de Batabano* in no time and by early afternoon at the southerly end of the *Archipelago de los Canarreos,* they had taken a westerly tack toward *Nueva Gerona* on the north coast of *Isla del Pinos*. By nightfall, they were safely docked in *Nueva Gerona*. The next day they unloaded their freight, and the following day they took on cargo for *Cienfuegos*. The boys struggled in the hold with hugc pallcts of finc-grained, crystalline, colored marble from the mines of the *Casas Range*. That evening, they set sail for *Cienfuegos*, exhausted from two days of freight handling.

The *Juana Mercedes*, filled to capacity, lumbered out of port under the weight of her load. Fortunately, the weather held good and she made way steadily, albeit slowly, back toward *Cienfuegos* to the northeast.

That evening, Alberto and Jose sat at the bow of the schooner, legs hung over her side, watching the sparkling phosphorescence of the passing salt water as the *Juana Mercedes* cut her path toward *Cienfuegos*. Eventually Alberto, exhausted from the day's labours, retired to the fo'c'sle for sleep. Jose, still excited and enthralled with the serene beauty of the night under sail, moved quietly back toward the stern and laid down on a hatch cover to watch the clear sky above, jeweled as it was with a million brilliant stars. It took only minutes before he was sleeping soundly.

Some time during the night Jose was startled to consciousness by the muted sound of voices on the stern of the ship behind him. He immediately recognized the voice of the Spaniard who said:

"Do you have it?"

"*Si.*"

"Then go and get it. I want to see it."

Jose did not immediately recognize the second voice, but he saw the dark figure of Antonio Rivas pass him walking softly up the deck to disappear down the forward companionway. Jose was at first fearful that he would be detected and accused of eavesdropping, but curiosity compelled him to roll slowly and silently off the hatch cover and crawl on his stomach and elbows into a canvas tarp heaped at the foot of the mizzen mast. He covered himself with the canvas and lay on his side, head resting on one elbow as he peered back in the darkness toward the stern of the ship.

Jose could make out the form of the Spaniard at the ship's wheel. He was smoking a cigarette and from time to time its glow cast a faint light on his face. Again, his eyes were dark hollows and his visage looked to Jose like a death mask. Jose shuddered and found himself barely breathing. The minutes seemed like hours before Jose heard the footsteps of Antonio Rivas returning to the stern.

"Where is it?" said the Spaniard.

"Here."

Jose could not make out what they were handling in the darkness, but soon he heard the Spaniard hiss, "You fool, you will only kill *yourself* with this ancient cannon!"

"No, Pablo, no....it is old but I have tried it. It is an American Navy pistol."

"You idiot, I told you to get a *good* weapon!"

"Honest, Pablo, this *is* a good weapon, you will see......"

"You had better come through when I need you, Rivas, or *I* will kill you myself. Now put it away and take the wheel until the next watch."

Then the Spaniard walked silently to the main companionway and disappeared below deck. Rivas stood motionless at the wheel and Jose quietly pulled the tarp up over his head. Eventually, he fell into a restless sleep.

Chapter 6

En route to Cienfuegos, Cuba

Jose awoke at dawn to the gentle sway of the *Juana Mercedes* under sail in a light wind and the tuneless whistling of Cristobal Gual, who was on watch at the wheel when Jose stirred and looked from under his canvas cover. The sky was breaking orange on the eastern horizon and a light breeze kept the schooner on course toward a barely visible dark shore to the north.

Jose rose from under the canvas and tried to slip quietly to the fo'c'sle but Cristobal caught sight of him and shouted, "*Buenos dias muchacho*, come and help me with the wheel."

Afraid that any resistance might raise suspicion, Jose returned reluctantly to the stern and took a position beside Cristobal.

"Here, Jose, take the wheel. Now look at the compass, you see we are on a course of 15 degrees, north northeast, do you see?"

"Yes *senor*," Jose responded submissively.

"Now you keep the ship on that same course while I get coffee, do you understand? Try it for a while before I go below."

Cristobal stood by long enough to assure himself that the boy beside him could keep the *Juana Mercedes* on point before he went to the galley for Angel's fresh morning coffee. Soon Alberto emerged from the fo'c'sle, rubbed his eyes and stretched, and joined Jose at the wheel.

"Where were you last night little brother?" Alberto inquired. "I know you were not out of the fo'c'sle before me this morning."

"I slept on deck Alberto."

"You do not look good, little brother. Why did you not come to bed?"

"I cannot speak of it now, Alberto, I may be heard...."

Cristobal returned with a steaming cup of coffee in his hands, smiling broadly at the boys.

"Keep her on course *muchachos*," he said, "we will be in *Cienfuegos* before the end of my watch."

The rest of the crew began to stir and at 6:30 Angel served breakfast on the crew table at the stern. The boys took turns at the wheel under the watchful eye of Cristobal Gual while the rest of the crew ate. As always, Angel served *El Capitan* in his cabin. The Spaniard and Antonio Rivas sat across from each other at the crew table, but neither spoke.

"There it is *muchachos*, the entrance to the bay, *La Bahia de Jagua*, the most beautiful bay on the south coast of Cuba!" Cristobal took the wheel and pointed out the broad channel entrance to Alberto and Jose.

"See, there is *Punta Colorados* to port and *Punta Sabanilla* to starboard!" The bay entrance was about a mile wide but quickly narrowed as they made entrance. "There it is!" exclaimed Cristobal, in a flourished announcement to the boys, looking at them expectantly with raised eyebrows: *"El Castillo de Nuestra Señora de los Angeles de Xagua!* It was there that many a pirate and captured marauder was hung high from the gallows and left for the seabirds to pick out his bulging eyes!" He kept watching the boys intently, awaiting their reaction, but they had little more than passing interest in the ancient ramparts of the old stone fort. Cristobal did not notice the furtive glances between Konig and Rivas, and probably would not have given them any thought had he seen them. After all, the days of piracy and looting and violence on the high seas were mostly ancient history and myth and couldn't even raise a comment from two young deckboys.

It was still eleven miles across Cienfuegos Bay to the city, so the boys walked up to the bowsprit and sat in the shade of the taut foresails. To Jose, the cool soft breeze and the hiss and foam of the bow cutting the crystal water of the bay was almost hypnotic. Alberto had taken to whittling a tobacco pipe bowl out of a piece of black mahogany root, so Jose said nothing to interrupt his concentration. Low clouds and mist obscured the tops of the blue mountains to the east, but the mountainsides ran down into the deep green jungles of tropical valleys below and then further down into the lower endless rolling fields of the cultivated sugar cane plantations.

Finally, the foot of the mountains tumbled down to the white strand of the bay where numberless king palms held court over the beach, swaying in unison with each push of the breeze.

Despite the breathtaking beauty engulfing him, Jose was troubled. He wanted to tell Alberto what he had seen and heard, but he did not want to interrupt Alberto's concentration. Besides, it was nothing anyway. Perhaps all crewmen carried handguns to sea, he did not know. So he turned and lay on his stomach and looked over the toe rail at the bow and looked into the water below. It was so clear that he could see the sandy bottom and the thousands of strange and colourful fish passing below. As they approached Cienfuegos, he watched the myriad of green islands in the bay, and coral keys and promontories, and the bright scattering of shoreside cottages and villas that became more and more frequent as they approached the great port city.

Finally, Jose rolled over and sat up. "Alberto?" he said quietly. Receiving no response, he crabwalked over to Alberto and said again, more urgently, "Alberto!" Alberto looked up impatiently, unhappy with the interruption of his work.

"What is it, Jose?"

"Alberto, *Senor* Rivas has a gun."

"What?" Alberto responded, only now starting to pay attention.

"I said *Senor* Rivas has a gun."

"What are you talking about Jose?" Alberto's interest was finally piqued and he laid aside his knife and mahogany root to concentrate on Jose's words.

"I saw them last night, Alberto, when I was on deck. I was hidden in the dark. Rivas went below and got a gun and showed it to the Spaniard."

"What kind of a gun was it Jose?"

"It was a pistol… I could not see it well in the dark, but Rivas showed it to the Spaniard and they spoke about it. The Spaniard was unhappy with *Senor* Rivas and cursed him……What does this mean Alberto?"

Alberto was quiet for a few moments, contemplating Jose's words. "Jose," he said quietly, almost in a whisper, "are you sure this is true?"

"It is true Alberto," said Jose, lowering his voice to the same confidential pitch as his friend, "I will never lie to you. Is this thing wrong, to have a gun on the ship?"

"Any gun must be reported to *El Capitan* and secured in his locker for the voyage. Only in emergency will such weapons be brought out for the crew, it is the rule! It has always been the rule! We must report this to *El Capitan*."

At no more than a mile off Cienfuegos, a small sloop came alongside *Juana Mercedes* and delivered a harbor pilot for the docking. The harbor pilot was curt and efficient, taking immediate control of the schooner and issuing the orders that would bring her safely and quietly to dockside within half an hour. Compared to Batabano, Cienfuegos was a large port city, with some huge steel steamships at the quays alongside the schooners and other larger sailing vessels. Still a novice in docking, Jose sat quietly on the fore cabintop watching as the crew went efficiently about their work, responding immediately to the various orders of the harbor pilot from the helm, repeated to them immediately in the resounding voice of *El Capitan*.

Within minutes of reaching her assigned dockage, the *Juana Mercedes* was made fast and the harbor pilot, having gone over some papers with *El Capitan*, departed the schooner and walked up the long wharf, back straight and uniform still fresh and pressed. Jose thought momentarily: that is the kind of captain I will be, in a handsome uniform with much authority, so everyone will admire me and answer to my orders.

Jose was still imagining himself a great sea captain when Alberto, now finished helping dock the ship, walked back to find Jose. Finding him still on the fore cabintop, Alberto said in an urgent whisper, "Jose!" Then, receiving no response, he repeated "JOSE!!!" in a muted shout.

Jose's head snapped around and he focused his attention on Alberto, who was standing on the foredeck trying to get his attention. He immediately rolled off the cabin top and ran forward to Alberto. "*Oye*, Jose, we must tell *El Capitan* what you have seen. Come with me, we will wait for him on the dock." Alberto knew that the captain was always required to report to the harbormaster and port customs official immediately upon making port, so he planned to catch him up the wharf, out of earshot of the rest of the crew. So the boys jumped across to the wharf and ran to sit in some freight boxes on the dock, awaiting the captain's arrival.

In a few moments, however, a long open touring car with its top down drove past the large frame chandler's warehouse at the head of the dock and continued right down the wharf, chauffeur dodging stacked freight and ships' tackle strewn along the way. In the back seat of the limousine sat a portly gentleman in a black suit coat and white shirt and black full tie with a shiny black top hat perched precariously on his head. They passed the boys without noting their presence and drove out the pier to stop alongside the *Juana Mercedes.*

*El Capita*n emerged immediately from his cabin and walked to the side of his ship. He wore his best uniform in navy blue, with gold braid on the epaulets of his waistcoat and white captain's hat, trimmed in red and gold, placed jauntily on his head. But then to the surprise of the boys, he disembarked and walked directly over to the gentleman in the back of the limousine and greeted him warmly. The chauffeur jumped immediately from the front seat to open the rear door for *El Capitan* to be seated beside the gentleman in the top hat.

Initially the scene caught Alberto by surprise, but when he realized that *El Capitan* was about to depart in the limousine, he snatched Jose off the crate where they were sitting and ran to catch the captain with Jose hot on his heels. The chauffeur had reseated himself and turned the automobile to drive back off the pier by the time Alberto and Jose arrived alongside.

"*Capitan*!" Alberto shouted with urgency, "We must speak with you sir!"

All three of the men in the limousine went silent in surprise, then *El Capitan* smiled and said, "Stand at attention when you speak young sailor! You too, little one!" Both the boys snapped to attention, shoulders squared and legs together. They presented a curious sight, Alberto shoeless and wearing only a ragged pair of canvas shorts, and Jose also naked except for his rumpled shorts, crucifix on chain and the scuffed pair of leather shoes that were too big for his feet.

Then the older gentleman in the top hat began to chuckle, "Juan!" he said jovially, "It must be terribly difficult for you to find a crew these days!" Then he laughed out loud, obviously amused with his own humor. Then *El Capitan* began to chuckle as well and responded, "But you would be surprised Ramon, these two boys work harder than any man on the ship!"

"If that is the case," said the man in the top hat, smiling broadly, "perhaps I should find another ship for my cargo!" With that response he had so amused himself with his own humor that he laughed loudly, slapping his knees as his belly shook with his mirth.

El Capitan was still smiling as well and he turned and said to the boys, "*Muchachos*, meet *Senor* Ramon

Fernandez. It is he whose cargo we will be transporting for his plantation outside *Tunas de Zaza*."

Both the boys, still standing stiffly at attention, saluted *Senor* Fernandez in unison, the sight of which caused *Senor* Fernandez to laugh even harder. "Juan," he shouted, still laughing heartily, "did you prepare this show for me? Really, where did you find these ragamuffins?!"

The captain, now tiring of the joke at his expense, turned and said to the boys, "You are dismissed. I will speak to you when I return."

"But *Capitan*," Alberto started to speak but was cut off by his captain, "Alberto! I said I will speak to you upon my return!" Then he turned back to the chauffer and motioned for him to depart.

As the limousine driver motored back off the wharf, *Senor* Ramon Fernandez was still speaking loudly and laughing, but *El Capitan* sat stiff and resolute, obviously ready to move on to other business.

Chapter 7

Cienfuegos, Cuba

Angel Perez was standing at the rail of the *Juana Mercedes*, wiping his hands on a stained white apron. He had watched the episode of *El Capitan's* departure with a smile of amusement on his round face. But when the two boys slumped and turned reluctantly back toward the ship, he straightened his face and called out to them. "Come, *muchachos*, it is time to eat. I know you are hungry!"

When the boys came back aboard, however, they barely acknowledged him, so Angel said cheerfully, "*Muchachos*, come and help me with the food. It is *El Capitan's* order!" With that said, Alberto and Jose followed him down the companionway to the galley. There, Angel served up plates of fried battered fish and fried hominy corn patties and fresh sliced tomatoes with a guava jelly and hard bread on the side, and the three of them sat at the small bench table in the galley and ate. The boys were still quiet, so Angel pressed, "*Amigos*, what is so important that you must speak to *El Capitan*?"

The boys glanced at each other briefly but continued quietly to eat. Then Angel said, "Is it not me who is always here when you need help? Why do you not speak to me?"

Jose had felt a special kinship with Angel since the latter had befriended him on the train to *Batabano*, and had become his confidant. So after another moment of thought he blurted out, "Rivas has a pistol!" Alberto looked back to his plate and shook his head. Then Alberto said, "Jose, this is a matter for *El Capitan* only." Angel Perez paid Alberto no attention and pressed on: "Jose, how do you know this?"

Jose was aware of Alberto's disappointment that this matter should be reported to a mere cook, but he felt compelled to speak of it to an adult, any adult, since the captain had left the ship.

"I saw him with it last night, Angel. When I was on deck, Rivas was on watch and he had a pistol. He showed it to the Spaniard and the Spaniard cursed him about it."

Angel thought for a moment and said, "Do you know if the Spaniard has reported this to *El Capitan*?"

"No, we do not know," interrupted Alberto, "that is why we tried to tell him before he left..." Alberto was visibly irritated that Jose's report had been made to the ship's cook rather than directly to *El Capitan*, "...but we will report to him immediately upon his return."

"Well, that may be a few days, *muchachos*, for he is not to return for several days...when the ship is ready for departure. Rivas and the Spaniard have now probably left as well and will not return until it is time to leave. In this port, stevedores do all the offloading and loading, so we have only to sit and wait. Our orders are to stay aboard and attend the ship and cargo. We must protect it. Those are our orders."

After that, they continued to eat quietly with no more words spoken.

Antonio Rivas disembarked the *Juana Mercedes* almost immediately after *El Capitan* was out of sight. He waited another few minutes until Angel Perez and the deck boys went below to eat, and then he jumped the rail and walked briskly up the wharf toward the shore. He carried his sea bag with the pistol inside so that it could not be found by anyone aboard the schooner. His job, assigned by the Spaniard, was to find his cousin Giddy Ebanks and to get him in line for the work to be done. Rivas knew that his cousin would go along with the plan because he knew that Giddy was running out of choices. The word had spread that Giddy's drinking and fighting and brushes with the law had made it almost impossible for him to hold a legitimate job aboard ship anymore.

Evans Rivers—Antonio Rivas as he now called himself—was born and raised in West End, Grand Cayman, and grew up with his cousin (his father's sister's son) Gideon Ebanks being raised in a house not a stone's throw up the beach from him. And like his cousin Giddy, Evans had spent most of his life on the sea, first turtling and later crewing foreign sailing ships, where Cayman expertise was in high demand. But Evans had the added advantage of having had a whole branch of his family living in *Isla del Pinos*, Cuba, where he could visit regularly and where he became proficient in speaking the native Spanish tongue. Work was easy to get in Cuba, he had found, but later it had become more apparent that the Cubans mistrusted—even disliked—the notoriously independent Caymanian seafarers who were displacing them in the important positions aboard all the larger Cuban cargo ships. So Evans Rivers had decided to adopt a Cuban persona. Antonio Rivas he now called himself, and he spoke virtually flawless Spanish, so he could hardly be detected as a Caymanian. Only his complexion gave him away—white ruddy complexion and Aryan features—made him stand out among his Cuban sailmates. But mostly, no questions were asked and he had gotten by without detection for several years.

So now to find Giddy, he thought, as he scurried up the pier. Giddy had written him more than a month ago to say that he would arrive in *Cienfuegos* on October 16th, but now it was almost the end of October and God knows where he might be by now. But the first place to look, of course, was the *Cantina del Mar*. When he was in *Cienfuegos,* Giddy would be there or he would be in the ratty flophouse next door, *Las Estrellas*, with some frowzy Cuban bitch. The one thing about Giddy is—or so thought his cousin—Giddy is predictable.

At four o'clock in the afternoon when Evans Rivers arrived, the *Cantina del Mar* was empty. Except for the stale, sour bar smell and the bartender stirring behind the bar, making ready for the evening traffic, nothing was even notable. Evans searched quickly, looking around at the dark corners of the bar and across the open patio to the bay, but the tables were empty and the bar was completely quiet except for the clinking of the glasses that the bartender was rearranging and occasionally polishing with a dirty rag behind the bar.

"Manuel! Manuel, *mi amigo*!" Evans shouted across the bar to get the attention of the bartender, "*Que pasa amigo*?"

Manuel the bartender looked up and squinted in the bright reflection of the afternoon sun off the bay. He couldn't see Rivers' face in the sun's glare, so he grunted unintelligibly and continued with his work behind the bar. Rivers satisfied himself that nobody was in the bar, and then he walked over to where Manuel was working and pulled up a barstool. "Manuel…Manuel," he said, "…you know me… Antonio Rivas!" The bartender knew him no better than a thousand other nameless faces, but he smiled mechanically and said, "So what will it be, *mi amigo*?"

"Rum straight," Rivers replied, "with a piece of lime."

Manuel poured a neat double shot of dark rum in a glass and put it on the bar in front of Rivers along with a quartered slice of lime. "So, Antonio," said Manuel, "when was it that I saw you last?"

Rivers took a long pull on his rum and looked Manuel directly in the eyes. "Manuel," he said, "you will remember me only by my cousin, Giddy Ebanks. We have been here many times together." After only a moment, Manuel's eyes lit up in a flash of recognition. "Giddy, the son-of-a-bitch!" he said in English, a smile broadening on his face, "the son-of-a bitch!"

"You know him, of course, you know him…" Rivers said, searching for recent information on his cousin.

"Yes! Yes, he was here only two weeks ago, the son-of-a-bitch!" Manuel chuckled and looked up at Evans Rivers with a mirthful grin on his face. "The son-of-a-bitch is in jail again!" Then Manuel shook his head and laughed out loud again, wiping the counter with his dirty rag.

"What are you saying, Manuel?" Rivers snapped, "What are you saying?"

Manuel chuckled and said, "This crazy Caymanian bastard, your cousin, he tried to smuggle three Chinamen aboard an American freighter bound for New York and he was caught! They all were caught and put in jail!" He was still chuckling to himself as Rivers walked out of the *Cantina del Mar*.

The cell was dark and cramped and smelled of urine and human excrement. It was eight feet long and eight feet wide and was furnished only with two wooden bunk type beds—one against each side wall—and a single slop bucket placed between the bunks against the back wall. The front of the cell was secured with rusty iron bars overlooking a long dim hallway lit only by a few hanging oil lamps. The only sounds were the echoed grunts, grumbles and epithets emitted occasionally by the prisoners.

Giddy Ebanks was laid back in the shadows under one of the lower bunks, his arms folded back to rest his head. There were no pillows or sheets on the bunks—

only dirty canvas mattresses stuffed with dried leaves and straw. Ebanks had suffered through the worst of his alcohol withdrawal during the first several days of imprisonment and now could only concentrate on scratching and picking the lice that had infested his body. He couldn't carry on an intelligent conversation since the police had put the Chinamen in the same cell with him. So about all he could do was lay on that stinking bunk and think.

Now that the alcohol induced euphoria that had seduced him and kept him going for so long was gone, his thoughts had gone completely dark. He could think only of the many ships and the many voyages he had been on, and the many captains and ships' officers he had served under. To a man, there were none as good a sailor as he. Every one of them, he thought, were cocky and overbearing, but none as good a sailor as he. Most of them were ships' officers by way of family ties and family money, not by skill and experience. *Damn them all and their fancy uniforms and their connections and their money...*

His thoughts were interrupted by the clank and rattle of keys in the iron door at the end of the dark hall. He didn't think it was time for another serving of the indescribable slop that was pushed under the door occasionally by the guards, but it was impossible in this god forsaken place to determine whether it was night or day, much less whether it was mealtime. Then the door down the hall creaked open and he could hear the footsteps of several people in the hallway. As always, the other unnamed and unknown prisoners up and down the dark hallway began to scream and beg, at the same time cursing and entreating the guard for help and for mercy.

Ebanks was mildly interested when a group of three men stopped at the bars to his cell and peered in, but it was too dark to see their faces, so he stayed still in his bunk. He could tell that the third man, who stood behind the other two, was a guard, because the dim light identified his uniform and round, billed cap. The other two stood close to the bars and peered in, eyes trying to adjust to the darkness.

"Giddy! Giddy, is that you?" one of the voices inquired in English.

Ebanks sat up immediately, now surprised in earnest to hear English words spoken.

"Who is it?" Ebanks said, standing up, "Who are you?

"It's me, Evans Rivers."

"Cousin! How the hell did you find me?"

Rivers chuckled audibly and said, "You son-of-a-bitch, you leave a path a mile wide! Everybody on the waterfront knows where you are!"

Ebanks had stepped up to the bars and now looked Rivers in the face. Then he glanced over to the shadowed face of Pablo Konig, who was studying him in silence. "Who's your friend?" he asked simply.

"This is Pablo Konig, I am working for him now. We want you to work with us too." Then Konig whispered a few words to Rivers in Spanish, who in turn asked Ebanks in English:

"My friend Pablo wants to know why you are in here, Giddy."

Ebanks glanced back at the silent guard for a moment and then responded to Rivers, "I went out to this American freighter that was about to leave for New York. I was talkin' to the guard at the gangway—you know, about gettin' a job aboard the ship—when these three Chinamen tried to come aboard from a rowboat on the other side of the ship. They would've made it, too, if a deckhand sleepin' out on deck hadn't caught 'em comin' over the rail. The dumb asses stumbled right over him—can you believe it? Then all hell broke loose, so in the confusion I just went back to the *Cantina del Mar* for a drink and the police come and got me. They say I was helpin' these Chinamen to stow away to New York, but they can't prove it…I mean, I didn't do it. And then they put these Chinese sons-a-bitches in the same cell with me! Evans, I need you to help get me out of here! I'll come to work for your friend, I promise…"

Evans Rivers turned his head to Pablo Konig to see if Konig had understood, but got no signal. Then he whispered a few words in Konig's ear, and the Spaniard's hard face broke briefly into a slight smile. Then he rattled some Spanish to Rivers and turned to walk back up the hall toward the iron entry door.

Rivers glanced back around to Ebanks briefly and said, "Giddy, it's on! I'll be back to get you!" Then he turned on his heel and ran to catch up with the Spaniard.

Late the next morning Rivers returned to the *Cienfuegos* jail to request his cousin's release. Earlier that morning, the Spaniard had located the local Chief of Police and paid the necessary bribe, thereby procuring Ebanks' immediate release. After receiving and counting the tendered money in the privacy of his office, the Chief had given Pablo Konig a crooked smile and conceded that there had been insufficient evidence to convict Ebanks anyway. After all, he had concluded, who could trust the story of a Chinaman, or even three of them.

So Konig gave Rivers the handwritten release order signed by the Chief and sent him immediately to fetch his cousin. Within a few minutes after Rivers arrived at the jail and presented the paper to the jail keeper, Ebanks was pushed out of an iron door at the jail entry, which was quickly slammed and locked behind him.

"Jesus, Evans! How did you do it?" Giddy Ebanks exclaimed, blinking his eyes and shielding them against the sun with the back of a hand.

"The Spaniard did it, Giddy, the Spaniard did it! He bribed the Police Chief and sent me to get you…I told you I'd be back for you."

"Who is this Spaniard, Evans? How do you know him?"

"He's the Mate on the *Juana Mercedes*, the Cuban schooner I'm decking on. I met him in a bar in *Batabano* and we ran around together for a few weeks. Then he told me he would get me a job aboard the *Juana Mercedes* as a deckhand if I would agree on a partnership deal with him, so I did, and here I am……"

"So what about me, Evans, what does he want with me?"

"He wants you to be a partner too, Giddy! I told him you would be a good man for the job. We need another partner to make the deal work. You said you'd do it yesterday…that's why Pablo got you out of jail."

"What's the deal, Evans, what's he want me to do?"

"It has to wait until we meet Pablo this afternoon, Giddy, he wants to explain to you himself so that there won't be any misunderstanding."

By that time they were walking briskly down the Prado, a narrow flagstone promenade running through the center of the *Avenida de la Independencia*, the main thoroughfare of the central city. The Prado was lined with blooming trees and shrubbery, and upscale stores, shops, residences, movie theaters and hotels gracing either side of the *Avenida.* It was crowded with locals and tourists strolling among the marble busts of local and national notables that flanked the flagged walkway. Evans Rivers diverted his attention to the passing strangers who were gawking at them—two obvious *gringos* speaking English—one of them dressed in the same rumpled, now filthy clothes he had disembarked in several weeks earlier.

"Goddamn, Giddy, you stink like shit!" Rivers said to his cousin, suddenly realizing the stir they were creating.

"What did you expect, you bastard?" Ebanks responded quickly, "I've been laid up in that shithole jail for more than a week now."

"Alright, Giddy, alright. Let's just get to the hotel so you can get that smell off you....then we'll talk about it."

"What hotel are we goin' to, Cousin?"

"*Las Estrellas*, right next door to the *Cantina del Mar*."

"That's good Cousin," Ebanks said, "you can buy me a drink along the way."

At 3:30 that afternoon, Ebanks and Rivers were sitting in the bar of the *Cantina del Mar*. Ebanks had bathed at the hotel where he was given a spare set of clothing from Rivers' seabag, and they were already working on their second hour of rum drinks. Manuel had brought Rivers up to date on all the latest waterfront gossip, and Rivers was passing it along to Ebanks in English. Finally, Rivers asked Manuel for the time, and Manuel pulled a gold pocket watch on a chain from the lower right pocket of his buttoned vest. He squinted at the watch and recited the time to Rivers.

"Giddy, we got to go," he said to Ebanks, "we'll be late to our meeting with Pablo."

"Why don't Pablo just come here, Evans, we can talk right here."

"Goddamit, Giddy, I told you, if we're gonna work together we got to do what Pablo says. That's the deal. Now come on."

Rivers got off his barstool and tugged at Ebanks' shirt.

"Alright! Alright!" Ebanks shook his cousin's grip from his arm and stepped off his barstool as well. "Let's go."

Rivers put money down on the bar for Manuel and they walked out the door into the sunlight. The whole bay seemed a bright aqua pool except for the darker blue hues of deeper spots and green browns of submerged sea grasses. Rivers and Ebanks walked quietly, both watching the bustle of the bayfront and the ships beyond.

Finally Ebanks said, "Where we goin'?"

His cousin responded simply, "*Parque Marti.*"

"Why there?" Ebanks inquired.

"Because Pablo wants a quiet place to talk about our deal."

After that, they walked on quietly until they reached the *Parque Marti.* It was the largest, most beautiful public plaza in *Cienfuegos.* Located in the southwest quarter of the city, not far from the waterfront, it had been less than a fifteen minute walk for Rivers and Ebanks from the *Cantina del Mar.* The park was manicured and landscaped with flagstone walkways, fountains, flowerbeds, blossoming trees and an ornate, bright white covered bandstand for its centerpiece. Ebanks, who had rarely left the waterfront in *Cienfuegos,* was awestricken at the beauty of the place and said nothing when Rivers led him to the Spaniard, who was standing at the foot of the bandstand smoking a cigarette. Rivers and Pablo Konig spoke a few words in Spanish and then continued walking through the park, with Ebanks following behind.

The Cathedral of the *Purisma Concepcion de Cienfuegos* was the largest church in the city at the time, overlooking the *Parque Marti* at its northeast quarter. Unlike most Catholic cathedrals of its genre, it had a plain but imposing, severe grey façade and clock-tower looking down over the park. But rather than enter the huge wooden doors at the front of the church, Konig led Ebanks and Rivers around to a side entry on *San Carlos* Street, pulled open the door and without knocking, motioned for them to follow him into the dark interior.

They walked through the shadowy sacristy and then through a massive wooden door into the giant, vaulted and pillared nave of the cathedral. The only light within came in muted colors streaming through twelve large, arched stained glass windows, each separately depicting one of the twelve apostles. After his arrival

Ebanks, who was the last to enter, stopped short. He glanced up and across the high altar. There, a picture above the transept on the opposite wall transfixed him. In the picture, the Angel of Mercy was reaching out to an array of demented and tortured sinners below her in an effort to rescue their souls from the anguish of purgatory.

The message of the foreboding scene above in this dreary place was lost on Giddy Ebanks, who saw it only as a depiction of human horror and chaos. But it so surprised and intrigued him at once that he stood motionless in place. Rivers and the Spaniard passed in front of the altar and turned to walk down the central aisle. It was only then that Rivers realized his cousin was no longer behind him, so he paused and looked back. When he realized Ebanks was still in the shadows at the sacristy doorway, he turned and quickly returned to where his cousin stood. Then he whispered urgently:

"Giddy! Giddy! What are you doing—why did you stop?"

Ebanks, still staring at the picture of purgatory as if in a trance, quietly responded, "Evans…what the hell are we doin' *here*?"

"Jesus, Giddy, you know what we're doin' here—we gotta go over the plan with Pablo—we gotta work out the details."

"Yeah, Evans, but why here? Why do we have to do it here?"

"Because it's quiet here.....because nobody can hear us. Besides, this is where Pablo said we're gonna work out the plan. Come on, Giddy, he got you out of jail. You said you would be our partner. Come on." Rivers turned and walked back to the aisle and turned to walk toward the back of the church where Konig was waiting.

After a moment more of hesitation, Ebanks walked out of the shadows and quietly stopped in front of the altar. *It really is quite beautiful*, he thought, *maybe I should have come here before now…* The elevated altar was supported by eight fluted and gilded Corinthian columns and golden trim. It was surrounded by richly coloured statues of the saints, with the Virgin Mary in a blue robe and golden crown standing at front center. Above and behind the altar was a magnificent organ loft and again above and behind that was a twelve foot high depiction of Christ in stained glass, his arms outstretched and beckoning.

Ebanks turned his head to look for his cousin and the Spaniard. He could see them sitting in a dimly lit pew toward the back of the cathedral. They were talking in subdued tones, and he couldn't hear anything they were saying. Then the Spaniard looked up at Ebanks, eyes obscured in the dark shadows below his brow, but Ebanks could see that he was smiling. The Spaniard signaled with his right hand for Ebanks to join them.

Ebanks looked briefly back over his shoulder at Christ in stained glass behind him, and then walked toward the back of the cathedral. The only sound to be heard was the click of his heels against the cold marble floor.

Chapter 8

Departure for Tunas de Zaza
October 30, 1922

Jose was awakened from a sound sleep by muted footfalls and whispering voices on the deck above him. It was dark in the fo'c'sle with the overhead hatch opened only to a crack because of rain earlier in the evening. When his eyes adjusted to the darkness, he could see that Alberto was not in his bunk. No doubt Alberto would be helping cast off, Jose thought groggily, and turned over to go back to sleep.

But the whispering voices and small noiscs on dcck persisted, so he reluctantly rolled on his back and rubbed his eyes. He knew that tonight the *Juana Mercedes* was to sail for *Tunas de Zaza*, and that he should be on deck with Alberto learning his job. He snatched back his blanket and sat crouched in his bunk, for the overhead bunk was too low for him to sit up straight. Finally the whisper of the voices on the cabin top above captured his attention. His curiosity overcame his desire to go back to sleep and he climbed to the top bunk to peer out into the dark night.

The moon had not yet risen, but still there was enough glow of twilight to distinguish two men sitting on the cabin top close by the fo'c'sle hatch. They were slumped over and whispering in barely audible breaths that Jose could hardly make out even at his perch in the hatch next to them.

"Giddy's on board…." said one of the voices.

"I didn't see him, where the hell is he?" whispered the other.

"You'll never see Giddy, he's good at it. I told you. He's under the canvas tarp at the foot of the foremast…"

Then they were quiet, scanning the deck and the wharf for any movement.

Jose found suddenly that he had not been breathing and he dropped quietly down to a sitting position on the bunk, sucking in a breath of air, instinctively aware that he should remain undetected. He had a prickly feeling between his shoulders and up his neck to the base of his skull. The voices, the slight movements…he knew it was Rivas and the Spaniard. What were they doing? Who were they talking about?

Jose was torn between the desire to run up the companionway and out of the fo'c'sle to find Alberto, and the wish to hear more of the secret conversation above. He had the presence of mind to realize that if he came out on deck at this moment he would be detected, and maybe not make it to Alberto or the others… so the logical conclusion was to find out as much as he could to pass on to *El Capitan*.

It had been momentarily quiet above, and Jose could smell the faint odour of cigarette smoke through the hatch. He mustered his courage and rose again to the small slit in the hatch opening, barely able to get his eyes high enough to make out the backs of the slouched men sitting beside him. He could see their profiles in the intermittent glow of the cigarettes they were smoking. Rivas and the Spaniard. He was right, but what were they doing? What were they talking about?

Finally, the Spaniard flicked his cigarette overboard and Jose could see the wide arc of its light before it disappeared.

"So where is the old man!" This was the Spaniard's voice, and although it was still whispered, it had an urgent and menacing tone. "How can we know he brought the old man and the money?"

"He must be on board with *El Capitan*...nobody saw them when they came aboard because it was raining and dark and he didn't speak to anyone. Everybody was below decks. But I saw the big black car leaving the wharf and the light is on in *El Capitan's* cabin. The old man will berth with *El Capitan.* He must be there. Pablo, look, I will go down and knock on *El Capitan's* door and ask if he and the gentleman want coffee or food before we depart."

"All right!" the Spaniard said audibly, flailing out with his arms as if impatient or disgusted with the conversation.

After a moment passed silently, the Spaniard said, again at a whisper, "Where is your pistol? Do you have it?"

"*Si*, Pablo, it is in my belt, covered with my jacket. It is ready."

"What about your cousin, does he have a weapon?"

"No, only a knife," Rivas whispered, "but he does not need one. He will use anything for a club. He is a fighter."

The Spaniard thought for a brief moment and then said, "Go make sure *El Capitan's* guest is aboard and report back to me."

Rivas rose with a silent nod of his head and started toward the stern of the *Juana Mercedes*. Jose noticed that the moon was rising and Rivas was now clear in the twilight as he made his way through the stacks of covered cargo strapped to the deck.

But then, unexpectedly, the loud, clear voice of *El Capitan* rang out:

"Come *muchachos*, all men on deck! Prepare to set sail!"

At that, Rivas froze in his steps amidships, and looked back toward Pablo Konig. The Spaniard's gaze had likewise turned to Rivas, but they were both without words. Then Jose bolted without thinking. He knew somehow that this may be his only opportunity to escape the fo'c'sle without being detected, so he jumped barefooted to the cabin sole, unlatched the fo'c'sle door and bounded up the companionway stairs to the deck hatch, which was propped partially open. Jose looked about in the darkness and seeing no movement, scuttled through the hatch and made his way down the deck on the opposite side of the ship from Rivas and the Spaniard, trying to stay obscured behind stacks of deck loaded cargo.

At the stern of the ship, *El Capitan* was talking to the uniformed harbour pilot about expected weather conditions, so Jose turned back to the galley to find Alberto, Angel Perez and Cristobal Gual coming out on deck laughing and talking loudly.

"There he is!" shouted Angel, motioning toward Jose, "He's been avoiding work since the sun went down! Come on Jose, we're finally going back to sea!"

The three of them pushed by Jose and continued toward *El Capitan's* position at the wheel. Jose grabbed at Alberto's sleeve and tried to talk to him, but Alberto, like the others, was enthralled with the animation and excitement of his shipmates and the prospect of beginning another cruise. He shook Jose's hand from his sleeve and then pulled Jose to the stern by his wrist along with the others.

The Spaniard and Antonio Rivas were already there now, watching *El Capitan* intently.

"Gentlemen! Gentlemen, be seated on the cabin top please. Attention to orders!"

El Capitan was at the wheel facing his crew, the starched harbour pilot standing beside him. When the crew had settled, he said:

"Men, this is *Capitan Garcia*. He will be our pilot until we are well in sight of the lighthouse at the channel entrance to *La Bahia de Jagua,* where he will depart on his own craft for return to *Cienfuegos*. His pilot boat has preceded us and will be on station awaiting our arrival. Since we have an onshore breeze to assist us, we will not need auxiliary power to depart the wharf. When our lines are loosened, Mr. Gual and Mr. Rivas will push us back along the wharf. Alberto, you will take the lines up and throw them aboard. Then you will come back aboard and help Jose store them properly. Once we are at the head of the wharf, put out the main jib and let the breeze turn us. The wind is light enough that we can then hoist the main and mizzen on our jibe to the south."

El Capitan paused a moment to scan the faces of his crew for questions, and then continued:

"Incidentally, gentlemen, we are to expect some weather from the northeast before we make harbour again. It is expected to be nasty, but not overwhelming. Since we will be in the lee of the island until we reach *Tunas*, the wind will not be able to push the seas high enough to harm us. I apologize for the inconvenience, but our employer and benefactor, *Senor Ramon Fernandez*, considers it urgent to have our cargo for his plantation outside *Tunas* by the end of the day tomorrow. Are there any questions?" He hesitated briefly, "...Thank you. Prepare to cast off."

The crew broke immediately, each to his own station. The circumstances had been such that Jose had been caught up in it, unable to slow Alberto long enough to relate the conversation he had overheard. So he took his position on the rail, opposite Alberto on the wharf, waiting to receive the tossed lines.

Almost as soon as they set sail the rain came again. It was driving in sheets, slashing the sails and washing the deck. *El Capitan* and the pilot had donned slickers and remained at the helm, with Cristobal Gual at post on the bow and Evans Rivers on the crosstrees of the foremast spotting for channel and lights through the wet darkness.

Angel Perez, Alberto and Jose retreated to the small galley of the *Juana Mercedes*, drying themselves briskly with dishrags that Angel retrieved from a cabinet. No sooner had they seated themselves than the Spaniard appeared in the companionway and took a place on the bench at the small galley table across from the two boys. He was dripping wet and made no effort to dry himself except to wipe his brow with his forearm sleeve. Angel's black iron potbellied stove was glowing in the corner with a tarnished metal pot of coffee boiling on top.

The Spaniard was in an unusually good mood it seemed to Jose: he smiled broadly, and his silver tooth gleamed in the scant light of the single oil lamp swinging above their heads in the galley.

"Angel, Angel! *Mi amigo!*" Pablo Konig was at his amiable best. "What will it take for me to get a cup of your best coffee?"

Angel Perez, who held no grudges toward any man, smiled broadly as well. Any compliment brought out the best in him, and he quickly replied, "The best will be yours, *Senor!"*

Angel took out four mugs from the pantry and poured them full of his opaque, black coffee from the stove. Then he served thick cream and sugar, which the boys added greedily to their cups. The Spaniard, on his part, sipped his coffee black, and still smiling, said to Angel: "*Mi amigo*, this is the best you have made yet!"

The ship's cook beamed in the light of his success, and took a seat on the tight bench beside Konig. "My place is but to serve, *mis amigos*!" he said, still smiling broadly.

Jose was uncomfortable and wanted to speak out, but he was afraid of the Spaniard. He glanced furtively at Alberto, but Alberto was engrossed in downing the creamy, sweet concoction he had made of Angel's coffee. So he turned his glance back to the Spaniard, who was obviously focused on Angel.

"So, Angel," Konig said, " have you yet taken some of this delightful coffee to our guest, *Senor Fernandez*?"

"No, *Senor*," Angel replied, "*pardoneme, por favor*, but *El Capitan* came aboard with him so quietly that I am yet to meet him. Then, of course, we set sail…and the rain…I am yet to meet him and serve his needs…"

"But *Senor Fernandez* is to buy the *Juana Mercedes* on this trip, am I right Angel?" Konig said, not meeting the eyes of the cook.

Angel Perez was quiet for a moment, caught off guard. "*Si, Senor,*" he said hesitantly, " but *El Capitan* tells me that we will all retain our jobs. *El Capitan* says that nothing will change, except that we will sail exclusively for *Senor Fernandez.* He is very wealthy, you know, and his plantations are all in need of the supplies we will deliver…"

"Yes, but what of the money?" Konig queried, "I hear that *Senor Fernandez* is to pay a full Twenty-Five Thousand American Dollars for the *Juana Mercedes…* am I right?"

The small galley was suddenly very quiet. Even Alberto had been diverted from his coffee, and raising his eyes to Angel's face, he silently awaited the response. Jose had pushed back in the corner of the galley bench and waited also, hardly breathing. After a brief hesitation, Angel stood up and began to scurry again around his galley. He said:

"Money! Finances! I know nothing of such matters! I am only the ship's cook, how could I know of such matters?"

"Jose, how could you not tell me this before we departed!" Alberto had jumped off his bunk in the darkness of the fo'c'sle and now held Jose tightly by his shoulders. The two of them had left the galley immediately after taking coffee with Angel and the Spaniard, and then in the quiet of the fo'c'sle Jose had related the particulars of the whispered conversation between Rivas and the Spaniard that he had overheard earlier.

"You should have told me this before we left, Jose! Why did you not tell me before we left?"

Alberto's urgent words cut Jose like a knife to his heart. He felt he had betrayed his friend—his brother—Alberto, and the rest of the crew as well. He said:

"Alberto, I had no chance. I tried but I had no chance to speak!"

The rain had blown over and the sky had opened to a million gleaming stars. The wind was brisk and steady, and the *Juana Mercedes*, all sails out, was running with the breeze, churning trails of sparkling phosphorescence in her salt wake.

El Capitan and the pilot were still tending the wheel, searching attentively for the port entrance channel light. Evans Rivers—*Rivas*—had already spotted it, and called it out from his vantage up in the crosstrees on the mainmast, but it was not yet visible to those below.

Shortly Rivers called out again, and off to starboard *El Capitan* picked up the running lights of the pilot boat. He could now easily see the channel light to exit the bay. He ordered the crew to shorten sail and assist the harbour pilot in his disembarkation aboard the swift auxiliary pilot sloop that was now coming up alongside the *Juana Mercedes* for the pickup. The transfer went perfectly, the pilot saluting *El Capitan* and then scrambling quickly over the lee side on to his sloop for departure.

The Spaniard was back out on deck in time to see the pilot boat turn out to starboard and disappear quickly into the darkness. In minutes, the *Juana Mercedes* was passing the channel entrance lighthouse to port, moving quickly into the open waters of the Caribbean. Shortly thereafter, *El Capitan* brought his vessel up into the wind on a broad reach to the east toward *Tunas* and turned the helm over to Konig. He gave instructions for Konig and Rivers to take the midnight watch, and he retired to his cabin without further comment.

By that time, Jose and Alberto were back on deck, hidden in the shadows. Alberto was intent on finding an opportunity to speak to *El Capitan* and relate what Jose had heard, but the companionway to the captain's cabin was no more than fifteen feet in front of the ship's wheel, where the Spaniard stood at watch.

Chapter 9

October 31, 1922
Caribbean Sea

Shortly after midnight, the weather had taken the anticipated turn for the worse. Unable to get past the Spaniard and Evans Rivers–*Rivas*—to *El Capitan's* cabin, the boys retreated to the fo'c'sle when the first heavy squall crashed in out of the northeast, it being only the advance warning for an even harder windstorm chasing behind the squall. There was too much deck cargo aboard to carry much canvas in this blast, so the main had been gathered in as soon as *Juana Mercedes* had made open water.

Even so, water was rolling over her decks as she crashed through the steadily rising seas. No matter, *El Capitan* had assured them that everything was battened down securely and the worst of this mess would pass by morning. So the boys lay quietly in their fo'c'sle bunks, unable to sleep. Between the raucous sounds of thundering seas over their heads and all around them, and the persistent, grinding snores of Cristobal Gual in the small fo'c'sle bunk under them, neither clear thinking nor conversation were options at the moment.

At the helm of the *Juana Mercedes*, the Spaniard and Rivers held station on either side of the wheel. The Spaniard was using a leather strap to help hold the helm steady in the buffeting wind and seas. Finally, when he felt the wind had steadied and she was holding her course, Konig leaned over to Rivers and said, "Get Ebanks. Now!"

Without hesitation, Rivers left the helm and started to move forward, clinging to a lifeline that had been hastily hung along the deck. In the midst of the stormy, overcast sky, the night was pitch black and the only glimmer of reality for the Spaniard came down to the muted glow of the compass light under cover of the ship's binnacle standing before him. Without it, he thought, they might as well be swirling mindlessly into the menacing black vortex of the surrounding sea.

It seemed only moments before Rivers, still following the lifeline, reappeared out of the darkness. This time, however, he was followed by Gideon Ebanks, who appeared to be surprisingly dry and unruffled. In fact, Ebanks had spent his evening in relative comfort nestling beneath a heavy oilcloth cover strapped over some cargo boxes arranged so as to make a quite comfortable stowaway space. He had managed to get some sleep and to belt down some rum, so he was in high spirits. This adventure, he had concluded, was to be his opportunity for money and glory—and long overdue it was in his view.

Once the three of them had gathered back around the helm, the Spaniard looked at Rivers and said, "Antonio, did you latch down the fo'c'sle?"

"I did, Pablo, and Giddy checked behind me to make sure. I don't know if any of them were awake, but I didn't hear anything."

"All right, *mis amigos*, here is what we will do now..."

El Capitan was still seated behind his desk—the chart table—at 1:30 a.m. when he heard a knock at his cabin door. At first, he was not sure he had heard anything at all through the symphony of sounds that the *Juana Mercedes* was offering up at the moment. High wind and rough seas had her singing with creaks and groans and the clanks, slams and rattles of equipment and tackle working on deck. It was only when the second knock sounded that he focused on his cabin door and shouted, "Enter!"

The cabin was almost completely dark. Only *El Capitan's* small, gimbaled desk lantern was lit, and it was turned down to a low flicker. It cast a dim circular light out over the chart table, but left the rest of the cabin dancing in dull shadows. Konig could hear his heart throbbing as he stepped over the threshold and pushed the cabin door closed behind him. *El Capitan* looked up at him only briefly and then continued studying the chart before him.

"What is it, Mr. Konig?" he said quietly.

Konig's eyes darted around the small cabin trying to adjust to the scant light. He had expected to find Ramon Fernandez sitting with the captain, or perhaps lying in a nearby bunk, but he could see no one else in the small cabin. He stammered slightly and said, "Sir, we thought you and your guest might like some coffee this foul evening."

"My guest?" the Captain responded quizzically. "Of what guest do you speak?"

Konig was at first dumbstruck, caught without words. His eyes now adjusted better to the dim light, and he confirmed for a certainty that there was no one else in the cabin besides himself and *El Capitan*. Then he panicked, his face flushed and he broke out into a sweat. Words would not come…

"Konig!" *El Capitan* snapped, "Are you ill?"

"Yes, sir." Konig mumbled. "May I sit sir?"

"Of course…take the chair across from me."

The *Juana Mercedes* was still bucking high wind and seas, and the combination of shock and rolling deck beneath his feet had made Konig faint, his stomach queasy. He sat down and waited a long moment quietly, hoping his nausea would pass.

Finally, *El Capitan* said bluntly, "Mr. Konig, why are you here?"

Konig squirmed in his chair and finally responded, "We were under the impression that you had a guest for this voyage, sir."

The Captain tapped the bowl of his pipe in his ashtray and then began to refill it out of a leather tobacco pouch. He was slow and deliberate forming his next words:

"Mr. Konig, who gave you the impression that I might have a guest for our voyage this evening?"

The Spaniard could think of no excuse, so he told the truth: "Sir, it is common knowledge on the docks in *Cienfuegos* that Senor Fernandez has arranged to buy the *Juana Mercedes* from you. It is said that she will serve his interests and plantations not only in Cuba, but also in *Isla del Pinos* and Central America. Surely you did not think that your own crew was too ignorant to hear and understand these rumours?"

El Capitan lit the fresh tobacco in his pipe and inhaled a long breath. Then he let it out softly across the chart table into Konig's face, where it clouded up in a haze.

Again, Konig felt sick and queasy, and turned his face away. *The son of a bitch, he's baiting me,* Konig thought, trying to remain calm.

"So, Mr. Konig, has rumour told you when this sale is to take place?"

Slowly but surely another different feeling was rising with the bile in Konig's stomach. That feeling was rage, as pure and simple as it must have been in the most ancient of mankind... Konig felt the heat in his face as it flushed.

"And the purchase price," said *El Capitan,* "does rumour also tell you the purchase price of my fine schooner?"

Finally Konig's rage outweighed his temerity and caution, and he pulled his M1911 Colt semiautomatic pistol from his coat pocket and pointed it squarely into the captain's face. He said in a throaty growl:

"I am told the price is Twenty-Five Thousand American Dollars, which should be burning a hole in your pocket as we speak!"

"Very good, indeed, Mr. Konig! Your facts are all straight, so far as they go."

A long moment passed with no further comment between the two men. Then, after another pull on his pipe, *El Capitan* blew another stream of smoke into Konig's face.

Holding his temper as best he could, Konig said, "So where is Senor Fernandez and where is the money?"

El Capitan leaned back in his chair and enjoyed the movement of his ship beneath him. *Strange*, he thought, *that my only anchor to the earth should be so transitory and unsteady. But, so it is for all of us, even in the best of times.*

"Pablo, my friend, the money is already in the bank for my wife and children, and *Senor* Fernandez was afraid to make this passage with bad weather predicted. So here we are, just you and me. No money, no *Senor* Fernandez."

"You're lying!" Konig screamed, for the first time losing complete control of his emotions. "The money is here! You're hiding it! Where is it?!"

At that same moment, a rogue wave hit the schooner's port quarter and she quivered with the thud and rush of water over her deck. *El Capitan* stood quickly and started to move around the chart table, but Konig recovered quickly and pushed the Colt back up to the Captain's face.

"Sit down, God Damn you!" Konig muttered, this time with a menace and hatred in his face that *El Capitan* had not seen before. At the same time, recovering his balance, Konig shuffled back to the cabin door and pulled it open. He snatched out in the dark companionway and jerked Evans Rivers into the cabin. Rivers stumbled at the threshold and almost fell face first into the cabin. Konig snatched him back up by the collar of his oilcloth poncho and raising his pistol again to the Captain's face said, "I told you to sit down you son of a bitch, I will kill you now if you don't!"

Capt. Bautista y Silviera realized for the first time—this instant—that his life and the fate of his ship and crew were in the hands of a madman. He sat down quietly and tried to think…

The Spaniard screamed at Rivers, "Search the cabin, now! Everything! Everywhere!"

Rivers set about the search in earnest, not wanting to test the Spaniard's threats.

El Capitan leaned back into his chair and struck a match to revive the tobacco in his pipe. After a quiet moment, he said thoughtfully, "Pablo, assume for a moment that I am telling the truth. Assume that the money is not aboard, as I am telling you. If that is true, you will have made the biggest mistake of your life. Mutiny…do you know the punishment for mutiny? And now, look at poor Rivas…you have him in on it too and there is—by my word to you—no money aboard the ship to be taken. A few dollars for port fees, that is all…"

"Shut up, goddamn you! Shut up! If you speak again before I ask I will kill you!"

By now Rivers was sweating profusely under his oilskin, yanking open drawers, boxes chests, looking under mattresses in a panicky quest to find the money…*it has to be here,* he thought, *that was the plan…it has to be here!*

Again a rogue wave ran over the *Juana Mercedes* on her port bow and she quivered with the first impact, then she rose abruptly and slammed down in the following slough. The sound of rushing seas thundering over her deck, breaking and moving deck loaded cargo brought the captain's cabin back into a brief silence. Streams of seawater were beginning to find their way into the ship through every hatch, crack, portlight and opening now, and rivulets of brine were running back and forth across the floor of the captain's cabin with every roll and wallow of the ship.

"Pablo," *El Capitan* said in a level voice, "is anyone sailing my ship or do you plan for her to go down with us?"

Before Konig could respond, Rivers rose to his feet and said, "Pablo, he is right, Giddy cannot hold the ship by himself. We must assist or we will all die!"

Then the beginnings of a wide grin started to spread across the Spaniard's face. He said to Rivers, "Antonio, where is that ancient, rusty pistol of yours? Get it out!"

Rivers reached compliantly beneath his poncho and pulled out the old Navy .45 Colt single action, staring down briefly at it in his hand.

"Now Antonio, explain to *El Capitan* that you will kill him if he doesn't tell you this minute where the money is."

Doing as he was told, Rivers raised his pistol slowly toward *El Capitan* and said, reluctantly, "Please, Sir. Tell us where the money is. We'll let you and the rest off the ship at the nearest land…this can be over with."

The Captain turned slightly to face Rivers. "Antonio, I have already explained to Mr. Konig. There is no treasure—no money—on the ship. The plans were changed at the last minute. Antonio, you must stop this madness while you still have a chance…"

This last statement convinced the Spaniard that either *El Capitan* was telling the truth or that he would never reveal where the money was hidden. *In either case*, Konig thought, *he is of no further use to me.* So he raised his pistol again and started firing.

Konig's first round struck *El Capitan* high in his torso and slammed him violently back against the cabin wall, but his victim rebounded immediately and lunged across the chart table with his arms outstretched in a vain attempt to grab the gun in his adversary's hand. At the same time, the Spaniard took a step back and fired twice more into *El Capitan's* body before he crashed to the floor at the Spaniard's feet. Then Konig shot him twice again in the back where he lay. The last two shots were unnecessary, for Juan Bautista y Silviera was dead when he hit the floor. Konig's second shot had found *El Capitan's* heart.

The deafening explosion of gunshots in the small cabin had so shocked and surprised Evans Rivers that he had stumbled backward and dropped the old Navy Colt from his hand. It clattered loudly on the cabin sole, adding to the noise and confusion.

Eyes wide, Rivers shouted out at the Spaniard:

"Pablo! Mother of God, Pablo! You have killed him! What are you doing!"

The Spaniard turned slowly then toward Rivers, his pistol still in his right hand.

"Shut up Rivas! Shut up!" he shouted back, raising his pistol as if he intended to shoot Rivers as well.

Evans Rivers cowered back into the corner, and then slumped down into a sitting position on a bunk behind him. He lowered his eyes again to see a pool of dark blood now forming under the body before him, some mixing with the seawater sloshing around on the cabin sole. He sunk his face in his hands and slowly shook his head.

Then Konig reached in his pocket and extracted a handful of bullets. He diverted his attention from Rivers momentarily and started reloading his weapon. Finally

Rivers looked back up at Konig and said in a shaky but controlled voice:

"Pablo, you said we wouldn't have to kill anyone. That was not part of the plan. We were just going to take the ship and the money and maroon them on some island…"

"The plan has changed Antonio," Konig replied simply, not looking up from the reloading task at hand. When he finished, he sat down on the bunk beside Rivers and put a consoling arm around his shoulders. In a confidential voice, Konig continued: "Now, Antonio, you must see that we have to kill the rest of them so that they can never tell what has happened here."

Rivers turned his head slowly to look directly into the Spaniard's eyes. Konig's face broke involuntarily into a smile. He was amused with the incredulous, astonished look on Rivers' face. Then his tension broke and he laughed outright at Rivers, and he said:

"Antonio, my friend, did you think we came here for a party? Now pick up your pistol and let's go."

Chapter 10

1:35 a.m.
October 31, 1922

Even with the furious sounds of the wind and seas raging all around them, Alberto and Jose could clearly hear the loud reports of gunshots being fired aboard the Juana Mercedes. In less than a breath they were both out of their bunks in the darkness trying to open the companionway door out of the fo'c'sle. When the door didn't immediately give way, Alberto leaped to one of the top bunks and tried to push open the overhead hatch, but it would not budge. He returned to his bunk and, scrambling briefly through his seabag, found matches and a candle, which he immediately lit and took down to the bottom bunk where Jose was now sitting quietly. Across from them in the other bottom bunk, the flickering light of the candle danced on the prone figure of Christobal Gual, who was still asleep and snoring noisily.

Alberto sat down on the bunk beside Jose. Trying to calm his young friend, he said, "You remember what I told you, Jose," motioning toward Cristobal, "this one sleeps like a stone. If the grim reaper comes tonight, someone will have to wake him up to die." If Jose found any humour in Alberto's comment, it didn't show in his solemn demeanor.

After some moments in silence, Jose said, "Alberto, I am sorry I didn't tell you sooner. I knew they had guns, I knew things were not right. I didn't think you would believe me…I didn't think anyone would believe me…" His voice trailed off and tears welled up in his eyes.

"Listen to me now, Jose, and never forget this no matter what happens. I am older than you and I know much more what should have been done. *El Capitan* had me swear to protect you and to teach you, and I have failed you both. Whatever has happened is my fault for not forcing my way to see *El Capitan* and warning him of the things you had seen and heard. So, whatever happens to us now, take it out of your mind that anything is your fault. The question is, what can we do now? Before we awaken Cristobal, we must have some idea, some plan…"

After a few moments, Alberto continued, "They have bolted us here in the fo'c'sle…that means they wanted to make sure we stay out of the way while they take over the ship. Why would they need us, they have their extra man aboard for extra help with the ship. They may plan to maroon us and take the ship and the money."

"But Alberto," Jose interrupted, "we know who they are. If they let us live, we will surely tell the police who they are. What if they kill us all? Then they can sail away and nobody will ever know what happened to us or the *Juana Mercedes*."

Alberto thought for a moment and said, "If they kill anyone, it will surely be me. The Spaniard hates me and he knows that I would kill him in a moment if I could. So here is what we will do…" Alberto reached in his pocket and pulled out his bone handled knife. He flicked it open several times and closed it back. Then he put the knife in Jose's hand and said, "Jose, do you know how to open and close my knife?"

Jose finally smiled slightly. "Of course Alberto, you have taught me to use it for many things."

"That is right, Jose, so here is what I want you to do. Hide my knife in your clothes where it will not be easily found. They will expect me to have a knife because I always carry one. If they come for us they will surely search me, but not you. Then, when the time is right, either you or me, or maybe both of us, can use it to escape."

"What about Cristobal, Alberto, can't he help us?"

Alberto thought for a moment and responded, "We must wake him now and tell him the whole story but you know him…he will not believe us. He will think we are afraid because of the storm. Besides, he cannot fight his own shadow. We will see what he says, but don't tell him about the knife!"

Shortly after the shooting, Konig and Rivers rejoined Ebanks at the helm. Despite lack of assistance on the wheel, Ebanks had held the schooner on course and was actually singing—or more like yelling—a profane seafaring ditty into the roaring wind. He laughed at the Spaniard and Rivers as they fumbled to take his place, and shouted out, "I thought you boys were going to leave me here to drive this boat straight to hell!" Then he laughed again and took a long pull of rum from his flask.

"Wha'd you boys do down there Evans…take on the whole damned Cuban Navy?" Ebanks raised his flask to Rivers as in a toast, and continued, "Shit! Ya fired enough shots to take out the whole goddamned crew, is that what you did?"

Rivers responded in words barely audible, "Pablo killed the captain."

Ebanks grinned slightly and sidled over beside the Spaniard, and put an arm around his shoulders. Then he put his face close enough to Konig for him to smell the liquor on Ebanks breath despite the raging wind engulfing them. Lopsided grin still on his face, Ebanks said "Damn boy! You changed the plan a little didn't ya?" Then he started laughing again.

Angel Perez had been startled from his sleep with the sound of gunshots. It took him only a moment to realize that the gunfire was coming from *El Capitan's* cabin and he leaped from his small cot in the galley and started to move in that direction. But then he stopped short… In a flash he recalled Jose's report of Rivas and his pistol. Yes, he told himself, he had taken the boy's words seriously, but he had not had the opportunity to report to *El Capitan* before departure. My God, he thought, what have I done?

Now Angel knew that he must shake the sleep from his head and think this situation through before barging out of the galley. Who fired the shots? Where is *El Capitan*? Does he need help, and what can I do…a mere cook? Unconsciously, Angel was backing up—away from the galley companionway. Still struggling with indecision, he instinctively opened one of his utility drawers and took out his huge honed meat cleaver and a large cutting knife. Then he shut off the oil lantern in the galley and crouched in a corner behind the galley door. His heart was beating wildly and he was sweating profusely. His mind—usually carefree—was abuzz with questions without answers. Although he did not realize it, he was caught up in the throes of a new life experience: *Terror*.

The Spaniard, Rivers and Ebanks were all still at the helm holding course, but seas and wind were still building, and the fully loaded *Juana Mercedes* was near submerging herself in every roller that hit her. By this time, the seas were not just washing over her deck, but literally burying them in walls of water that crashed over hatches and swirled about her masts. Stout though she was, the *Juana Mercedes* groaned and creaked with each rising sea that assaulted her.

In a slight lull between gusts, Ebanks yelled out in the Spaniard's face, "What you gon' do now Pablo, deliver your dead captain up to the dock in *Tunas de Zaza?!*"

Konig was enraged at this drunken, crazy Caymanian screaming in his face, but, the truth was, he didn't know what to do. He knew the three of them were capable of holding the *Juana Mercedes* on course, and unless she broke up in the storm they could make landfall back in Cuba. But what then? They had no money to run with, and a dead captain to explain, and a boatful of potential witnesses to hang them.

Then Ebanks—now deadly serious—yelled out to his cousin: "Evans, I ain't waitin' any longer. Tell that asshole we're gonna make a Cayman cross! If he shoots me, you know this bitch is goin' straight down to hell for sure! Get his ass out there on deck to help bring in some more sail. I'm takin' the helm!" Ebanks pushed the Spaniard roughly to the side, causing him to stumble and fall on his knees in the foaming seawater surging across the deck. Before Konig could react, Evans Rivers had him under one arm pulling him forward to help with the sails. Whatever else his cousin may be, Rivers knew Ebanks was the best seaman he had ever known.

Buffeted by the rising seas, wind screaming in the rigging, it was all Rivers and the Spaniard could do to hang on to shrouds, waiting for Ebanks to make his move at the helm. Ebanks, locked in mind and body to the ship's wheel, handled the *Juana Mercedes* as if he were a part of her, completely attuned to the elements around him, anticipating the right moment for his move. That moment came with a brief lull between rollers, and Ebanks jammed the helm down hard to pull the ship's bow up into the blistering wind, hoping for enough time to shorten sail and come around.

The *Juana Mercedes* first balked and wallowed, and then slowly, begrudgingly nosed around into the wind. Ebanks screamed out orders to bring the sails in, all but the main jib and the staysail. Rivers and Konig fought and cursed in the dark as they lowered and pulled the sails in and lashed them in a struggle against the gusting wind, sloshing sometimes knee deep in the seas running from time to time over the deck.

Ebanks kept the wheel over and slowly but surely the gale in the remaining foresails dragged the bow of the schooner around until she groaned and creaked, finally starting to run with the wind. Even with most of the sails in, the wind in her rigging continued a high, steady whine and her port shoulder set in as she began to gain speed, wind and seas now behind and driving her forward. This time, however, she was settled into a course of west southwest which, according to Ebanks' dead reckoning, would take them directly to the Cayman Islands.

Now with the fury of the storm driving the *Juana Mercedes* forward from astern, she settled in to a steady downwind run in concert with the seas and the elements.

Ebanks remained at the helm, instructing Konig and Rivers to relash and batten down some of the deck loaded cargo that had been torn away and scattered in the maelstrom. After that, he had them furl and stow sails and make fast all the deck lines and tackle in the sparse light of lanterns fetched from below decks.

All the while, Ebanks continued to sing, swigging periodically from his flask. *God*, he thought, *I'm good at this. Damn that Spanish bastard!*

Chapter 11

1:45 a.m.
October 31, 1922

Cristobal Gual was not at all amused being awakened from a sound sleep by Alberto and Jose. To make things worse, the stated reason for this intrusion was to listen to a frantic, outrageous story about gunshots and piracy and stowaways… *Ridiculous,* he thought, still groggy and rubbing his eyes in the candlelight. In his mind, the tale told by the boys made no sensc at all. Pure fantasy. But Cristobal was a good-hearted, friendly person, and he genuinely liked his young bunkmates—these boys trying to grow into manhood, without mothers, on the sea.

So he decided to humour them. He listened intently, trying to make sense of the fragmentary information spilling out before him in the candlelight. Outside, the wind was still screaming in the rigging and the schooner was bucking on a following sea, but none of that was alarming to Cristobal Gual. He was one of those rare persons, even among seamen, who had no fear of the sea. She was his life, his friend, and it simply never crossed his mind that she might take his life during one of her tantrums. It was not that Cristobal was a particularly brave or fearless person; it was simply that he was in his element—comfortable—when he was at sea.

After hearing out the disjointed story told by Alberto and Jose, Cristobal scratched the stubbled whiskers on his face thoughtfully.

"Listen, *muchachos*," he said, "it's just this stormy weather's got you on edge. Lightning and thunder, that's what you heard. The cabin door was locked by mistake when they battened down the hatches for the storm. Antonio will be here soon to find me for the change of watch. Why don't you put out that candle and get some sleep. I'll make sure you get a chance to talk to *El Capitan* first thing tomorrow morning, I promise."

Alberto and Jose exchanged glances. It was exactly as Alberto had said: Cristobal would never believe them. They were wasting their breath.

It was five minutes before two in the morning when Antonio Rivers pounded on the fo'c'sle door and yelled, "Cristobal! It's time for your watch at the wheel! Come on, and bring the boys with you to help clean up the mess on deck!"

Alberto and Jose had pushed back in the lower bunk and were still sitting quietly in the candlelight. They heard the outside latch slide open, but the door did not open.

Cristobal had not made it completely back into a sound sleep, so he rolled over and swung his feet onto the deck, cursing under his breath. He hoped Angel had coffee made in the galley. This night, he knew, would be a nasty one against the weather on deck. He pulled on his trousers and sat back down on his bunk to put on his boots. Then he noticed the boys, still awake in the lower bunk across from him.

"*Muchachos!*" he said, "Did you not hear your orders?"

The boys remained silent while he laced and tied his boots. Then he got up and pulled his oilcloth poncho out of the locker. "Come on, *muchachos*," he said, "You're not still afraid, are you?" He put his hand on the fo'c'sle door and pushed it slightly. It opened to his touch.

"You see *muchachos*," he said, "it is open as I told you it would be. Get your weather gear and let's go!" But still, the boys were unresponsive.

Cristobal had never had children, and he really didn't know how to handle young people. He simply felt, subconsciously, that friendship and camaraderie were inevitably the solution to all personal relationship issues. So again he sat down on his bunk and thoughtfully scratched his stubbly whiskers. Then he said, in a confidential tone:

"*Muchachos*, this is a very serious matter for a sailor. Did you know that refusal to obey orders is considered mutiny? I know this weather has you spooked, but we must obey *El Capitan's* orders."

"That was not *El Capitan*," Alberto responded quietly, "it was Antonio Rivas."

"But Alberto, you know all orders are set by *El Capitan*. And even if it was the Mate who gave the orders, we must obey him too when *El Capitan* is not on watch. And remember, *El Capitan* has a guest on board. He is probably below deck attending his guest through this ugly weather. So let us go and make him proud!"

Before the boys could make any response, Rivers' voice rang out again from the darkness of the fo'c'sle companionway, "Goddamit, Cristobal! Are you coming or not? *El Capitan* awaits your attendance at the helm!"

"*Uno momento, Antonio!*" Cristobal yelled back up the companionway. Then he looked back quickly at the boys, a slightly distressed and pleading look on his facc. Jose turned to look into Alberto's eyes, awaiting his instructions.

Finally, Alberto leaned over to Jose and whispered closc in his ear, "Jose, I don't think they will do you any harm, at least not yet. I'll make an excuse to stay here a few more minutes and then I'll sneak out to find you. If you can do it, come back and unlatch the fo'c'sle hatch so I can climb out that way…and keep my knife hidden as I have told you. *Comprende*?"

Jose nodded his understanding and moved out of the bunk to the locker for his weather gear. Alberto said:

"Cristobal, I truly do not feel well. Take Jose and give me a few more minutes. I will follow shortly. *El Capitan* will not mind me being late if I am sick."

Cristobal was relieved and replied, "*Muy bien, muchacho*, but don't take long. You know I have to deal with the asshole Spaniard as well. Let us go, Jose, quickly!" He had taken a kerosene lantern from the locker and lit it while Jose dressed and donned his slicker.

"You go ahead of me, Jose, so I can hold this lantern above to see the way."

Jose stepped out into the darkness of the fo'c'sle companionway and started to ascend the stairs with Cristobal, lantern held above their heads, following close behind.

Suddenly, in the midst of a blinding flash and thunderous resounding boom, Cristobal crashed backward down the companionway stairs and landed on his back with a thud at the entrance to the fo'c'sle. Somehow, the lantern that he was holding had landed alongside him without breaking. It was standing on the deck beside Cristobal's head and still cast a dim flickering light up the small stairwell.

The moments that followed would later play back in Alberto's mind as if they were hours apiece—horrible framed images in his mind that would never be forgotten:

When he heard the shot, Alberto had instantly lurched forward in the bottom bunk to look down at Cristobal's face staring up into nothingness at the fo'c'sle doorway. Cristobal's eyes were still wide, slightly rolled up, and his mouth was agape. There was a ragged black hole in his forehead and smatterings of brain, blood and bone fragments were sprayed across the companionway deck, bulkheads, stairwell and fo'c'sle floor. Glancing now up the stairs in the scant light, Alberto could see that

Cristobal's arms and legs were unnaturally askew on the stairs, and he was still as stone. Finally, at the head of the stairwell, barely visible in the last glow of the lantern was the face of a stranger. The man had a vacant look in his eyes and a quirky smile on his face. At the end of his outstretched arms, gripped tightly in both hands, was a big, black pistol pointing directly at Alberto's face.

In less than a heartbeat Alberto lunged across the doorway just as another shot rang out. Splintering wood exploded at the door frame where Alberto's face had been a split second before. In a single catlike movement Alberto grabbed the fo'c'sle door and slammed it shut, slapped the inside bolt latch home to lock the door and dove into Cristobal's bottom bunk, back pressed against the hull of the ship, where he hoped the next bullet could not find him.

But then all was quiet in the fo'c'sle. Dark and quiet.

Evans Rivers had a viselike grip on Jose's thin upper arm. He yanked the stumbling boy back along the wet deck toward the helm, holding on to a lifeline with his other hand. Rivers had not stayed to watch the rest of the scene unfold at the fo'c'sle companionway after he snatched Jose away from Cristobal Gual. He knew that Giddy had shot Cristobal point blank in the face, and he didn't want to see the rest. His cousin was drunk, he knew, and there was no telling what Giddy might do when he was that way. When the second shot rang out Rivers ducked instinctively but didn't stop.

Konig was at the helm now with only the faint binnacle light before him to throw a muted glow on his face. Rivers made his way back beside the Spaniard, but didn't release his lock on Jose's arm.

"So, what is the report?" the Spaniard said to Rivers nonchalantly.

"Gual is dead. Giddy shot him in the head. I don't know about the other boy. You'll have to ask Giddy about that."

"I'm starting to like your cousin, Antonio. I guess that goddamned old cannon of yours does work after all. Here, take the wheel while I light a cigarette. And let go of the little one…where the hell do you think he'll run away to? Your crazy cousin will kill him too if he goes back up forward. You think the boy's gonna jump overboard to feed the sharks? Let him go…we'll need him to help clean up the blood."

The Spaniard stepped aside and let Rivers replace him at the wheel. Jose slumped to a seated position on the deck beside them, his legs too weak with fear to support him. Konig was still smoking the same cigarette when Ebanks reappeared out of the darkness to join them at the helm. He took out his flask, took a long pull, and said to Konig in English, "Gimme a cigarette, Pablo."

Konig didn't feign stupidity this time. He took out his cigarettes and lighter and handed them to Ebanks, who quickly lit up and took a long drag. "I didn't kill the other boy…I missed him," he said matter-of-factly.

"I'll tell you what you *did* do Giddy," Rivers commented, "You goddamn near blew my eardrums out. Couldn't you wait until I had pulled this boy out of the way?"

"Damn you, cousin," Ebanks responded in a level voice. "If you weren't such a chickenshit you would have done it yourself. And the other boy, you told me yourself he has a knife and knows how to use it. Why don't you get your ass on back down there and take it from him yourself?"

"We weren't supposed to have to kill anyone anyway," Rivers grumbled, "that wasn't the plan in the first place."

"Well, you'll have to talk to your goddamned Spanish *amigo* here," Ebanks responded, indicating with his thumb toward Konig, "the two of you cooked up this shit stew to start with and now you're complainin' you forgot the biskits! I'm jus' doin' what I got to do now to get away with it. I've been in jail before and I don't plan on goin' back."

Chapter 12

3 a.m.
October 31, 1922

Angel Perez had been crouched for what seemed to be hours in the darkness of the galley. He clutched the meat cleaver in one hand and butcher knife in the other, his mind racing through interminable minutes—hours perhaps—of doubt about what was happening outside the small realm of his galley. The echo of two more gunshots still rang in his head, and he was frozen in place. He could not bring himself to move. He could hardly breathe.

In one moment, he thought that he was in the midst of a nightmare that he hoped might soon end. In the next, the clarity of what the deckboys had told him was true. *The Mate, that goddamned Konig, I should have known he was up to this...I should have warned El Capitan...and Rivas, that weasel, he does whatever the Mate tells him...*

Angel had thus been cramped in his dark corner of the galley for well over an hour. He had been a seaman for many years, and knew that the *Juana Mercedes* had taken a turn and was now following the wind to the southwest. He had no doubt that *El Capitan* could have and would have maintained course and brought them safely to *Tunas de Zaza* as scheduled, so now he knew that something had gone dreadfully wrong. Beyond that, he had only doubt and fear.

Not long after four o'clock in the morning Rivers shouted down into the galley, "Angel…*Angel!* Get your ass up here, we need coffee!"

Angel jerked upright, back pressed against the galley bulkhead behind him. He was too frightened to utter a word in response.

Less than a minute passed before Rivers, now screaming, cried, "*Angel, Goddamit, get your ass up and bring us some coffee!*"

Angel Perez was conditioned to the sea and his station and duties as cook and galleyman. Guilt immediately overwhelmed him for his assumed dereliction of duty, and he thought for a moment that perhaps this night—this Halloween night—and this storm and tempest had clouded his mind beyond reason. That instant of doubt caused him to utter a loud but hesitant response, "Where is *El Capitan*?"

Rivers responded immediately, "He is asleep with his guest. Mr. Konig is at the wheel. Now bring us some coffee!"

Angel Perez had never aspired to rise above his station aboard *Juana Mercedes*. His wages were small, but his family was privileged among the other *campesinos* living in and around his home in *San Felipe*. *El Capitan* had been good to him, and for the first time in his life perhaps, he would not back down.

"Damn you, Rivas!" he shouted, "What have you done *with El Capitan?!*"

To that there was no response.

Back on deck, Rivers and Konig were now huddled with the stranger that killed Cristobal, all speaking anxiously but in hushed tones. Jose knew that Cristobal and *El Capitan* were dead because he saw Cristobal shot in the face point blank, and the three conspirators were discussing the murders before him as if he were not there. Jose was nothing to them, he knew—less than nothing—as he sat quietly on deck near the helm, shivering with cold and fear. He could not hear what they were saying, but he knew they were discussing Angel Perez and what they would do with him because he heard Angel's name in fragments of indistinct conversation among them.

Their voices rose and fell in the crescendo of the wind and whipping rigging, and they cursed each other, and shook their heads, and even shook their fists at each other, but Jose already knew what they would do…they would kill him and Alberto and Angel just as they had killed *El Capitan* and Cristobal. Strangely, that reality had come to him immediately in their presence, much as if he had been a small bird crouched in the presence of vultures. It was an unspoken thing of nature, he knew that. They would continue killing in order to protect themselves.

Now they were talking more about Jose, making gestures toward him, grinning and finally nodding their heads in accord.

The Spaniard walked over to Jose, grabbed him under one arm and yanked him up off the deck. Rivers had taken the helm and was concentrating on the dim glow of the ship's compass in the binnacle. The stranger whose name Jose did not know, the one who had shot Cristobal, pulled the heavy black pistol back out of his belt from under his slicker. He said to Konig in words Jose did not understand, "What now Pablo, you want me to finish him too?"

"No! No yet!" the Spaniard blurted in garbled English. Then he said to Jose in a low growl, "*Muchacho*... Where is your beautiful silver crucifix now, *chico*, just when you need it the most?" The Spaniard grasped the chain at Jose's neck and pulled it, with silver cross suspended at the end, over Jose's head. "You will not be needing this anymore," he said, placing the chain over his own head and leaving the large shiny cross to dangle outside his jacket. "Besides," he said, grinning broadly, "it will look better on me anyway!"

Then Konig pulled his pistol from his pocket and pressed it painfully in the center of Jose's spine, pushing him toward the galley companionway. Jose stumbled over lines and deck debris, but the Spaniard's lock on his arm was like a steel band, the hard steel gun barrel urging him forward. Jose could not see him, but he knew the stranger was behind them, following the Spaniard, also with the big black pistol in hand.

When they were within a few feet of the galley door, they stopped, and the Spaniard crouched down on one knee partially behind Jose. Then he yelled out:

"*Angel*, come out immediately! This is the Mate! You will be charged with mutiny for disobeying your direct orders!"

Then came the response from Angel, shouted in a loud but discernibly fearful voice, "Damn you Konig! I take my orders from *El Capitan*. Where is *El Capitan*?"

Konig had now moved his free hand up to cover Jose's mouth so that he could not shout out, but the pistol barrel was still pressed firmly against his spine.

"*El Capitan* is presently indisposed, Angel. He is quietly awaiting departure from the ship. You see, I have taken the ship and will put you and the rest of the crew ashore at the first landfall. Neither you or *El Capitan* have any further choice in the matter."

"Damn you Konig, I have weapons! If you come in here, I will take your head off at the shoulders with my cleaver! You pig, I will kill you!"

Konig paused for a moment, and then shouted in a more patronizing voice, "Angel, you misunderstand my intentions! I simply want to put you and the others safely ashore so that I can be about my business...I mean you no harm."

"You are a liar, Pig! You swine, where is *El Capitan!?*"

"Angel, look, *El Capitan* is a big man. He had to be restrained for his own safety…you know that. How could I bring him here to persuade you? Look, I have the boy here—Jose—and he is safe and healthy…take a look for yourself."

For a few moments, all was quiet except the wind and passing seas.

Angel was still huddled in the darkness, his thoughts a scramble of doubt and uncertainty. If this were the truth, he told himself, they will put us ashore at the first landfall and this nightmare will be over. *After all, what gain do they have killing a mere cook and young boys? And El Capitan, perhaps he is well as the Spaniard says…*

Finally, a plan formed in Angel's mind. He screamed out, "Konig, you give me the boy, so I know he is safe, and we will wait here together in the galley until it is time to get off the ship…those are my terms!"

"That is fine, Angel, but first you must open the door to let him in the galley. He is here with me now!"

"Then let him speak out, tell him to let me know he is there!"

Konig gritted his teeth and pressed his pistol harder into Jose's spine. Left hand hard over Jose's mouth, the Spaniard pressed his mouth to Jose's ear and whispered in a snarl, "If you wish to live little one, you will tell Angel you are well and that you wish to come to him…"

Then he slipped his left hand from Jose's mouth down to his throat, and moved the hard barrel of his pistol up to the nape of Jose's neck, "Tell him now!"

At first, Jose thought that no voice could rise in his throat. What could he say…what could he do? The answer became clear. He could do nothing but what the Spaniard had ordered. Hesitantly he said, in the loudest voice he could muster, "Angel! Angel, it is me, Jose! I am well…I want to come to you…"

At that the Spaniard again crushed his left hand over Jose's mouth and glanced to his right where the stranger was crouched in the darkness, peering intently at the galley door.

"Konig!" Angel's voice now seemed a little more self-assured, "I'm going to open the galley door only a little. Have the boy reach his hand in slowly so that I know it is him…."

"That is fine, Angel…but open the door very slowly because it is dark and the boy must see when I release him…"

In the darkness of the galley, Angel laid his butcher knife carefully on the floor and moved quietly behind the galley door. He still wielded his meat cleaver in his right hand and used his now free left hand to lift the latch on the door and pull it slowly open to a crack.

Outside the galley door, with no warning, the night was lit with a kaleidoscope of light and sound and movement. Jose found himself slung to the deck, but with eyes open taking in each frame of horrible flashing light and the roar of gunshots assailing his ears. When the galley door had first opened slightly, Konig and the stranger began firing their pistols, at first into and through the door and then, as if in slow motion, at and into Angel Perez, whose meat cleaver slung back out of his hand as he sprawled backward, eyes wide with horror. Each flash of light and sound brought the sight of more blood splatter in the galley. Then, it was over. Jose heard the rattle of spent cartridges rolling on the deck and smelled the acrid scent of gunpowder. His ears were ringing and he felt numb and sick, but he was jerked on his feet fiercely and pushed, stumbling, back to the helm. There, he fell on the deck in a fetal position, eyes tightly shut, and covered his muted, ringing ears.

The first faint light of dawn came late under the heavy, roiling cloud cover. The rain had stopped, but the wind was still shrill in the rigging.

All had been quiet in the fo'c'sle since the last frenzied barrage of gunfire some hours earlier. To Alberto, time had lost any meaningful reference. He had been crouched in the fo'c'sle of the *Juana Mercedes* since the murder of Cristobal Gual, hardly moving, muscles tense with anticipation of what his move would be when they came for him. He had heard the mumbling voices, grunts and curses as they dragged Cristobal's body up the companionway stairs, but all else was quiet until the fusillade of gunfire that had cracked and reverberated from the galley area some time later.

Alberto had fear, but only of the unknown. He had no fear of the Spaniard, because he knew the Spaniard. He knew the Spaniard was a man, flesh and blood, and he knew the Spaniard was a coward, a jackal… an animal who could only feed in a pack. Now, he knew, the Spaniard had that help…the pack he needed to take the ship and perhaps the help he needed to kill them all. But how to stop it. He had no answer.

The fo'c'sle hatch was still bolted from the outside and there was no doubt he would be shot like Cristobal if he ventured out of the fo'c'sle companionway. So now, there was nothing to do but wait.

The muted daylight was a diffused grey through the fo'c'sle portlight when Alberto next heard movement on the deck. Then the voice of the Spaniard:

"*Negrito!* It is me, your friend Pablo. Are you there?"

"I am here, *cabron*," Alberto immediately replied, "waiting for you so I can cut your throat!"

"Alberto, this is such a shame that our relationship should come to this. Do you not appreciate the guidance of a man better than yourself? Think of the things that I have taught you!"

"You are a pig, Konig! You have taught me nothing but to hate you. Come in and get me you coward, I will tear your eyeballs out before you see me!"

"Now, Alberto, you must calm yourself. I have decided to give you the chance to show us if you are the man you think you are. How would you like that?"

"You're a liar and a pig, Konig. You think I trust you and your whores to let me have you by myself? It is you who is the fool."

"But Alberto, what choice do you have? You see, I have your little friend, Jose, right here beside me, and if you do not agree to come out and fight me, I will slit his throat and let you listen to him gurgle in his own blood. If you do come out and fight me, at least you and your little friend have a chance…if you beat me. So, what do you say?"

"How do I know that Jose is there…that you have not killed him?"

Konig shifted in his sitting position at the head of the fo'c'sle companionway and took his hand from Jose's mouth. He said loudly, smiling, "Jose! Tell your friend you are here with me and that I will cut your throat if he does not come out to fight!"

Jose stood silent and said nothing until the Spaniard slapped him violently across his face, causing him to buckle to his knees, holding his cheek in his hand.

"Talk to him now, little *amigo*," Konig said, "or you have taken your last breath."

"Alberto," Jose said, standing up straight and squaring his shoulders, "I am here. They will kill you if you come out, like they did the others…"

Konig struck Jose again, this time with his fist, knocking Jose to the deck in a crumpled ball.

"So you see, *Negrito*, you have no choice except to come out and fight me. So what will you do?"

Alberto felt suddenly hopeless, as if he had lost his right hand. He had given his knife to Jose, and didn't know if Konig had found it. He had no weapon—no chance—except perhaps an opportunity on the open deck that he knew so well… Then an idea came…

"*Cabron!* I will fight you only under one condition. That we fight with our bare hands. But I know you will not do that, because you are a coward!"

Rivers, who was crouching back behind Konig, heard the challenge and screamed back to Ebanks who was now at the wheel:

"Giddy! Giddy! You should hear this! The little bastard wants to fight Pablo with his bare hands! Can you believe that?"

Ebanks was in another world and could have cared less... He could literally smell and feel his homeland, the Cayman Islands, within reach. He was drunk and exhilarated. He was, for the first time in years, almost euphoric. Everything was fine, in his mind, and he had a ship of his own. The Spaniard was worthless but he could be dealt with. *Everything is finally coming around*, he thought…

"Giddy, Goddammit! Did you hear me? This little wild boy wants to fight Pablo bare handed!"

Ebanks was suddenly tired of the drama still playing itself out on the *Juana Mercedes.* He disliked the Spaniard intensely and had no stomach to watch him beat a thirteen year old boy to death for nothing but personal gratification. "Damn the Spaniard," he shouted back to his cousin, "I hope the boy cuts his balls off!"

Pablo Konig heard and understood Ebanks' comment, but he held strangely silent. He was beginning to understand this enigmatic Caymanian, Ebanks. *Perhaps*, he thought, *we are too much alike.*

Finally the Spaniard yelled to Alberto, "Never mind, *Negrito*, I cannot bring myself to kill an unarmed child. Stay down there until you starve!"

Then he turned and returned to the wheel, disgusted and ignoring Ebanks' cheerful whistling and insolent grin.

The pale light of a shrouded rising sun began to break the gloom in the east at about seven o'clock that morning. All had remained quiet aboard the *Juana Mercedes* since Alberto's earlier challenge to the Spaniard. The sea was still rough and grey, and the wind blew a thousand sprays off the tops of rising whitecaps. The sky was overcast and gloomy, but the wind had subsided significantly below the roar of the previous night.

Evans Rivers and Giddy Ebanks were rolled up in rain slickers, sleeping fitfully on the stern cabintop. Pablo Konig was at the wheel holding the course that Ebanks had given him an hour earlier, and Jose Martinez still sat quietly on the deck at his feet, shivering in the chill of the wet overcast.

The Spaniard was lost in thought, paying no attention to either the boy or his sleeping shipmates. He was consumed by desire to make his escape good, but could think of no way to do it without the continued assistance of the Caymanians. Then it came to him that he was more likely to succeed by playing to their egos rather than confronting them with his own demands. *After all*, he thought, smiling slightly, *I can always dump them when I know I'm safe*.

It was 10 o'clock when Ebanks awoke and shook his cousin. Evans Rivers rolled over on his back and looked up, sleepy confusion in his face.

"Get up cousin," Ebanks demanded, "our work ain't finished yet. We can't afford to get home with this boat all messed up and covered with blood." Then he looked over to the Spaniard and pointed a forefinger at him. "You, Pablo," he said, "*you* stay at the wheel."

Ebanks took a handful of Rivers' slicker at the shoulder and dragged him up into standing position. The two of them walked up to midships, where Ebanks turned to face his cousin and started talking to him in a low voice, pointing several times to the fo'c'sle companionway toward the bow of the ship. After several minutes Ebanks took off his boots and left them on the open deck. Then, barefooted, he crept quietly toward the fo'c'sle stairwell and motioned for Rivers to follow him.

When they got to the stairwell, Ebanks silently motioned Rivers down toward the fo'c'sle while Ebanks crept forward to hide behind the open companionway hatch. Rivers went only several steps down and yelled, "Alberto, listen to me! We mean you and the boy no harm. We're not far from land. You and the boy can take the dinghy. I put some food and water in it for you. We're all gonna be back at the ship's wheel. I'll send the boy back to you when you come up." Rivers then made a point to back heavily up the stairs in his boots and tromp back to the stern to join the Spaniard, who had by now grabbed Jose again and covered his mouth.

After that, the minutes seemed like hours for Ebanks. He didn't move, and he hardly breathed. It reminded him of the many times he had stowed away to make passage from one place to another. He smiled slightly to himself, amused at the thought. He was not the least bit ashamed to be a perennial stowaway. In fact, he was good at it. So he waited. Time was on his side.

It was almost an hour before Ebanks heard the inside latch on the fo'c'sle door slide open and the door swing free on its hinges. He knew the boy Alberto was checking out the companionway stairs to make sure it was clear. Then all was silent again. Ebanks could see only a small sliver of the companionway stairs through the crack at the hatch hinges. Now, more than ever, he knew that he must not be seen or anticipated…

Eventually, Ebanks saw the back of the boy's head as he slowly ascended the stairs. He could hear his heart pounding and wondered if the boy had unsheathed his knife. But there was no time to look back or change his mind. In a single swift motion, Ebanks swung his torso out around the hatch cover, his arm drawn back with the wooden club in it. Alberto sensed movement behind him but had only the split second it took to yield up the left side of his face as he looked around toward Ebanks. But the club found its mark before Alberto even saw it coming.

Alberto crumpled in the companionway, blood spewing from a huge open gap down the left side of his head and face.

Chapter 13

11:00 a.m.
October 31, 1922

Ebanks' blow to Alberto's head was so solid that the impact could easily be heard at the stern. Pablo Konig immediately started yelling joyfully and slung Jose off to the side where he stumbled and fell on the deck. Konig ordered Rivers to take the ship's helm and then he ran forward to congratulate Ebanks.

When he arrived at the fo'c'sle companionway, the Spaniard looked down to see Ebanks at the bottom of the stairs huddled over the sprawled, limp body of Alberto Monson. Blood had splattered and ran in vertical rivulets down the stairway paneling, and a pool of dark blood had formed at the foot of the stairs under Alberto's head.

"*Bueno! Bueno*!" Konig shouted down to Ebanks, who turned slowly back toward the Spaniard and said, "Get your ass down here and help me you goddamned chickenshit bastard!" The Spaniard understood and instantly heeded the Caymanian's command. He sensed that this was not a time to cross this crazy *Ingles*—he was wild with booze in his belly and fire in his eyes...not a good time to test his temper further.

Ebanks and Konig each took one of Alberto's arms and dragged him up the companionway stairs and back down the deck toward the helm. Alberto's head was lolling about and blood covered his face and the front of his shirt as he was dragged back to the stern of the *Juana*

Mercedes. Rivers was still at the helm holding tight to their compass course, and he forced himself not to look at the battered boy dragged within three feet of his station. Ebanks said to Konig, "Get him up and over the rail." As they lifted him, Alberto groaned and in an instant, Jose grabbed a life ring and dove over the stern rail at the same time Ebanks and Konig released Alberto's limp form to fall in the wake of the *Juana Mercedes*.

Jose crashed into the dark sea awkwardly, arms flailing, landing on his face and stomach and knocking the breath out of himself. As he descended in the brine the life ring wrenched his right arm back and turned him over under the surface. On reflex, he released the life ring, but then instantly began to flail around, instinctively trying to regain his hold on it. He surfaced gasping for air and then blowing salt water out of his nose and mouth.

The life ring was there beside him and he grabbed it, turning his body toward the hastily retreating *Juana Mercedes*. By the time he had rubbed his eyes enough to clear the salt water from them, the *Juana Mercedes* already looked small in the distance, flying as she was with the stormy northeast wind. Jose could see the Spaniard at the stern rail grasping a backstay and pointing at him. The Spaniard was screaming imperceptibly against the force of the wind, and Jose realized that he still had the pistol as he saw several pops of smoke emitting from the Spaniard's free hand. The reality of the shots being fired at him only came to Jose with the whack of a round into the swell in front of him and the plume of water that splashed from it.

Jose kicked his feet and retreated behind the life ring, exposing only enough of his head now to watch the continued retreat of the *Juana Mercedes*. He saw a large wave crash into the starboard bow of the schooner, sending a sheet of spray over her entire deck. She shuddered, lurched and rolled to port with the force of the impact. The Spaniard, still at the stern, lost his balance and crashed to the deck, almost falling over the rail. He tried to rise momentarily but slipped again and floundered on the wet deck. Then he was gone, along with the *Juana Mercedes*, into the rainy mist, running wildly on the wind.

It seemed to Jose that it had all been a nightmare, all happening in slow motion, and that he must now awake. But the reality that came to him then was the endless gray sea surrounding him, and the roar of the wind and frothing whitecaps on the dark swells upon which he was rising and falling. His first well formed, conscious thought after the disappearance of the *Juana Mercedes* was to remember that he must find Alberto. Although it seemed like an eternity, it had only been minutes since they had gone overboard. Jose sensed that they had probably hit the sea at the same time, and he immediately began to spin around the life ring, kicking with his feet, trying to spot his friend.

He was rising on the swells and falling in the troughs of the waves, making it virtually impossible to survey even the immediate sea around him. Then he found Alberto's name rising in his throat, coming out in screams of desperation. Almost immediately he heard his own name returning with Alberto's response, rising weakly above the din of the wind and waves surrounding them. Jose's heart leapt in his chest, and he was immediately swept up in a feeling of relief that Alberto could rescue them from the nightmare into which they had been forced.

In immediate reaction to Jose's cries, Alberto began swimming toward the sounds, barely maintaining consciousness from the blow he had suffered at the hands of Ebanks. Then he briefly spotted Jose in the life ring rising on a wave and then disappearing in the following trough. *I grew up in the waters of this sea*, he groggily told himself, *I can do this now*. He felt terribly sleepy and his peripheral vision was fading to gray. He swam on toward Jose, now feeling warm and secure in the dark swells, swimming easily even in the rough sea. Then, painlessly, everything turned to darkness.

Jose had been watching Alberto's strong strokes with an irrepressible feeling of joy, elated with the sense of security that came with knowing his older friend—his brother—would save them from this horror. Then, at no more than twenty feet away, Alberto simply stopped swimming. At first Jose was frozen with fear, and then he struggled momentarily with the thought that Alberto was teasing him. But then Alberto disappeared in the valley of a dark swell, floating face down in the water. Jose panicked and began flailing with his arms and legs, moving horribly slowly toward Alberto with the life ring.

Jose lost track of air and sea and beat violently against the elements to reach Alberto. He felt everything dragging him back—his clothes, his shoes, and the life ring… But he made it. Time stood still for the long moments before he seized Alberto under both of his arms and jerked him into an embrace, Jose inside the life ring and Alberto's arms and head lying over it. Jose coughed and choked on the seawater he had breathed, and then struggled to make sure Alberto's face was above water. Then he saw the open cut running from Alberto's left temple and across his left cheek, laid open to the bone. Although the wound was only barely bleeding now in the cold salt water, Alberto's flesh was swelling angrily from his lips all the way behind his left ear. His left eye was swollen to a bulging slit.

Finally, Jose truly felt lost. He was helpless, like a baby, a small speck in an endless sea. Then he began to sob, trying to shake Alberto out of death, riding up and then down the dark swells like any other floating debris tossed into the sea, soon to sink forever into the depths.

But then Alberto lurched and vomited seawater.

Pablo Konig had been caught off guard when young Jose Martinez snatched a life ring and jumped overboard. Konig was completely occupied and distracted with his attempt to murder the insolent *negrito* and then to get his unconscious body overboard, so the quiet white boy had momentarily escaped his attention. By the time Konig and Ebanks had gathered up the blood-spattered Alberto by his arms and his feet, and positioned to roll him over the stern rail, Jose's leap left them dumbfounded. They spontaneously let go of Alberto and he simply rolled off the rail and into the passing sea.

It took Konig a moment to gather his wits before he could curse his crew and jump for the wheel of the *Juana Mercedes*. Evans Rivers was still struggling with the helm, trying to keep the schooner upright in the full blast of the northeaster. His face was grey-white and his hands were frozen on the wheel as if for dear life. Giddy Ebanks continued his unsteady stance at the rail as if mesmerized by the unfolding events.

Then the Spaniard stopped and moved back to the stern rail, grabbing a backstay for support and digging in his pocket for his pistol. The weapon came out in a second and he spread his legs, trying to steady his aim against the movement of the deck beneath his feet. He spotted the small boy and life ring well behind him, raised the pistol and started firing randomly, unable to hold his target even a second at a time.

Then the *Juana Mercedes* hit an unusually large swell on her starboard quarter. She laboured up the wave and then crashed down in the slough below, sending brine and white spray over the entire deck. Konig went up with the schooner on the top of the swell and then felt the deck fall from under him when she fell back down in the trough and rolled away from the wind. From the high point of the crest Konig crashed back down against the stern rail and rolled on the wet deck, never letting go of the pistol.

When he tried to rise, the excruciating pain on his right side and the wet, rolling deck caused him to collapse. He knew immediately that he had broken ribs, and his fury rose in his throat. He rolled around to face Rivers, who was still struggling to hold the wheel. Konig raised the pistol in an effort to hold a point on Rivers' chest and screamed in Spanish, "Turn! Turn! Turn!" Rivers saw the gun pointed to his midsection and thought he would faint. He had no breath and he struggled to remain conscious.

"Pablo, No!... No! We cannot! We *cannot*! We have full sail! We cannot turn! She will go down under the wind!" Rivers flinched and turned a shoulder to Konig, believing that he would be shot and dead in the same moment that he spoke. But Konig held, glancing around to Giddy Ebanks, who had by then shrunken down against the stern rail, fedora hat pulled close over his eyes. *Why—why?* thought the Spaniard, *should I always be accompanied by incompetence?* Konig rolled back flat on the deck and clutched at his broken ribs, but only for a moment.

He pulled himself up and screamed to Rivers at the point of his pistol to hold the present course. Ebanks was watching from under the brim of his dripping hat, and Konig motioned him forward to help with the sails. After a struggle, they managed to douse the flying jib and reef the main, and the *Juana Mercedes* slowly came back under solid control of the helm. They did not know how much time had passed in the process, but Konig knew that it was too late in this weather to go back to try to find a young boy in this rough, endless sea. One boy was dead, he told himself, and the other would soon follow.

Alberto shuddered and coughed out the salt water in his lungs. He was groggy and did not know where he was, but he sensed Jose's arms around him and Jose's young voice coaxing him to response. He felt his face against the coarse white canvas covering of the life ring and the salt water splashing in his face. He lifted his head and tried vainly to focus. Then he decided complacently that he must sleep some more, and so he did.

With the realization that Alberto was still alive, Jose had become more or less comfortable in the life ring, riding the swells with Alberto's face held next to his in an effort to shelter against the wind and the breaking whitecaps coming off the mountainous crests. Alberto opened his eyes occasionally, and looked around, but Jose sensed that he saw nothing of the reality surrounding them. Then it became almost dark. The misty humidity enclosed them like a pressure cooker, and then the skies seemed as if they would burst.

The wind rose rampantly, and then subsided, and then the rain came in torrents. It was so intense that it stilled the wind and whipped down the surface of the sea, making it virtually flat but for the billions of droplets splattering on the surface. Jose lifted his face to the heavens and thought for a moment of Sister Elena. The deluge stung his eyelids and washed the salt from his face and he opened his mouth and drank in the cold, fresh water from a hand cupped at his lips. After drinking for himself, he cupped a hand at Alberto's lips and helped him to sip the fresh water from the sky.

Finally the rain and what was left of the wind subsided. The squall had passed and the day had become almost still and very overcast. It seemed to Jose that the whole earth had been reduced to the black water and grey sky that surrounded them. With Alberto drifting in and out of consciousness, Jose had little to think about but to keep them afloat and breathing. When he was overtaken by fright, Jose would talk to Alberto as if Alberto was listening, Jose telling the stories of their friendship and speculating on their adventures yet to come. So long as Alberto was with him, Jose knew he would survive. Occasionally, he would reach down into the right pocket of his canvas trousers just to find comfort in Alberto's bone handled knife resting there.

By the end of the day the sky was clearing and splashed over in orange to the west. But to his left, the south, Jose could see the dark outline of a low lying coast in the approaching darkness. He had no idea where they were, but he knew instinctively that they had to make landing on that distant shore in order to survive. Thankfully, the sea had flattened considerably and the overcast had broken into shards of clear blue and pink scattered amongst huge billowing dark clouds signaling the end of the passing front.

On the *Juana Mercedes*, the crisis had lapsed with the passing of the rainsquall, and the Spaniard, Ebanks and Rivers were all silent, acknowledging each other without speaking for several hours. With Ebanks at the helm, Rivers and Konig reset the sails and policed the deck. Konig went to the Captain's cabin and surveyed the damage—the blood spilled on the chart table, splattered and dragged across the cabin floor. It was all surreal, he thought, but *El Capitan* is gone and I am not. So much for the crew as well—they were dogs. He was elated, empowered with the realization that the *Juana Mercedes* was his and the remaining crew, for what they were worth, was his as well. Despite the throbbing pain in his right side, his lips curled into a smile, or perhaps a smirk, as he thought: Now *I* am *El Capitan.*

Chapter 14

6:30 p.m.
October 31, 1922

As the last rays of orange and yellow light died in the sea to their west, Jose and Alberto clung quietly to their life ring in unspoken fearful anticipation of the darkness falling over them. It was not just the dark, for neither of them had any inherent fear of the dark. It was, perhaps, the enormity of the darkness, not only coming in the sky above but also in the black sea that engulfed them and the huge dark spectres of swells that encircled and danced in shadows around them, slowly but surely drowning the last life and light from the descending sun.

For some time after the last mist of light faded, it seemed to Jose that the entire world was reduced to blackness, with the only sounds being that of his resounding heart and the soft whisper of the breeze in the silent swells surrounding him. Even the shadowy sight of distant low lying land that had earlier encouraged him was now gone, and there was only nothingness surrounding them.

It seemed also that Alberto was leaving him, no longer speaking, fading in and out of consciousness before the last light and now silent completely. Jose ventured close to him on the life ring occasionally just to hear his breath or to feel the warmth of it on his cheek. With the setting of the sun Jose felt a marked decrease in the water temperature, and he began to feel chilled and began to shiver occasionally. He shifted in the life ring as best he could and huddled with Alberto to share warmth. His legs and feet were cold despite his canvas trousers and heavy leather shoes, the weight of which began to drag and pull at him.

After what seemed an eternity of pitch blackness, the moon and stars started to break out among the scattering dark clouds, finally casting a misty aura of light over the sea surrounding them. Jose was filled with new encouragement in the dim but rising light of the moon and stars, and began to kick his legs and feet in an effort to stave off the shuddering chills that had almost overtaken him completely. Occasionally, he would speak to Alberto, giving him encouragement and making sure that his breath and his grip on the life ring were still firm. And as the endless minutes and hours passed, the clouds and overcast passed as well, and the sea continued to lay down until Jose could see the long shaft of the moon's broken reflection across the water, interrupted only occasionally by the intermittent shadows of retreating clouds.

As the hours of darkness fled in slow motion, Jose drifted into a sleepy euphoria. Between the chill in his body, and the exhaustion and shock of the events of the preceding night he slipped into moments—or even minutes—he could not tell, of dreamy escape. He occasionally jerked backed to conscioness only to slowly drift back into the same catatonic state. In a lucid moment he thought wearily that he must give up his grip on the life ring so that he could float lazily into the comfort of sleep. But each time he snapped back, he saw Alberto in the reflection of the moon, face damaged and swollen almost beyond recognition, barely holding on, and he knew that he must not fail Alberto. So he held fiercely, determined not to let his brother down.

At some time during what seemed like the endless dream of that night, Jose sensed the trace of a change in the sea. He stirred from his complacency and began again to look around him and listen. At first, he saw nothing, but he continued to concentrate and he knew there had been a change, but he could not distinguish it. Eventually, he realized in the darkness that the change in the sea around him was only the sound of the sea itself. As he listened he heard a muted but steady roar much like the sound in the conch shell that Alberto had put to his ear in *Batabano*. And ever so steadily, it had grown from a whisper to an audible hiss, like the sound of breaking surf, rising on the light breeze in the darkness.

And then he saw it: Now breaking the sparkling track of the moon over the water was a moonlit halo of light reflecting from the canopy of not so distant treetops, and the white frothy reflection of the moon on even closer breaking surf. He knew immediately that it was land, probably that which he had seen just before the preceding nightfall, and his energy and excitement were immediately restored in a rush of adrenaline. He yelled out to Alberto and shook his arm, but got no response.

"Alberto, you must wake up!" This time he screamed and Alberto stirred but did not open his eyes.

Jose moved beside Alberto and put an arm around his shoulders. With their faces only inches apart, Jose again shook Alberto and yelled in his face, much like a small child trying to wake his father. “Alberto, please, you must wake up and help me swim! It is land! I cannot make it without your help!”

Alberto’s eyes fluttered and he pulled himself up slightly, looking around dimly as if he had awakened in a strange place, almost surprised, with no memory of how he had gotten there. His face was horribly swollen and distorted, and he could not seem to find words to speak, but Jose saw his recognition of the moonlight on the treetops of nearby land. Without speaking, Alberto looped his left arm around the life ring and started to swim with his right arm and feet. Jose fell in time with him, clinging to the life ring and kicking his feet with all the strength he could muster.

In less than half an hour—although it seemed hours to Jose—their exhausted efforts together with the black rolling swells that were lifting and pushing them, had brought them close to the crashing surf. Through the broad shaft of the moon’s reflection, Jose could see the clear green and frothy white crests of the waves, and the rising spray and mist as they crashed just beyond his vision. The sound of the sea had risen to an ominous roar and the valleys between the rollers were getting deeper, with the undertow from the surf pulling and tugging at their legs as they clung desperately to the life ring.

It was only the very moment they were tossed upon the reef that they saw the field of black crags rising just above the surface of the churning water. The crest of a breaking wave finally carried them crashing down into the foam and razor sharp limestone rock and live coral of the reef. They kicked and struggled to maintain a foothold, but with each effort came the frothing tail of the wave and the rise of the next wave, tossing them down again into the horrible, cutting maze of hateful pinnacles, each of them banging and scraping against the submerged alien surfaces with every new push of the breaking surf. The low tide and darkness had combined to make it impossible to negotiate the reef by floating on the surface, so the boys struggled blindly to get away from the surf.

Finally they found themselves in flat water inside the reef, still clutching the life ring desperately between them. Again there was no bottom below them, but they could see the soft aura of misty moonlight in the palm tops and thick brush not far across the still water of the lagoon. Silently, now, they kicked and struggled until they found a sandy bottom beneath their feet, and they pushed on up in the darkness until they came to rest, backs down on a wide strand of white sand, the life ring still between them. Still without speaking, they fell into exhausted unconsciousness.

The clear, bluegreen water of the lagoon was gently lapping at his feet when Jose awoke. During the night he had curled into a fetal position and nudged a comfortable nest into the sand, but when he sat up he had sand in his mouth and hair and on his face, so he spat and brushed his eyes. He tried to open his eyes, but it was so bright that he raised his right forearm to cover them, squinting to adjust to the sunlight.

At first he was confused and disoriented. He couldn't remember where he might be or what he was doing here, but a quick glance around at Alberto still sleeping and the life ring between them brought the whole horrible memory back to him in a rush. Quickly he closed his eyes again and put his face in his hands, but when he did, he tasted the salty grit in his mouth and he heard the sound of the surf on the reef, and he realized that he was alive. Perhaps it had all been a bad dream, a nightmare to be sure, but he was alive here with Alberto and it was over. Suddenly he felt elated, like he and Alberto were on a new adventure, and it was just starting. So he opened his eyes again and looked back out over the lagoon.

In the bright morning sun, the sky was a spotless, seamless light blue expanse running down to a dark blue horizon in the sea. The ocean ran in royal blue from the horizon to the reef, where it churned white for a moment and then transformed into a rainbow of greens and blues until it lapped, crystal clear, on the white sand of the beach at his feet. He looked down and smiled to see his soggy, scuffed leather shoes still on his feet. But then he saw that his canvas trousers were in tatters, and his indigo cotton shirt was little more than a rag draped on his shoulders.

Beneath these rags, he also realized, were cuts and scrapes and bruises, and for the first time he became aware of pain. His whole body was sore and stiff and burning with salt and sand in his wounds…but still he felt good. He was alive…and he felt sure *El Capitan* would be proud of them. So slowly, painfully, he stood up and began to brush away the sand that covered him. Then he looked around at the beautiful white beach with its armies of sand crabs scurrying about their business, only stopping occasionally to note his presence. At the top of the beach were coconut palms and huge sea grape trees and beyond, a tangle of brush and brambles beyond his recognition. And nowhere—anywhere—was there any sign of human life.

This last revelation caused Jose immediately to want to wake up Alberto, for suddenly he felt very small and insecure in this new world that they had washed up in, and he needed Alberto's companionship. So he walked around to Alberto's side and dropped down to his knees in the sand and looked at his sleeping friend. It was only then that the enormity of Alberto's injuries became apparent to him. Alberto's face, at least the left side of it, was still swollen beyond recognition, and now his cut was laid full open and oozing fluid. He had taken on a grayish pallor in his skin, and he was burning with fever when Jose touched his brow.

Now also Alberto's feet, legs and trunk were covered with cuts and abrasions from the reef. He had only his canvas shorts on when he was thrown overboard by Ebanks, so he had had no protection at all from the sea and the reef. Many of the cuts on Alberto's body had bled, but were now obscured by crusts of sand and congealed blood. At first, Jose had not seen these wounds against the dark texture of Alberto's skin and the covering of sand, but now he became frightened. Whether it was so or not, Jose was convinced that he could not survive without his friend—his brother. So again he put his face in his hands, and this time he cried.

Jose might have sat terrified in that same position until they both had starved—were it not for the rising tide. Slowly, but as surely as God made the earth and the seas, the tide rose up to Jose's knees and began to lap around Alberto's body. Alberto stirred and groaned unintelligibly, and Jose snapped back to reality and realized the urgent need to move his companion off the beach and out of harm's way. So he got up and came around behind Alberto's head. He squatted and put his arms under Alberto's armpits and stood up, lifting only his friend's upper body to a sitting position. When Jose tried to drag him, however, he did not have the strength. But when he fell back with his arms around Alberto's chest, Alberto moved a few inches back with him. So, stubbornly, deliberately, Jose continued to wrap his arms around Alberto's chest, then stand up, and then fall backward, using his body weight to move Alberto inches at a time up the beach and finally under the fringing palms in the shade.

Exhausted, Jose sat puffing at Alberto's head without any idea what he would do next. But then Alberto's eyes fluttered and his head lolled over and he tried to speak. His mouth and throat were so dry that all he could manage was a raspy choking sound, and Jose sensed immediately that he must have water. It took Jose only a moment to realize that there were green coconuts scattered on the ground all about them, and that he had Alberto's bone handled knife in his pocket.

In no more than five minutes, Jose had hacked a hole in a coconut—just as Alberto had taught him—and was holding up Alberto's head, letting the liquid from the coconut trickle over Alberto's parted lips. Again

Alberto's eyes opened and fluttered, and he began to drink down the coconut milk steadily until it was gone. Jose then laid Alberto's head back and found another coconut. Jose carved a hole in it, and gave Alberto more of the fresh liquid until he ceased drinking. Only then did Jose drink the rest and open another to slake his own thirst. Jose then began cracking open the same coconuts and cutting out the pure white meat to eat.

Not long after he had taken the coconut milk, Alberto began to stir and look around him. He could not open his left eye, and he had difficulty getting his right eye to focus. He could see Jose on his knees beside him and the blur of swaying palms above. He had no memory of where he was or how he and Jose had gotten there. He started to sit up, but everything went white with the explosion of pain in his head.

Now, with his eyes both closed, he began to focus entirely on himself—his own body. His head was throbbing in pain with each pulse of his heart, and the left side of his face and head was so swollen that it felt alien, as if it were not really a part of his body. The pain in his head was so great that he could hardly feel the rest of his body, but when he tried to move slightly he felt as if every muscle were stone bruised. During his thirteen years he had been cut, bruised and battered from time to time, but he knew instinctively that this was different. For the first time in his young life, he sensed that his body might be damaged beyond repair.

He contemplated that thought for a long moment before he opened his right eye again and attempted to focus on Jose.

"Where are we little brother?" he whispered.

"Alberto, are you alright? Will you be alright?" Jose responded with urgency in his frightened voice.

Then Alberto heard *El Capitan's* voice in his mind: *Alberto, this boy will be your ward—your responsibility. You will teach him and you will protect him like I have done for you, do you understand?* Alberto tried to smile but the pain in his swollen and lacerated lip stopped him short.

"Jose, I will be fine," he said in a weak voice, hardly moving his lips, "but you must listen to me…you must do as I say…do you understand?"

"*Si*, Alberto, *Si*…what should I do? What can I do?"

"Listen to me carefully. First tell me where we are."

"I do not know Alberto, honestly, we washed up on a beach last night...you were hurt again on the reef… but I do not know where we are…"

"Alright, Jose, do not be afraid. Tell me what happened when we were fighting on the ship."

"When you came out to fight the Spaniard, the man they called Ebanks hit you from behind with a board and they threw you in the sea. I went in after you, but I had a life ring and we held on to it until we washed ashore last night. Do you not remember this Alberto? We did it together, you and me…we did it together!"

Alberto laid his head back and tried to think, tried to unscramble what had happened, but he could not. The pain in his head was too great. He vaguely remembered his last confrontation with the Spaniard, but nothing more.

"But the others, Jose, where are the others? Where is *El Capitan?*"

Jose bent his head down and closed his eyes. He was still on his knees beside Alberto, but the bloody memory of what had happened on the *Juana Mercedes* had suddenly muted him.

Alberto reached out and snatched the sleeve of Jose's tattered shirt, "Jose, where is *El Capitan!*"

"He is dead, Alberto. They all are dead."

Alberto's eyes were still closed. He had heard Jose's words, but it was all too incomprehensible to fathom. He felt very tired again, and he drifted back into unconsciousness.

Chapter 15

George Town, Grand Cayman
November 1, 1922

In 1922, the Cayman Islands were virtually unknown to the outside world, being little more than three small, isolated, low-lying limestone rock platforms, graced with sandy beaches and coral lagoons, floating lazily in an isolated reach of the Caribbean Sea. To a mariner, these Islands are the three highest peaks of the Cayman Ridge, a range of submarine mountains extending from the Sierra Maestra mountain range of Cuba, and running west southwest in the direction of British Honduras, with only three weathered tips of the submerged mountains emerging above sea level. The submarine slopes around the Caymans are steep, dropping immediately to great depths just beyond the protective coral reef perimeters surrounding each of the islands.

The Bartlett Deep, eighteen miles south of Grand Cayman, descends to a depth of 20,000 feet extending in an east and west direction from the Gulf of Honduras to Western Haiti. East of the Caymans is the Cayman Trench, which at more than four miles deep, is the deepest water in the Caribbean.

Grand Cayman is the largest of the three Cayman Islands, being over 21 miles long and four miles wide, and is separated from the two smaller Caymans by 70 miles of open sea, which reaches a depth of 7000 feet between Grand Cayman and her sister islands. Cayman Brac and Little Cayman lie to the east northeast of Grand Cayman, and are separated from each other by only 5 miles of open water. Even so, in 1922, the separation between the remote smaller islands could have been a thousand miles even to many of the inhabitants, since many had never set foot off island, or in some cases, outside of their own isolated communities, during their lifetime.

The largest community in the Cayman Islands and the center of government was George Town, located on the southwest coast of Grand Cayman. There, a single Commissioner appointed by the British Government resided. He served under the immediate direction and control of the British territorial Governor in Jamaica. The Cayman Islands had been colonized by the British in the 18th century from Jamaica, and had been administered by Jamaica since 1863 as a British Crown Colony. But in 1922, being completely isolated and of no recognizable strategic value to the Crown, the Caymans were largely forgotten and left to their own devices for government and subsistence.

The only communication the Caymans had with Cuba, Jamaica, the coasts of Central America or the southern ports of the United States was by occasional trading schooner, or by the belated news of world affairs brought back to the islands by the crews of local turtling schooners. Communication between Grand Cayman and her sister islands, Cayman Brac and Little Cayman was virtually non-existent. Only sporadic visits to the smaller islands by Grand Cayman sailing traders disseminated news of the outside world, and the smaller islands were left on their own without significant interest or interference from the government in George Town.

In 1922, the Cayman Islands had no radio or wireless communications with the outside world, no newspapers, nor any ship-to-ship or ship-to-shore communications. And because there was such infrequent and unreliable news from abroad, most Caymanians lived their lives with little concern or interest in what was happening in the rest of the world. So, inevitably, George Town was a sleepy, slow paced tropical community. Her inhabitants, generally, were industrious, devout, gentle Christian souls, most with family histories dating back several generations of life and isolation in Cayman. To the extent that the citizens were more than normally naïve to the ways of the outside world, the trait harkened back to several generations of simple honesty and innocence in the way that they lived their everyday lives.

At three-thirty on the afternoon of November 1, 1922, the *Juana Mercedes* rounded the northwest point of Grand Cayman about a mile offshore and still under full sail in the light breeze. At that same moment, Albert E. Panton was sitting in his office on the upper floor of the Government House on Elgin Avenue in George Town. The stormy weather of the preceding several days had passed and the clouds had dissipated, leaving the bright sun and a cooling breeze to make the afternoon one for daydreaming.

As he looked out his open second storey window toward Hog Stye Bay, Panton watched the several local catboats working the bright azure water offshore for their catch, but the waterfront market was silent and he couldn't see anyone at work or moving in the sunlight. *Oh, well, it was that kind of day*, he thought, *not one to be working anyway.*

Reluctantly, Panton averted his gaze from the bay front back to the scattered papers on the scuffed wooden desk before him. For a number of years, Mr. Panton had been the local British Government Agent for Customs and Immigration, and he took his position quite seriously and responsibly. He knew that His Majesty's appointed British Commissioner, Hon. Hugh Hutchings, was the figurehead of British rule in the Cayman Islands at the time, but just as realistically he knew that he, as top civilian employee of the government, made Cayman government work on a day-to-day basis in the Cayman Islands. He was a local, born and raised, with impeccable Cayman roots and contacts, and he appreciated that the weight and responsibility of the local Government rested on his shoulders. Not only was he the supervisor of customs and immigration, but also from time to time Justice of the Peace, Postmaster, Tax Assessor and Tax Collector, and for all practical purposes, the chief financial officer of the Cayman Islands. So he forced himself once again to focus his attention on the papers before him, back to his duties.

Some moments later, Mr. Panton jerked to immediate attention when he heard a long, shrill cry from the bayfront: "Sa-a-i-l h-o-o-o-o!" The first scream sounded like the voice of a young boy, but soon everyone within earshot in George Town picked it up until the news of a pending arrival had risen to an almost eerie cacophony of shouting voices. With this traditional first news of the arrival of a ship, the entire community of George Town had come alive. Everyone within earshot of the news was stepping out from homes and shops and looking with anticipation toward Hog Stye Bay. The townspeople were dropping whatever they had been doing and were wandering, as if mesmerized, out into the sandy marl streets and toward the bay.

Mr. Panton, "Bertie" as his close friends called him, stood up and stepped back to the hat tree in the corner of his small office. He took down his brown double-breasted suit coat and put it on, and then took his cream-colored fedora hat and placed it on his head. Then he picked up his Customs and Entry Journal, walked out of his office door without closing it, and walked down the hall and down the stairs into the bright sunlight of Elgin Avenue. It was only a short walk from the Government House to Shedden Road and then down to the bayfront, but within moments he felt beads of perspiration breaking out on his face. *No matter,* he thought, *it is simply one of the disadvantages of a responsible Government position.* From the beginnings of his career efforts, Mr. Panton had felt that the weight of his responsibilities required formality in dress and demeanor, notwithstanding the general informality of the Cayman community. He strode briskly past the white frame Court House facing the bayfront down to the Hog Stye barcedere and stood on the limestone rock formation overlooking the bay.

He immediately focused on sails, not much more than a white mirage off the distant North West Point, apparently on a turn toward George Town. While Panton stood quietly watching the approach of the vessel, townspeople gathered on the jagged bayfront limestone formations called ironshore, but Panton disregarded the gathering crowd assembling along the shores around him. The few stores in the town had not actually closed, but they were left with few attendants, and little if any business, as almost everyone in the small community gathered by the sea awaiting anxiously the news, mail, goods or loved ones who may be returning under the distant sails.

At that time in the history of Cayman, almost all goods, mail and returning seamen and visitors arriving on the island came on native Cayman-built schooners. Normally they were returning from various regular ports of call—Tampa, Florida, direct or by way of Nueva Gerona, Isle of Pines; Kingston or Montego Bay, Jamaica; Mobile, Alabama; Cayman Brac or Little Cayman; ports in Belize, Nicaragua, Honduras, or Costa Rica; or from the Banks off Central America where Caymanian schooners went to catch and harvest turtle. It was only very infrequently that a foreign flag vessel, even if passing close by the islands, would take the time to divert from its regularly scheduled ports of call. The dates and times for returning local schooners were purely speculative, and sometimes totally unexpected.

So it was not necessarily unusual that on this bright, sleepy afternoon, Bertie Panton would be required to perform his customs and immigration inspection and assess whatever small tariffs might apply in the circumstances. It was his standard protocol to board every arriving ship before anyone could disembark, even though the clearing process was normally leisurely and informal, since Mr. Panton knew every local seaman and vessel. Any unknown passenger had to present identification, a birth certificate or a passport, but foreign visitors going ashore on the island were exceptionally rare, so identification was not normally an issue in the process.

Ebanks and Rivers doused and stowed all the sails except a small staysail for steerage when they reached Hog Stye Bay. Then Giddy Ebanks took the helm of the *Juana Mercedes* from the Spaniard, who stepped aside without protest. At the perfect moment, Ebanks brought her up easily into the breeze and stalled the ship no more than a hundred yards offshore. Without any command, Evans Rivers let go the anchor and watched it fall through the crystalline water of Hog Stye Bay. The anchor went straight down and set itself on the bottom among the litter of old rusted anchors, chains and other lost and discarded ships' tackle and timbers that marked the passage of the past several centuries of maritime traffic and commerce in George Town. The Spaniard stood at the forepeak studying the village of George Town for the first time, becoming increasingly concerned as he realized that virtually all of the inhabitants of the settlement had turned out shoreside to watch their arrival.

After Rivers had let out and adjusted the scope of the anchor line, he and the Spaniard both walked back to the stern and stood beside Ebanks at the wheel. Trying to maintain his composure, the Spaniard said to Ebanks and Rivers under his breath, "Goddamn you both! This attention is the last thing we need. You told me it would be safe here."

"We know these people, Pablo, and they know us," responded Rivers in Spanish, "we will be safe here until we sail for Mexico. They know nothing of the *Juana Mercedes.*" But as he heard his own words, Evans Rivers felt a sudden dread and emptiness rise in his breast, and he turned and walked back up the deck to mask his emotions.

The Spaniard and Ebanks stayed at the wheel and watched intently as several men held a small launch alongside the rocky shore. A well dressed gentleman in a pressed brown suit and crème fedora hat climbed aboard the launch and took a seat on the middle bench. The others cast off and began to row her out to the *Juana Mercedes.* Ebanks took the flask out of his back pocket and took a long pull on it. "Bertie Panton," he said simply.

It seemed an eternity to Rivers before the government launch reached the side of the *Juana Mercedes.* Even the crowd that had gathered on the shore had now fallen completely silent, waiting curiously to discover why this unknown ship was here and who was aboard. In most cases, arriving vessels in George Town were Caymanian, with their neighbors and loved ones aboard. But this schooner was unknown to them, and one by one the spectators had fallen silent as they realized she was a complete stranger.

When the launch came alongside the *Juana Mercedes*, one of the men aboard tied off her bow line, and they all helped Mr. Panton climb aboard the schooner. Evans Rivers stepped up to the rail and lent a hand to help Mr. Panton aboard. Then, his crewmen followed Mr. Panton out of the launch and onto the deck of the schooner.

Bertie Panton was immediately surprised to find Evans Rivers and Gideon Ebanks aboard the visiting schooner. He had known them since their boyhood, knew they were cousins to each other and that they had grown up together at West End. In fact, Inspector Yates, one of the only three policemen on the island, had spoken of Ebanks and Rivers often, telling Mr. Panton occasional stories of their youth at West End and their earlier schooner sailing days together. The Customs and Immigration Inspector was at first at a loss for words, but then he held out his hand and said, "Giddy…Evans! It is a pleasure to see you again!"

Ebanks stepped up immediately and shook Mr. Panton's hand vigorously, as did Rivers more reluctantly a moment later.

Then Ebanks turned and motioned toward the Spaniard, "Bertie, this is our Captain," he said simply. Pablo Konig stepped forward briskly, shook Panton's hand and introduced himself, "Juan Bautista y Silviera, *Senor*." Rivers averted his eyes and looked down at his own feet, hands in pockets, but Ebanks was animated, shored up and feeling quite jovial from the rum in his blood.

"He can't speak any English, Bertie," Ebanks said, motioning again toward Konig, "he's a Cuban." Panton was smiling and polite, but felt curiously uneasy. Not only was it rare for a Cuban vessel to land in Cayman, but never would he have expected to find a Caymanian crew aboard such a vessel. He broke a long moment of total silence by smiling again and asking Ebanks, "Giddy, how in the world does it happen that you and Evans have returned home on a Cuban vessel?"

"Well Bertie, it's a long story but I'll make it short for you. I was on the *Lady Marian* in *Cienfuegos* a couple of weeks ago when I run into Evans there. He's my cousin, you know, an' he and this Captain needed another man to crew a short trip over to *Tunas de Zaza*. Well, I'm damned if we didn't get in one helluva storm and it blew us way the hell on back down southwest, almost back here, so we decided to come on in here and lay over for a few days. I mean, the Captain here said it would be alright since me and Evans wanted to visit home anyways. And besides, the Captain has got a lot of goods to sell and you might need 'em right here on the island."

Subconsciously, Panton concluded that Ebanks' explanation was plausible, so he decided to go on about his official business. "Well, Giddy, you and Evans know I'm the Customs and Immigration Officer and I'll have to inspect the ship, does the Captain know that?"

"Sure Bertie, sure," Ebanks replied, smiling broadly, "Evans speaks some Spanish and he's done explained everything to the Captain."

"Alright, boys, tell the Captain I'll need the ship's Articles and Manifest and I'll go on and do the inspection."

Evans Rivers then mumbled in Spanish to Konig and Konig produced several folded sheets of paper from his breast pocket. Rivers took them and handed them across to Mr. Panton, who in turn unfolded and looked at them briefly and put them in the breast pocket of his suit coat. Then he said, "Since you boys will be here a few days anyway, you might as well go on and take my launch and go ashore. I'll have them pick me up later. I know you've got family and friends looking forward to seeing you again. I'll find you after I've inspected the cargo and figured the customs charges. It might be a day or two, so enjoy yourselves, and, by the way, go ahead and take the Captain with you, if you like. He might like it here on Cayman."

"You hear that Evans!" Ebanks said almost gleefully, "Get your bag and let's go!" Then he looked over at Konig and said, "Tell him to come on with us. I can find him room at my sister's house." Within five minutes Ebanks, Rivers and Konig were in the government launch being rowed to shore to be greeted by the crowd assembled there.

Chapter 16

North Coast, Little Cayman
November 1, 1922

Late in the afternoon of November 1st Alberto regained consciousness for long enough to help Jose move him further back off the beach and up under a stand of huge sea grape trees. There, the canopy provided a shady shelter from the sun and a deep bed of dried leaves to rest in.

Once they had managed to resettle into a comfortable nest under the sea grapes, Jose went back to his work gathering coconuts to sustain them. He didn't know what else to do, and Alberto hadn't been well enough to tell him. So gathering coconuts was enough diversion to occupy him for a time.

Only after he had a small pyramid of twenty or thirty coconuts stacked in the campsite did Jose stop to rest. Alberto seemed to be sleeping so Jose did not disturb him. For a while, he sat silently beside Alberto while he slept, staring vacantly from their sea grape thicket out over the vacant lagoon to the ocean. There was no sign of life except for the constant scurrying of sand crabs on the beach.

Jose had felt lonely many times in his young life, even with the hordes of other children around him in the orphanage. But this was the first time that he had felt truly abandoned and helpless. As dusk was coming on, Jose cleared a sandy bed for himself among the leaves close to Alberto. He pushed a cover of the broad dry leaves up over Alberto, and then laid back and did the same for himself. He was asleep before dark.

Jose awoke during the night only once. He could not see the waning moon, but it cast enough dull light on the lagoon for him to see the vague reflection of white surf on the reef. And besides the constant sound of the sea, he could hear the faint noises of movement among the dried leaves around them, and occasionally in the limbs of the grape trees above them. The noises in the darkness around him caused the hair on the back of Jose's neck to stand up and he was alarmed, but he was not terrified. He knew that he must be brave, not only for himself, but also for Alberto. So he moved close enough to his friend to reassure himself from the warmth of Alberto's body, and eventually he fell back into a sound sleep.

Early the following morning, Jose awoke with Alberto's tugging on his shirtsleeve. "Wake up, little brother, wake up!" Alberto said, his voice still strangely weak and raspy.

Jose opened his eyes to a dreary, overcast morning. The sky was dark grey with roiling clouds and light sheets of rain falling in vertical columns out over the ocean. The grape tree thicket was cool, almost cold, and at first Jose wanted only to retreat back into the haven of sleep beneath his cover of leaves. But Alberto pulled his sleeve again and said, more urgently this time, "Jose, wake up! You've got to get up!"

With that, Jose sat up and brushed the sand and leaves from his clothing and arms and looked over to Alberto. Alberto was still lying on his back, but he had brushed the cover of leaves off his body. Jose's mouth fell agape at the sight of him, and he jumped to his feet.

Although some of the swelling had gone down in Alberto's face, his left eye had now opened enough for Jose to see the bloody orb in Alberto's swollen left eye socket, and the cut on his face was still open to the bone. And now, the many cuts and abrasions on Alberto's body had turned into festering sores, oozing pus and fluid. It was only then that Jose felt the pain and stiffness in his own body, and looked down to find infection setting in the several wounds in his own exposed skin.

When Jose looked back up, Alberto sensed the terror that had stricken his young friend. Then Alberto said, with as much strength as he could muster, "*Oye, Jose!* You must listen now and pay attention!"

Somehow, the forcefulness in Alberto's voice had a calming effect on Jose, who needed desperately to have some guidance from his elder. So Jose regathered his composure and squared his shoulders, and said, "Yes, Alberto, anything... I will do whatever you tell me."

"First you must listen, Jose. Only listen... The injury to my head causes me to be weak and to sleep. And I cannot stand or walk because I have many quills of sea urchins in my feet, so you must do as I tell you. Can you do this, Jose?"

"Yes, Alberto, I swear it! Tell me what I must do."

"First you must go into the lagoon and wash yourself, Jose. But take off your shirt and leave it here. Tear off a piece from your shirt as a rag to wash your wounds. These are cuts from the coral of the reef which are infecting and must be kept clean. And Jose, you must remember: The salt water will hurt terribly but you must endure the pain until your wounds are clean. And also, wear your shoes in the water and avoid the sea urchins…you remember, the round black sea eggs with quills that I have showed you before. They will stick in your feet and skin and hands if you touch them, and they will hurt you and become infected. These things have happened to me many times before, and my brother showed me what to do. Now hurry before it rains because we need the rain when it comes."

Jose took off his shirt without hesitation, ran to the lagoon and waded in, watching each step through the clear water to make sure there were no sea urchins in his path. At waist deep he stopped and squatted down in the water to his shoulders, ignoring the cold. But he could not ignore the pain in his wounds. It felt as if a hive of wasps had attacked him and set in all the sores on his body, but he remained still in the water until he began to quake from the combination of chill and pain. He had forgotten to tear a rag off his shirt, so he used his hands to gingerly rub his body, trying as best he could to get the sand and debris off his body and out of his cuts and scratches.

After several minutes the stinging seemed to subside, so Jose dunked his head and scrubbed his face and hair in the brine with his hands. Then he stood and scrambled back up the beach to Alberto.

"*Muy buen*, Jose," Alberto said quietly, "now gather up the coconuts you have broken open and use them like cups to fill with salt water and bring them back to me as quickly as you can."

Without a word Jose did as he was told. Within minutes he had placed a half dozen coconut shells beside Alberto, all filled with water from the lagoon.

"Now Jose, listen... I have torn the front of your shirt into rags. Take one and wet it. Then start pouring water in my wounds one at a time. Clean them out as best you can. You must do this for me, little brother, I can hardly sit up. Besides, I can't see well enough to help you. *Por favor*, Jose, you must do this to help me..."

Having heard Alberto's instructions, Jose went about his work without hesitation. He had never had to deal with anyone else's wounds before, so he went slowly, gently, trying not to hurt Alberto in the process. On his part, Alberto closed his eyes and locked his jaw. He said nothing and was completely still while Jose cleaned his wounds slowly, one at a time. Jose ran out of water several times, but ran back to the lagoon to replenish his supply each time without being told until he thought the job was done. Then he said quietly, "Alberto, what about your face?"

"You must do the same to my face, Jose. I will keep my eyes closed tightly, and you wash out the wound and then dry each of my eyes with a dry rag. And then

Jose…to this you must listen very carefully…I have torn a long strip from the front of your shirt…you see here, the strip from the front that has all the buttons on it. We'll put it on my chest and leave it there until you have finished cleaning my face."

Again, Jose did exactly as he was told, being as careful as he could to work gently with the horrible swollen wound on Alberto's face. But soon it was done, and Alberto looked remarkably better with his wounds cleaned and the caked sand, blood and debris washed away.

Then Alberto said, "Now Jose, take the button strip and put it around my head and face right at the level of my nose. There, that's good. Now take my knife from your pocket and open it…here's what you have to do: We're going to use the button strip to try to pull tight and close the gash on my face, do you understand?"

"Yes Alberto, but how do I tie it?"

"You will not tie it, Jose. When you get it tight enough to close the wound as best you can, you will cut a small button hole with the knife. Then button the strip tight so it stays in place right across the bridge of my nose, you see?"

"Yes Alberto, I understand."

So Jose followed Alberto's direction, wincing as he pulled the strip tight across his friend's swollen face. But immediately he saw that it would help close the gash on Alberto's face, so he pulled it tight, marked a spot between his left thumb and forefinger, and cut a small buttonhole on the marked spot. Then he pulled the strip tight again and buttoned it across the bridge of Alberto's nose. Alberto's lips were pursed and his eyes shut tightly, but he made no sound through the process.

When it was finished he said to Jose, "Now that it is tight, Jose, take the fingers of both your hands and pinch the entire length of the cut as closed as you can get it. Can you do this?"

Jose replied quietly, "Yes, Alberto," and then did as he was told. Only then did Alberto finally cry out in a guttural moan, but the worst of the effort was over.

After that, the boys were quiet for a long while. Finally Alberto said, "Jose, will you take a look at my feet now and tell me what you see?"

Jose nodded and pushed back to examine Alberto's feet. Then he looked back up at Alberto and said calmly, "Your feet are swollen, Alberto, and they have cuts and many of the black quills in them from the sea urchins."

"Alright, Jose, pull the spines out as best you can, but you won't be able to get them out. They will always break off in the flesh when you try to pull them out. But do what you can with them and then piss on my feet."

Jose had remained calm through the whole process of his ministrations to Alberto, but now again his mouth fell agape and he stood speechless. Alberto said again, more forcefully, "Jose, pull out the quills and piss on my feet! If I could stand up, I would do it myself!"

"Why do I do this?" Jose finally responded, "I mean, after I pull out the quills, why do I piss on your feet?"

"Jose, it is the only way to treat the quills of the sea urchins. My brother and I have done it many times in *Batabano*. The roots of the quills will come out in time, the body will push them out, but piss helps to take out the pain and infection. And all of these things that I have told you, you must do all these things three or four times a day for us both to heal, even if I am sleeping…can you do these things, Jose?"

Jose acknowledged his assigned duties with a nod of his head and then went about his work.

After enduring the pain and stress of his treatment, Alberto fell back into a sound sleep. Exhausted, Jose sat back against the gnarled trunk of a great sea grape tree, elbows on knees, trying to gather his thoughts. It was still overcast and humid, but the rain had not come ashore.

Eventually, Jose's hazy thoughts gave way to the commotion in the sea grape branches above him. A menagerie of bright green parrots with scarlet markings had settled in the branches above them, together with little yellow birds that he didn't recognize. The parrots were smaller than those he had seen in Cuba, but they were curious and slowly began to light on limbs so close that he could almost reach out and touch them. *These beautiful birds are our friends*, he thought, *and they will watch over us and keep us safe*. Soon his exhaustion overtook him, and pushed him into a deep sleep.

Chapter 17

George Town, Grand Cayman
November 1, 1922

Inspector of Customs and Immigration Bertie Panton was perplexed. He had scurried back to his office within an hour after he released the crew of the *Juana Mercedes* to take their leave in Grand Cayman. When he arrived at his office, Mr. Panton took off his coat and hat and sat down immediately at his scuffed wooden desk. He mopped the perspiration from his brow with his white handkerchief and put on his wire rimmed reading glasses. He had placed the ship's documents and the manifest of the *Juana Mercedes* on the desk before him and began feverishly rereading the translation that Miss Arch had handwritten for him, trying to make some sense of the happenings of that afternoon.

After Mr. Panton had released Ebanks, Rivers and the Spaniard for transport to shore, he had set about his ordinary task of inspecting and clearing the vessel's cargo. Immediately, however, he realized that the ship's documents and manifest were written in Spanish, a language he could neither read, write nor understand. The surprise of finding acquaintances Ebanks and Rivers on a Cuban schooner had caught him off guard, and he sensed that it had been a mistake to release them before the ordinary quarantine and thorough inspection that he usually conducted on foreign vessels. However, his strong sense of dignity and propriety had prevented him from crying out—signaling the government launch to return with the crew before it reached the waiting crowd on shore.

Under ordinary circumstances, Mr. Panton would have conducted his boarding inspection with much more formality. Typically, he would have lined up crew and passengers, and with ship's manifest in hand, he would have required each person on board to provide identification documents before transport to shore. In the case of foreign visitors, which was a relatively rare occasion, he would have required a financial showing of the ability to pay for expenses ashore and return fare for departure from the island. In this instance, however, when he realized his error, he stood silently, shook his head briefly and watched the crew of the *Juana Mercedes* land and disembark at the Town Barcadere—the main boat landing—and then melt into the bustle and excitement of the waiting crowd. He could do little more but check the vessel for stowaways until the return of his launch.

After a cursory search of the vessel revealed no obvious problems, he had returned to deck to find the government launch tied alongside and awaiting him. He boarded the skiff immediately and motioned for return to shore without speaking. He was disappointed with himself, and he couldn't help a nagging suspicion that all was not well with the *Juana Mercedes*. But he maintained his composure to the barcadere, while he devised a plan to cure his oversight. The moment the bow of the skiff touched, Mr. Panton stepped to the rocky shore and bounded up the rough stairway hewn in the jagged gray, coral and limestone rock. Up on Church Street he walked briskly across the bright white sand and marl street to the old two storey whitewashed frame Court House building overlooking the waterfront. There the only library in George Town was located in a very small, dark upstairs room. When he entered, Bertie Panton had been relieved to find Miss Jane Bond Arch seated at her small secretary desk in the corner, reading quietly as always.

Miss Arch was a sweet, soft-spoken and very British little gentlewoman who served as community librarian without pay. Most days, she spent her afternoons reading among the handful of worn out volumes in the tiny library and canvassing visiting ships and returning passengers for more books to read and to stock her little community library. Bertie Panton knew Miss Arch spoke, read and wrote fluently in the Spanish language, and he was relieved to find her there this late in the afternoon.

"Miss Arch," he had said, almost breathlessly, "I'm so glad to find you here."

She turned half way around in her chair and replied, "Why, Mr. Panton, the pleasure is all mine. I am so happy you have come. Just this week we have had three new works donated to our collection! Will you check one out this evening?"

"I'm sorry Miss Arch, this evening it is your help that I need..."

So now, an hour later, Inspector Panton sat at his desk reviewing again the translation Miss Arch had written out for him. The *Juana Mercedes* cargo manifest was unremarkable. It appeared to be consistent with the miscellaneous drygoods and other stores he had found on the ship. But the crew list was another matter. It contained the printed names, stations, ages and signatures of the crew of the *Juana Mercedes—all seven of them!* And to make matters worse, the names of Gideon Ebanks and Evans Rivers were *not* on the crew list. Mr. Panton had known that a crew of three was unusually small for a schooner of that size, not to mention that it was a Cuban ship with two out of the three crewmen being *Caymanian.*

Overlooking mistakes such as this were not typical of the way Bertie Panton worked. He was a careful and meticulous man. In fact, his hard work and diligence had made him the most powerful public service officer in the Cayman government—subject only to the British Commissioner—now Mr. Hugh Hutchings—the King's foreign service appointee to serve under the auspices of the British Governor of Jamaica. Panton placed his elbows on his desk and his head between his hands. To be sure, he was disgusted with himself. Nonetheless, there on the desk between his elbows was the crew list:

Captain—Juan Bautista y Silviera, age 41 years
Mate—Pablo Konig, age 25 years
Ordinary Seaman—Cristobal Gual, age 39
Ordinary Seaman—Antonio Rivas, age 28
Cook—Angel Perez, age 36
Deck Boy—Alberto Monson, age 13 years
Deck Boy—Jose Martinez, age 9 years

Mr. Panton shook his head and stood up. Darkness was approaching and he knew that Ebanks and Rivers would already be with their extended families in the small community at West End about eight miles up on the northwest end of the island. *Too late to do anything about it tonight,* he thought. *Anyway, I'm sure they'll have a reasonable explanation.*

He gathered up his coat and hat and left for the day, the *Juana Mercedes* papers clutched tightly in his fist.

Almost three days had passed and none of the *Juana Mercedes* crew had shown back up in George Town. Rumour was that they were all partying, drinking and carousing in the sparse settlement up toward the northwest end of the island while the *Juana Mercedes* rested quietly at anchor in Hog Stye Bay.

On his part, Bertie Panton had decided to keep his concerns quietly to himself until he had an opportunity to confront them. If he sent a Constable out to summon them back to George Town for questioning, it would reflect poorly on his decision to release them so quickly in the first place, and may raise unwarranted suspicions and gossip in this small island community. For years, Panton had presided over a quiet, virtually crimeless, closed society, and he was not inclined to let his impatience ruin that perception. *No*, he thought, *they'll be back soon enough*. And he was right.

On the morning of November 4, 1922, Mr. Panton had just strode into his office and hung his coat and hat when Police Constable Roddy Watler appeared at his door and requested leave to enter. Panton summoned him in with a wave of his hand and sat down. Constable Watler, an enthusiastic and promising young policeman, was at his usual immaculate best. He wore a spotless white tunic, blue trousers with broad scarlet stripes down either side, and white pith helmet with silver British coat of arms insignia gleaming above its bill. His shoes were spit shined in military style. As was his manner, Watler stood at attention and saluted when he stepped in Panton's office.

Although Bertie Panton was a practical man not given to pompous military formalities, he did expect the Inspector of Police and his Constables to inspire respect in the Cayman communities. After all, the sister islands had no military, so he felt that a disciplined police service reflected well on his leadership.

"Stand at ease, Constable," Panton said, "what can I help you with this morning?"

"Sir, I have an unusual circumstance to report," Watler replied.

"What is it Constable? I have Petty Sessions cases this morning."

Watler relaxed a little and said, “Sir, you know that Cuban ship out in the bay? Giddy and Evans and that Spanish fellow are unloading it.”

“What!?” Panton virtually jumped from his seat to look out his window to the bay.

Indeed, there was the *Juana Mercedes* with a barge type tender laid alongside. He couldn’t see who it was, but several men were offloading cargo onto the tender.

“When did this start!” Panton demanded.

“Early this morning, sir. I’ve heard that McTaggart and Bodden have agreed to buy thc whole store of cargo for their merchandise stores here on island.”

Panton’s earlier self-restraint gave way to outrage.
“Dammit, Constable! Why have I not been made aware of this earlier? You well know the cargo on that ship has not yet cleared customs or for import duties!”

“Sir, I’m sorry, sir.” Constable Watler stammered, straightening again into a stance of military attention. After a moment of silence, Watler continued reluctantly, “Well, you know Sir, it’s Giddy and Evans and we thought you might have approved it since they went through inspection. Besides that, Sir, the Spanish captain is staying with Inspector Yates while he’s here.”

The blood under Panton’s ordinarily mahogany complexion rose to a purple hue.

"Where the bloody blazes is Inspector Yates anyway?! Does the Commissioner know about this?!" he demanded.

"I don't think so sir. And Inspector Yates, I think he's at the Police Station, Sir."

"Then you'd bloody well better get it stopped and get everything back on that ship immediately! Tell McTaggart and Bodden that they'll have to wait until those goods have mustered customs first and get Ebanks and Rivers and their Spanish friend in here right now! Get Yates in here too. Do you understand me Inspector!?"

Constable Watler still stood at attention. He'd never seen Bertie Panton like this. "YES SIR!" he snapped, turning on his heel and leaving on a run.

Bertie Panton had been on a slow boil for almost two hours. He had canceled all court proceedings while he waited for Constable Watler to return with the others. He had watched from his window while the government launch made its way to the *Juana Mercedes* with Inspector Yates standing at the bow in a stance much like Washington crossing the Delaware. Constable Watler was behind him pulling oars as were two other men. Obviously, from Panton's tone, Constable of Police Watler had sensed the gravity of the situation before him and had passed it along to Inspector of Police Yates as well.

Now Panton sat at his desk, ship's papers from the *Juana Mercedes* laid out carefully before him, awaiting Watler to return with Yates and the others. Presently came a knock on his door and a voice: "Inspector Yates, Sir!"

"Enter."

When the door opened, it was Gideon Ebanks who entered first. He was followed by Evans Rivers and then the Spaniard. Inspector Yates proceeded only to the doorway and remained there standing at attention with Constable Watler close behind him.

Ebanks was first to speak. "Bertie, it's good to see you again! What can we do for you?" The three visitors looked much the worse for wear since their arrival in George Town. Their clothing was dirty and disheveled and stained in fresh sweat. The smell of stale alcohol and body odor settled in the small office. There was only one wooden visitor chair across from Panton's desk, and he did not invite anyone to sit down. Instead, he took a cigar out of the box on his desk and took his time lighting it and taking a few slow puffs.

"Gentlemen," he said, "I believe you already know that among my many other responsibilities, I am the Inspector of Customs and Immigration?" He asked the question but gave no time for response, "Therefore, you know you are responsible to me for the illegal import of goods from your ship before I have given you customs clearance papers." With that said, he took another slow pull on his cigar and awaited their response.

Again, it was Giddy Ebanks who spoke up:

"But Bertie, you took the ship's papers when we got here and we just thought everything was fine. You know, the captain don't speak any English, and me and Evans—we ain't captains—we don't know anything about those kinds of things…"

"Interesting you should mention your Captain, Giddy, what did you say his name was?"

Ebanks was stumped. How the hell did he know the guy's name except 'Pablo'? Anyway, he never even knew the real captain's name. As tortuous seconds quietly passed, Ebanks could feel the sweat coming even more profusely to his forehead and the rest of his body. "I don't know," he stammered, "you know I was only gonna make this one short trip before we was blown off course down here…like I told you before."

Sensing that his cousin couldn't talk them out of this one, Evans Rivers spoke up: "Mr. Panton, sir, you know Giddy drinks some and he don't keep up with details. Our Captain here is *Juan Bautista y Silviera.* I been sailing with him for a while."

Again, Mr. Panton made no immediate response. Instead, he leaned back in his wooden swivel desk chair and went through the motions of relighting his already lit cigar. Then he took another puff.

"Evans," he said, "I have reason to believe that the Captain of the *Juana Mercedes* is 41 years old. This person can't be a day over 25 or 30. What the blazes is going on here?"

Like Ebanks, it was now Rivers who was caught without words. Rivers looked at his feet and said, "Uh, I don't know anything about that sir. I mean, I'm just an ordinary seaman and I don't know anything about that."

Again, Panton let a few quiet moments pass. "Evans," he said, "I know you speak Spanish so tell the captain here that I'm the Inspector of Immigration for this Colony and that I want him to empty out his pockets on my desk for identification purposes."

Evans Rivers glanced nervously back and forth between the Spaniard and Panton, but then decided he had no choice but to comply. He spoke in Spanish to Konig while he was bobbing an index finger, pointing down to the top of Panton's desk. Konig replied in abrupt, quick epithets to Rivers, who continued to glance back and forth while he pointed to the desktop. In a moment, Rivers said to Panton:

"Sir, he says he has no identification with him. He didn't know he needed any when you let him off the ship."

Now Panton leaned forward in his chair, looking directly into the Spaniard's eyes. He said, still looking at the Spaniard, "Tell him to empty his pockets onto my desk right now or he will be held for immigration violation until the next ship heading for Cuba comes around. You might remind him how often that actually happens."

Rivers, now sweating again profusely himself, turned deliberately to Konig and began speaking slowly, deliberately to him in Spanish. His concern was evident in the tone of his voice and his demeanor.

The Spaniard took a long moment to consider his options. Then, unexpectedly, he smiled. It was not a half-hearted smile, but a full facial grin at Bertie Panton, his silver front tooth gleaming. He then commenced an animated conversation in Spanish as if Panton might understand every word he was saying. At the same time, he was digging in his pockets and dropping minutia on Panton's desk. Out came coins, a mixture of Cuban, British and American. Out came scraps of paper, some receipts and scribblings in English, some in Spanish. Then came a pearl-handled switchblade knife which he held up between his thumb and index finger, pointing at it with his other index finger and grinning, making inane conversation in Spanish as if explaining or apologizing for the knife. He placed the closed knife on Panton's desktop and turned toward Inspector Yates, who was still standing at attention in the doorway. Still grinning broadly he motioned for Yates to come to him, and held his arms straight out as if inviting Yates to search him.

"Mr. Panton", Evans Rivers interjected, "He says he will do anything you wish. When you let us off the ship, he didn't know you needed anything more, but he will cooperate fully. He will even get back on the *Juana Mercedes* and sail back to Cuba if that is what you wish. But he says he always heard that Caymanians were friendly and he thought he could cut the losses of this trip by providing much needed stores right here in Cayman. By the way, he says, his knife is strictly for maritime uses…all sailors carry them." In the background, Giddy Ebanks was now chiming in with his garbled observations and Inspector Watler still stood at the door, an inquiring look at Mr. Panton for instruction as to what he should do now.

Finally, Panton snuffed out his cigar and virtually yelled: "QUIET!"

"Here is what we will do," he said. "I am putting the *Juana Mercedes* in absolute quarantine until this mess is straightened out. If the three of you try to go aboard or remove stores from the ship you will be immediately arrested. In the meantime, I am sending an inquiry by the next mail packet to Kingston to get word about the status of this ship, the *Juana Mercedes*. Something is wrong. I can see it. I can smell it. And I'm having our police keep you three under observation. You are restricted from leaving the island. Are you all clear on this!?"

All three of the crewmen, including the Spaniard, shook their heads affirmatively, Pablo Konig still grinning brightly, his head bobbing up and down as if he understood it all or was simply stupid.

Panton's patience was gone. "Inspector," he said, "get them out of here!"

Chapter 18

Little Cayman
November 5, 1922

Alfred Lord Tennyson Scott was born and raised on Little Cayman, the smallest and most isolated of the Cayman triad. At thirty-two years old, he was big, brawny, and freckled with coarse, sandy blond, almost red hair. His father was the captain of a Cayman turtle schooner which accounted for his lifetime of knowledge of the sea and the sailing ships that rode upon her.

Alfred, or "Tenny" as he was called by his family and friends, was a simple, uncomplicated man. Not stupid by any means, Tenny was content with the life he led and the pleasures and treasures it offered each day. He had a wife, two young daughters and a home he had built with his own hands for his bride some years ago. He had provision ground for planting, and some cattle, goats and turtling to depend on, not to mention the daily bounty of the sea at his front door. The way he figured it, there couldn't be much more in life to enjoy.

Tenny was tall with a huge upper torso and broad shoulders and muscular arms from a lifetime of hauling nets and pulling lines, and his hands were thick and scarred. But his square face and blue eyes were uncommonly handsome in a rough cut way. Among his friends and family he was known for his sense of humor and mild, soft-spoken manner.

This November morning was particularly beautiful on the northeast coast of Little Cayman. Tenny awoke at first light with Lelia beside him, and a cool northeast breeze caressing them both through the open windows of their tiny bedroom. His wife looked so peaceful and beautiful beside him that his thoughts turned immediately to love-making, but she was sleeping so soundly he decided to allow her the rest. So he arose quietly, pulled on his tattered canvas trousers and stepped lightly out of the room. He found his broad-brimmed straw hat, placed it on his head, and crept out of the house, trying not to arouse Lelia or the girls.

As always, Lelia had the yard around the house swept down to spotless white sand with neat conchs, pink side up, lining the otherwise indistinguishable walkway under the coconut palms to the beach. *Dear Jesus!* he thought, *This is the day to die for!* As he strolled down to the lapping crystal water of the lagoon, he stretched, arms out, and smiled a wide grin.

"Lord," he said quietly, "what blessing is it you will give me today?" Searching the beach in the early light, his eyes set on his mahogany canoe, a gift from his father when he was just a boy. Like most Cayman canoes, it was a double-ended dugout fashioned in the Indian style, carved from a single mahogany tree trunk, and then brought home from the Miskito Coast of Central America on his father's turtle schooner when he was a young boy. He had virtually grown up on it—fishing, turtling inshore, gathering bounty from the endless sea—like his father, grandfather, and all known before him had done, except, perhaps, the earliest pirates from whom he was told he was descended.

This is a good morning for conch, he thought, as he walked to the canoe and pushed it into the lagoon, hopping aboard briskly and pushing it off the beach.

As the sun rose, this day was to be a typical one on Little Cayman. The prevailing northeast breeze was mild enough that the dark blue and purple sea beyond the reef was flat to the horizon. The vast, treacherous reef along the north shore ran as far as the eye could see in either direction, and the azure and jade waters of the lagoon fronting on the white sand beach were crystal clear and still as if frozen in time.

Tenny stood in the stern of his canoe and poled his way across the shallow, clear waters of the lagoon, watching the passing patches of crystalline sand and intermittent emerald green eel grass below the surface, trying to catch sight of easy conch for the taking. Before the sun was fully up and bright, he had filled the bottom of the canoe with conch and he continued to pole his way west inside the reef toward Bloody Bay. *I'll go as far as Sparrowhawk Hill*, he thought, *and then back to Mama.* He was whistling and intermittently singing gospel songs as he pushed along briskly in the early morning sunshine.

Jose had been drowsing for some time in the early light with Alberto in a fitful, feverish sleep beside him.

As hard as he had tried to help his friend, Jose was feeling more and more helpless. Although Jose had kept Alberto's superficial wounds clean with salt water and covered with fresh green leaves, he could do nothing with Alberto's swollen, infected face and feet. To make things worse, Alberto had fallen into a kind of delirium, sometimes speaking nonsense and mostly not speaking at all. Jose sensed that his friend was dying, but knew nothing more he could do to prevent it.

Jose remembered Sister Elena's faith, and he asked God why he and Alberto had been delivered from the *Juana Mercedes* only to die in this deserted place. *On the other hand*, he thought, *we have coconuts and occasional rainwater, and Alberto has told me how to gather whelks from the tidal ironshore places, and how to take the meat of this salt water snail to eat. But what now?* He sat upright, still and thinking about what he should do.

Before the sun was up clear from the sea, Jose snapped from his reverie when he heard the faint drift of a whistled tune from the distance, a long way up the lagoon. At first, he didn't know whether it might be the breeze in the sea grape leaves rattling above, tantalizing him with this light, foreign music. But then, no, it was not the breeze—it was a real tune whistled in the distance.

Jose rose quickly from his deep bed of sea grape leaves and scuttled, crablike, under the shroud of shoreside vegetation toward the foreign sound. After several hundred yards Jose came to an uneasy rest under the protective cover of a leafy young sea grape at shoreside. Looking to the east under his leafy cover—

toward the new sunrise—Jose saw a big man in a canoe, poling slowly inside the reef, leisurely moving toward their hidden thicket while whistling his solitary tune.

Jose froze immediately at the sight of this intruder and the hair rose on the back of his neck. For a moment he trembled, both in fear and in indecision. He suppressed his immediate inclination to run on the beach, flailing his arms to attract the attention of this stranger, but his recent brutal experience in the adult world suppressed him—caused him to crouch down out of sight—and study this foreigner.

The stranger was a big, powerful looking white man, muscles rippling effortlessly as he poled his canoe slowly through the shallows. His skin was dark tanned by the sun, but the bleached blond hair on his forearms and bare chest could be seen even at this distance. His face was shadowed by a broad-brimmed straw hat, and he spent most of his time studying the bottom of the lagoon as he poled along, paying no attention to the shore. Then the stranger began to sing in a deep, clear voice. Although Jose could not understand the language, he recognized the melody of the hymn immediately from his days in the orphanage, and it put him more at ease with the approaching stranger. But what to do now—he didn't know.

Jose scrambled wildly back to his campsite, hardly quiet as he ran upright ducking only for low lying limbs and brambles. Alberto was as he had left him, sleeping—or unconscious—Jose knew not which. Jose skidded to a stop on his knees beside Alberto and began immediately to shake him by the shoulders. "Alberto! Alberto! You must wake up. A man is here! You must help me! Tell me what to do!"

Alberto lolled his head and briefly opened his right eye with a glazed stare. Slowly, reluctantly, Alberto responded almost imperceptibly, "Jose, where are we?"

"We're still on the beach....Alberto, we will die without help! You're sick Alberto, you must have help! What will I do now with this stranger?"

Alberto seemed to focus on Jose's face with his right eye for a brief, lucid moment, and he said in a whisper, "Jose, do not tell this stranger who we are...do not tell him about the *Juana Mercedes*....if you do, the Spaniard will find us and kill us.........."

Tenny Scott was just starting to perspire. The sun was finally out in a brilliant glare, striking both from the sky and by reflection from the still water of the lagoon below. It was time to take a swim before his return home, but Tenny hesitated for an instant. There was a sound on the shore, barely audible, uncommon and unexpected in his experience. It was a rustling of brush and leaves, too noisy for birds and too fast for iguanas. Then it was gone. His curiosity piqued, Tenny decided to keep on poling toward Bloody Bay for a few more minutes.

Tenny's focus was on the treeline of coconuts, seagrape and the wild, thick brush beyond the strand of white, sandy beach. The lagoon was still and quiet except for a menagerie of brown and white red-footed Boobies swooping down and skimming the lagoon's surface, occasionally diving for a catch from the still water. They were common visitors from their habitat in the huge salt pond, mangrove fringe and woodlands on the south side of the island, known locally as the Booby Pond or the Rookery. Suddenly, a very large Frigatebird rose up from the nearby shoreline to attack and rob the Boobies of their catch. This was a particularly magnificent, glossy black male Frigatebird, with a wingspan of close to six feet, red throat pouch extended for the breeding season, forked tail and scimitar-like wings, gliding weightlessly in the light air, doing spectacular aerial combat stunts to steal his morning meal from the fishing Boobies.

Distracted as he was momentarily with the ongoing airshow above the lagoon, Tenny failed at first to see the small pale waif of a boy standing as still as death on the white strand of beach before him. It was only out of the corner of his eye that Tenny first glimpsed the boy, and he instinctively jerked around and stiffened to the sight.

As a young Caymanian boy, Tenny had listened wide-eyed to firelight stories of Caymanian ghosts or gremlins known as "duppies." In fact, his superstition was almost as strong as his religious bent, so he immediately froze at the sight of this pale, frail and ragged white duppy on the beach. His voice stuck in his throat as their eyes made direct contact. *Jesus, Lord, what do I do now?* he thought. Then he remembered what Old Man Bodden, the storekeeper at South Hole, had told him: *You must curse a duppy to make it go away*. The old man claimed to know this procedure from first hand experience, so it must be true. Tenny's mind was racing with such thoughts as the seconds, feeling like hours, passed.

Finally, with all the nervous energy he could muster, Tenny choked out a weak shout, "Damn you duppy, go away!" Then, seeing no response from the pale waif, he shouted again in a more commanding voice, "Goddamn you duppy, go away!" Then the ragged duppy stirred slightly and said in a hardly audible voice, "*Ayaudame Senor, por favor... Help...*"

Jose lowered his eyes and shifted his feet in the sand. The big man in the canoe was still now, studying him a long time without speaking further. Jose's black hair was unkempt and last vestiges of his indigo shirt and canvas trousers were nothing more than rags and tatters. *What must this man be thinking of me? He is a crazy Ingles, and he will surely kill me right here where I stand.*

Finally, the big man broke their impasse by poling his canoe to the beach at Jose's feet. Then he stepped out into the shallow water and walked slowly, but deliberately to within an arm's length of the boy. Jose lifted his eyes to meet those of the stranger, and he sensed immediately that this huge man was pale and slightly trembling. But the man's eyes, now shaded under the brim of his straw hat, were kind eyes.

After a silent moment, the man reached out and patted the boy's head.

"Jesus, Lad," he said, "I thought you were a duppy!"

Jose did not understand the foreign words of the stranger, but he sensed immediately the quiet relief in the big man's voice. Then the man took hold of Jose's arms at the shoulders and shook him gently, as if to make sure he was real flesh and blood.

"My God, Lad! What are you doing here? Where are you from?" Tenny said, clearly relieved now that the Lord had spared him from confrontation with a dreaded duppy.

"*No hablo Ingles, Senor. No comprendo.*" Jose responded quietly. Then, compulsively, Jose took hold of the big man's thick right hand and led him into the seagrape thicket to Alberto's side.

Tenny knelt down on one knee and studied the inert black boy sprawled amongst the leaves. Then he tentatively felt Alberto's forehead with the palm of his hand, and slowly shook his head. He looked up through the canopy and said in a murmur, "Lord, God, you brought me to these children just in time."

Tenny picked up Alberto's limp form in his huge arms as if Alberto were weightless, and then he returned to his canoe with Jose trailing at his heels.

Chapter 19

Northwest Coast
Grand Cayman
November 23, 1922

By the last week of November, 1922, Ebanks and Rivers had managed to squander their share of the little money they had pilfered from the bodies and personal effects of the victims of the *Juana Mercedes* before the remains were thrown overboard. The co-conspirators' subsequent grand plan to sell the cargo off the ship to Grand Cayman's merchants had also failed when Bertie Panton cut them off at the dock. He probably could have had them arrested then, but at least so far he had waited.

They were all just marking time before they would be arrested, and they knew it. Even though there was still no official word out of Kingston, even a Honduran schooner passing through George Town had left rumours of a lost Cuban ship, the *Juana Mercedes*. Time was short, and they all knew it.

Giddy's sister, Ettie, had gone to church that evening of November 23. She had left her house available to Giddy and his friends, as she had often done since her brother's return to the island. Mostly, the *Juana Mercedes* pirates had partied there since arriving in Grand Cayman. But their circumstances had taken a serious turn for the worse, and with no money or prospects in sight, Ebanks had called them together for a serious meeting.

Unlike the others, the Spaniard seemed still to have the money to do as he chose. That fact in itself enraged Ebanks, and led him to call this meeting with Rivers and Konig at his sister's house.

When the meeting started that evening, Gideon Ebanks was almost drunk and was nursing a drink of straight dark rum from a clear glass. Sitting with him at the same sturdy mahogany table in the light of a single candle were both Evans Rivers and Pablo Konig. The sun had faded into the early hours of evening and darkness was upon them. Even though the mosquitoes were mostly an issue for the summer months, Evans had lit a smoke pot of buttonwood by the door to ward off the evening invaders, and its glow had created a smoky haze in the room.

After a long silence, Ebanks took another gulp from his glass and said:

"Goddammit, Evans, this sonofabitch has got us in deep shit," he said, pointing an accusatory finger at the Spaniard "Now, the Government has the *Juana Mercedes* an' we can't even get away on the damn thing. We don't have food or money nor nothing to sell off the schooner. An' here your Spaniard is, dressed up like a pretty boy and still sportin' money and pretendin' he can't speak English. Damn him, he's tellin' the girls around here somethin' for 'em to swoon for 'em like they do."

Ebanks had his eyes on the Spaniard while he was speaking, trying to read some response in Konig's demeanor. But there was none.

After a moment of thought, Rivers replied, "Look, Giddy, I know we're in big trouble. I mean, I'll be honest…I can't hardly live with it no more. In fact, I told my family and the Preacher what we done and they said to own up to it and ask for repentance. What else we gon' do?"

"Evans, you stupid sonofabitch! If you told your family… you know the truth is over the whole island by now…you stupid sonofabitch!"

Ebanks slammed one fist on the table and buried his face in his other hand, shaking his head. Then he reached into his pocket and put the Navy Colt revolver on the table, holding it in his right hand.

"Evans," he said, now looking again at Konig, "tell this bastard I'm going to kill him where he sits if he don't tell us where the money is off that ship."

With that the quiet in the room became deafening. Whatever the Spaniard might have understood, he did not try to move his hands and arms off the tabletop. He looked over to Rivers and gave an innocent, quizzical look, turning the palms of his hands up as if to inquire what was going on.

Reluctantly, Rivers turned to Konig and spoke to him briefly in an even, quiet tone. Almost instantaneously, Pablo responded to Rivers with a surprised look on his face, but still with a low, controlled voice.

Ebanks took another deep pull on his drink. He was becoming all the more enraged by what he was now beginning to believe was a foreign language conversation of Rivers and Konig against him personally. He raised the old Colt and pointed it directly into the Spaniard's face.

Again, the room was silent as death for long moments. Eventually, the barrel of the pistol began to quiver.

The Spaniard, at first having looked fearfully back at Ebanks, now spread his face slowly into a broad smile, bringing his hands—palms still up—into an international gesture: *What did I do to piss you off?*

Finally, the effects of the alcohol took control of Ebanks' gun hand and it started to shake uncontrollably. He knew the moment was lost, so he lowered the pistol back to the table. If the Spaniard had found more money on the schooner, he wasn't about to admit it. At least not yet. Ebanks looked again at Rivers and said:

"Tell him to get out, and if I find he cheated us I'll kill him."

Hog Stye Bay
Grand Cayman
November 27, 1922

The Spaniard's luck and—*he* believed—his cunning, had saved him again.

Only four days after his last confrontational meeting with Ebanks—whom he had come to hate—Konig tossed his bag on a small skiff awaiting him at the George Town barcadere. Konig sat in the skiff's stern while an oarsman rowed him out to the sole schooner at rest in the harbour at Hog Stye Bay, the *Mary K. Hasty*. As the oars dipped slowly and rhythmically through the smooth, clear water, Konig smiled in a silent moment of self-appreciation. He knew it was only a matter of days, possibly hours, before their luck ran out. Word of their adventure on the *Juana Mercedes* was common gossip on the island now, and he felt sure that even the police and the British Commissioner knew about it.

When Konig and his oarsman arrived alongside the schooner, Konig scrambled up a rope ladder and was greeted on deck by the Mate, a Central American from Honduras. The rest of the crew was busily making ready to set sail.

Konig and the Honduran Mate spoke briefly about the required fare for passage to Honduras, and the Spaniard hastily paid the Mate in full with Cuban currency. Then he and the Mate proceeded toward Konig's transit passenger quarters. As they reached the companionway to go below deck, the Spaniard looked one last time back to the quiet, idyllic community of George Town. This time his smile was even broader—his silver tooth glinting in the blinding Caribbean sun. After a moment, he disappeared below deck and was gone.

Chapter 20

George Town
Grand Cayman
January 7, 1923

On Elgin Avenue in George Town, just up from the Court House, stood the Police Station and Jail. The Police offices were up a flight of outside stairs in a whitewashed, wood frame building sitting atop a carriage house. The jail, such as it was at the time, consisted of an attached ground floor roofless pen enclosed by a concrete wall, roughly twenty feet square in dimension. The surrounding masonry walls were no more than seven or eight feet high, topped with embedded shards of broken glass which had long since dulled and worn in the weather. In one corner of the jail enclosure was a tin-roofed shelter to provide cover for anyone who might be so unfortunate as to become an inmate. This honor, however, was reserved almost exclusively for the occasional drunk and rowdy citizen who breached the peace and needed some time to dry out. In fact, most of the time spent by the handful of Police Constables in the Sister Islands was dedicated to their dual role as postmen picking up and delivering the mail.

As it may seem, it was in fact for many years exceedingly easy to escape from jail in George Town. It was not so easy, however, to escape the island. Very few foreign ships entered the harbour at George Town, and fewer still stayed long enough or cared to take on passengers. Typically, they arrived and left in the span of a single day, generally under the watchful eye of Bertie Panton.

As for local vessels, everyone knew everyone and it would be difficult to escape the island in that fashion due to the vessel owner or captain's fear of reprisal upon return. Expectably, most prisoners sat out their short jail terms counted in days, if not hours.

In Giddy Ebanks' case, it had happened that not only his drinking, but more particularly his cousin's Navy Colt pistol had turned out to be his undoing. The escape of the Spaniard over a month earlier had so enraged him that he stayed drunk and disorderly, waving Evans' pistol around and threatening people with it on a regular basis. He was in and out of jail—even escaped once—but his rampages were finally more than the law—and more particularly, Bertie Panton—could allow him. This time he was arrested to stay, his bond set too high by Panton for him to make bail.

So in the early evening hours of January 7, 1923, Ebanks laid silently on the wooden rack and canvas covered palm frond mattress that served as his bunk in the George Town jail. Strangely, the thought of punishment for his role in the piracy of the *Juana Mercedes* wasn't on the forefront in Gideon Ebanks' thoughts that evening. That was just something that happened and was gone. It was more important to him at the moment that he was sober, broke and in jail. The combined total of those realities was enough to inspire him. He didn't need the complication of his part in piracy or murder to decide what must be done.

To make things better, he still had friends in Cayman and this night, he knew how he would escape. The schooner *Varuna* was to depart George Town at sunrise and he would be aboard her. He smiled as he thought how simple it would be: Scale the wall in the wee hours of darkness, sneak to the shore, swim to the schooner and hide himself aboard until the next landfall.

Being a stowaway was easy. If nothing else, he knew he was good at being a stowaway. *Really* good.

Northwest End
Grand Cayman
February 2, 1923

It was the day of her grandfather's funeral that Evans Rivers was arrested.

Little Vernice Ebanks had gone to the services for her grandfather that morning and she remembered standing on a solid wooden bench outside the front window of her Grandmother's house after she returned from the funeral. The Bougainvilleas were up and beautiful with their coloured flowers covering the whole front of the house. Her "Uncle Evans," who she loved dearly, was standing in the open front window of the house with his right arm around her waist. The service for Gandap' had been wonderful and the weather was perfect. At about eight years old, Vernice felt the beauty and the power of the whole world before her.

But then, as she gazed down the long sandy trail toward West Bay, Vernice could see Constable Roddy Watler approaching. At first, she thought he may be going somewhere else, and then she thought he may have some special mail or message to deliver. As it turned out, she was wrong.

When Constable Watler reached the Rivers' cottage, he turned in the path, approached the little frame house and stopped before them. He tipped his white pith helmet as a matter of courtesy to Miss Vernice. Then he said, "Evans, I'm sorry, but I have an arrest warrant to serve on you. You're going to have to come with me to George Town."

Evans Rivers hesitated a moment and then kissed his niece on the cheek. "Vernice," he said, "I won't see you again for a long time, but I hope you'll remember me. I love you."

He put on his straggly hat, left the house by the front door, and accompanied Constable Watler back out the path without another word.

Chapter 21

George Town
Grand Cayman
April 5, 1923

As it turned out, the piracy of the *Juana Mercedes* and the escape of two of the three perpetrators from Grand Cayman had become the worse diplomatic debacle in the history of the Cayman Islands. Clearly, the piracy had also included the multiple murders of Cuban citizens as well, and two of the three pirates had escaped the reach of justice right through the hands of Caymanian authorities. The incident was particularly troublesome and embarrassing for Hugh Houston Hutchings, the British Commissioner of the Cayman Islands at the time.

Commissioner Hutchings, who had received his appointment to the Cayman Islands in 1919, was a career British foreign service bureaucrat. To make matters worse, he was 53 years old and married with ten children at the time the *Juana Mercedes* piracy crisis played out.

Hutchings had originally agreed to take up the Commissioner's post in the obscure Caymans only after assurances by the Governor in Jamaica that it was a pensionable post. Furthermore, the living quarters provided for him in George Town was surprisingly well-appointed and had turned out to be a more than adequate home for him and his large family. The last thing he needed in his career was to become a sacrificial lamb for a political embarrassment to the British government.

Although he was generally easygoing, the dapper Commissioner could be abrupt and outspoken when it came to protection of his own career interests. Until now Hutchings had relied unconditionally on the work ethic and judgment of the chief officer of local Caymanian government, Mr. A.E. Panton, to cover him in all matters of local importance. Hutchings was savvy enough at this point in his career to understand that he was personally only a diplomat and the face of British government in the Cayman Islands. The real power of government in the Caymans was in the capable hands of his friend and confidante, Bertie Panton.

In fact, Commissioner Hutchings and Mr. Panton had hit it off right from the beginning after Hutchings' appointment in 1919. Panton was open and honest, and he knew everyone. More importantly, Bertie knew how to *do* everything, at least insofar as running government in the Cayman Islands was concerned. Bertie was also savvy enough to know that his position and power base could only be sustained with the confidence and support of his only boss, the Commissioner.

Now with the *Juana Mercedes* incident looming, Hutchings and Panton both knew that the Commissioner had to answer to his superiors in Jamaica for what had happened. More importantly for he and Panton both, the wily Commissioner knew that he had to do it in such a way as to diplomatically lay the blame where he believed it really should be: in the hands of his own superiors in Jamaica. With the assistance of Bertie Panton, Commissioner Hutchings wrote on April 5, 1923:

To His Honour
Colonial Secretary of Jamaica

Regarding the Cuban Schooner "Juana Mercedes"

Dear Sir:

In response to yours on the detention of the "Juana Mercedes" in November Past, the men Konig, Rivers & Ebanks were put ashore (I counted it unwise to leave them on board as the Police were directed to keep themselves informed as to their whereabouts which we believed to be a comparatively easy matter). They were reported to you for his Excellencies' information as being under Police surveillance. On the first subsequent arrival from Cuba, current rumour implicated the men in the commission of serious crimes outside the Dependency. Under my instructions, the Clerk of the Courts inquired of experienced Justices of the Peace as to whether, with such evidence as was available, it was desirable to arrest the men and possible to hold them. The advice given was that it was not possible and that it was wiser to await direction from His Excellency the Govermour before taking public action. With this I concurred. Your letter of 30th of Nov. last approved of my action with respect to the vessel but, to my surprise and disconcertion, gave no instructions or suggestions as to any action with respect to the men. 2 were natives and at home and the other,Pablo Konig, lived in the private quarters of the then Inspector of Police and appeared to be able to support himself. I took no steps in restraint of their liberties. I had no evidence against them of crimes committed within my jurisdiction and no notice that warrants of arrest had been issued or were in contemplation.

Gideon Ebanks was thereafter arrested for a breach of the peace and threats with a pistol. Failing to find security for good behavior, he was sent to prison for safe keeping but succeeded in breaking goal. Repeated efforts were made by the Police toward his recapture but without avail. He is believed to have hidden in a part of this island and to have been supplied with food by sympathetic relations.

Konig is supposed to have left here on the "Mary L. Hasty" for Honduras on Nov. 27th before I had received from you any communication on the matter of the "Juana Mercedes". Ebanks is supposed to have been smuggled from the island on the "Varuna" on Jan 8th, 3 weeks before I had received any instructions as to his arrest and 10 days before I was first advised by you that he and the others were wanted by the Cuban Govt. on serious charges.

We still however had Rivers and a warrant was issued for his conveyance to Sutton St. Station, Kingston, Jamaica, dated Feb. 2nd, 1923. He was duly conveyed there by schooner "W.M. Fulmar".

The Cuban Govt. applied for the extradition of the 3 men accused of piracy, murder and theft within Cuban Jurisdiction but only Rivers was left to send to Jamaica for delivery to Cuban police authorities there.

Cuban motor-schooner "Juana Mercedes" of 36 tons owned by Barbiete & Cia of Batabano, Cuba was built in 1917 in Cienfuegos. She cleared Cienfuegos for Tunas-de-

zaza Oct 30th with general cargo, rice, beans, dry biscuits, potatoes, gasoline, dry beef, salt fish, lard, machetes, empty sugar bags, and 30 railroad ties& 50 pkts of provisions for Ramon Fernandez, Tunas-de-Zaza.

Crew were Juan Bautista Silveira, Cuban, Capt. (2) Pablo Konig, alias Eulogio Paz, Spaniard, sailor, (3) Angel Perez, Cuban, Sailor (4) Cristobal Gual, Cuban sailor, (5) Evans Rivers, alias Antonio Rivas, British, Cayman sailor, (6) Alberto Monson, negro deck boy, (7) Jose Martinez, white deck boy (8) Gideon Ebanks, Cayman British, stowaway discharged from American schooner "Lady Marian" on Oct. 16th, 1922.

This Commissioner was out of town when the Juana Mercedes arrived but on return suspicions were roused by certain various facts; that the 3 men were not in lawful possession of the schooner and her cargo. They said she had been blown off the Cuban coast when on voyage from Cienfuegos to Tunas. We visited them and examined papers. Pablo Konig was soon identified. His friends called him Pablo, he could not sign Silvieras' signature though he said that was his name. A note described Silvieras as 41 years old and the man professing to be him was only about 25. Papers belonging to Pablo Konig were found aboard and a pawn ticket in his pocket. All these facts were duly reported. They had no accurate crew list and were disposing of a part of the cargo.

The cargo was landed and protected, The boat sent to the North Sound for safe harbourage and the men watched.

Under our remote circumstances, and without further communcation or guidance from His Honor the Governour, I believe that we acted in an altogether lawful and circumspect manner.

Your Faithful Servant,

Hugh H. Hutchings
Commissioner, Cayman Islands
British West Indies

No further action was taken thereafter by the Governor against Hutchings, Panton, or any other Caymanian authorities arising out of the *Juana Mercedes* incident. In fact, Commissioner Hutchings continued in office to become the longest serving of all Caymanian Commissioners appointed by the Crown (1919-1931).

As of 1931 when Commissioner Hutchings retired, Pablo Konig and Gideon Ebanks had simply officially vanished. As the years passed, the piracy of the *Juana Mercedes*, and the murders of her captain and crew, simply moved further toward historical obscurity.

Part Two

1937

The following front page article appeared in *The Daily Gleaner*, Kingston, Jamaica, January 7, 1937, edition:

Fifteen-Year-Old Crime On The High Seas Is Recalled

Caymanian, Arrested on Return to Native Land After Long Absence, Said to be Mixed up in Piracy, Murder and Theft: Carnage on Juana Mercedes

---

(From our Correspondent)

GRAND CAYMAN, January 1—On Saturday morning, December 26, the fishing schooner "Majestic," Captain D. Ebanks, arrived here from the Mosquito Cay fishing grounds, and shortly after she dropped anchor, it was revealed that among her passengers was Gideon Ebanks, from the West Bay district of this island, who escaped from jail in George Town during the month of November, 1922, where he had been detained pending further developments into charges of 'alleged piracy, murder and theft.'

According to the story told, the cargo schooner Juana Mercedes, flying the Cuban flag, got into Georgetown November 1, 1922. She had on board a crew of three men. Two of them were Cayman Islanders, and the third, who acted as master, was a Spaniard. They said they were engaged in the Cuban cargo trade between Batabano and Cienfuegos, and that on a voyage from the latter port, strong north easterly winds had blown them off their course and they had been forced to sail for Grand Cayman for refuge. In Georgetown the ship was detained until the mysterious absence of some crew members and the absence of ordinary ship papers was accounted for.

RUM LOOSENS TONGUES

Within a short time after their landing, however, the crew went on a carousal, and while in their cups, it is alleged, revealed bit by bit the story of a terrible crime—a story such as might have been told in the drinking dens of the Port Royal of 1633.

The story came to the ears of the authorities who were suspicious and placed the crew under surveillance. There was no wireless here in those days and it took a long time to get a reply from Jamaica on enquiries. Meanwhile the three men continued their drinking. Then the Spaniard managed to give the police the slip, getting away to Spanish Honduras where he disappeared. Gideon Ebanks was eventually arrested and detained in the local gaol from which he escaped and allegedly made his way to Tampa, Florida.

Evans Rivers, the third man, remained and when in late November definite news of the crimes was received, he was arrested and extradited to Cuba where he was subsequently tried and convicted.

PIRACY AND MURDER

At Evans Rivers' trial the full story came out. The charges laid by the Cuban authorities were piracy and murder and theft.

It appeared that when the schooner Juana Mercedes left Cienfuegos on October 30, 1922, for Tunas de Zaza she had on board Juan Bautista (Captain), Antonio Rivas (alias Evans Rivers), Pablo Konig, Spaniard, Angel Perez, Cristobal Gual, Jose Martinez and Alberto Monson (the latter two being children). There was also a stowaway, Gideon Ebanks.

From the evidence heard in the Cuban Court there was a mutiny immediately after the vessel left Cienfuegos and the master and two crewmembers were murdered. The children were kept until the following day when in sight of land they were forced to jump into the sea or were pushed over the side. Their bodies were never recovered.

For 15 years Gideon Ebanks has lived somewhere on the Nicaragua Coast.

Immediately on his arrival in George Town he was arrested and is being held there pending extradition to Cuba for trial.

Chapter 22

April 2, 1937
Christiansted
U.S. Virgin Islands

On the afternoon of April 2, 1937, the schooner *Black Hawk* was at anchor in the azure waters of Gallows Bay off the Dutch-American village of Christiansted at St. Croix in the Virgin Islands. Capt. Allie Scott stood on her fantail, one hand on a backstay, taking in the beauty of the quaint, cobbled streets of the town that had become his home between voyages.

Since American Prohibition ended in 1933, the rumrunning trade had dried up and turtling was no good in the Caymans anymore. Motor ships had taken up all the major routes for freight trade, so Allie's business had become somewhat limited. Schooner trade was still holding well in the out islands, but he knew that the days of real sail trade were numbered. But no matter—he reflected—he and his white brother Joe Scott had made a small fortune running liquor during the good times. For Capt. Allie Scott, sail was now for the freedom and challenge of the sea. Everything else had become secondary in his life.

At twenty-eight years of age, Allie Scott was just short of six feet in height, but his body had filled to 185 pounds of sheer muscle and sinew since he was the deck boy known as "Alberto" on the *Juana Mercedes*. It seemed like a lifetime since he and Jose Martinez had been "taken in" and adopted by Capt. Tenny Scott and his kind wife, Lelia—now "Daddy Tenny and Mama Lelia"—to their adoptive sons.

It wasn't long after rescuing the boys those many years ago that Daddy Tenny—completely baffled by his effort to learn some Spanish dialect—had sat his two refugee boys down at the table in his Little Cayman house. He looked them both carefully and seriously in their eyes. He reached across the table and poked the older boy, Alberto, on his chest with his index finger and said, looking the boy straight in the eye:

"From this day forever, you gon' be Allie Scott. You got that boy?" Allie gave a positive indication with a shake of his head.

Then Daddy Tenny looked Jose square in the eyes and said, just as seriously, "*You,* 'Joe-Say,' you jus' gon' be Joe Scott the rest of your life. You got that?" Joe smiled and nodded his agreement.

That was the adoption ceremony. For her part, Mama Lelia had just stood in the corner and cried tears of joy.

By 1937, with a life spent working on sailing ships since his rescue on Little Cayman, Capt. Allie Scott had toned to mechanical perfection in his body and features. But his yellow-green eyes remained his most striking feature. Those eyes, set in a handsome dark face with high cheekbones and a narrow nose gave away the Carib in his bloodlines. The only flaw in his countenance was the wide, raised scar that descended down his face from the hairline at his left ear to the corner of his mouth. But despite the fearsome appearance he took on between his scar and catlike eyes, he was, by reputation, the finest young schooner Master sailing the Caribbean and Central American routes.

There was no corner of the Caribbean where either the man, *El Tigre*, or his legend, was not known.

But on this day, he was thinking about his return to George Town and the anticipation of seeing his best friend—his 'little brother'—again. It had been almost three years since their parting and there was much to catch up on—much to do.

The freight for George Town and ports beyond had been loaded earlier in the day, and Capt. Allie had his crew making ready to weigh anchor. He had become almost fanatical with the maintenance and seaworthiness of his vessel, and he expected no less of his crew than he did of himself. But he was not a tyrant. As hard as he was, every man of his crew knew that he would be there for them in times of need, and often, he was. The admiration and respect of his crew was evidenced by the fact that most had served under him through their rumrunning days and had no plan or expectation of leaving.

Allie finally broke his reverie and turned to the companionway leading down to his cabin and descended the stairs. Years ago, he had had his cabin paneled and trimmed in finished, polished mahogany, and he kept it immaculate. When he entered, shafts of bright light falling through the portlights lit up the surface of his chart table at the rear of the cabin. He strode back to the chart table, pulled back his cushioned mahogany chair and sat down. Then he picked up and read again for perhaps the hundredth time the front page article from that morning's issue of the *Kingston Daily Gleaner*. It read:

Man Accused Of Piracy and Murder Escapes from Jail

GEORGETOWN Grand Cayman April 1 (Radiogram to the Gleaner by West India and Panama Telegraph Co Ltd from our Correspondent)

Gideon Ebanks, who had been under arrest here from early in January, on a charge of piracy and murder on the high seas alleged to be committed fifteen years ago, escaped from gaol yesterday morning, and in spite of an island-wide search, has not yet been recaptured.

Ebanks had been kept a prisoner pending extradition papers from Cuba.

After reading, Capt. Allie rose, ascended the companionway stairs, and returned to the deck. Then he shouted to his crew, "It's time! Weigh anchor Boys!"

Kingston, Jamaica
April 11, 1937

Joe Scott sat on the edge of the bed in his dingy Kingston hotel room as he read the telegram from Allie yet again. It read:

2 April 1937
Christiansted USVI

Dear Brother,

As always, I miss your companionship and hope that you are doing well as Master of your own ship. My ventures continue to be profitable, but only barely enjoyable since you have left to seek your own fortunes.

Without saying more now, I have sent you this telegraph to ask a favour. I am aware of the demands of your ship, but I wish and hope that you will take leave and come to George Town to meet me. Please let me know

by return wire, General Delivery George Town, when that might be.

I would suggest that you travel via Cimboco from Kingston. I ask you not to fail me in this. I need you once again.

Allie

Slowly, Joe refolded the telegram and put it in the left breast pocket of his khaki uniform shirt. He looked out the second storey window of the hotel room down bustling King Street toward Kingston Bay. Although he couldn't see her, he concluded that the *Cimboco* was probably already loaded with her freight, passengers and mail for the return trip to George Town. Although she would probably not depart until nightfall, he decided to go ahead and walk down to the wharf rather than to take a taxi. He had been awaiting her arrival for several days, cooped up in this ratty hotel room, and he needed the air.

He'd not slept well in the old wooden hotel with its raucous billiard saloon below and drunken planters and prostitutes laughing and tramping around the upstairs halls through the night. It seemed he found little peace these days except when he was aboard his own ship enjoying the freedom and quiet of the open sea.

He picked up his canvas sea bag and cap, left the room with the door open and walked down the stairs and through the dark billiard saloon, which reeked of stale rum. It was quiet now, with only a couple of players racking balls and a drunk sitting at a table in a dark corner, slumped over and sleeping, glass empty on the table. He smiled imperceptibly, thinking wryly that this might be any of a hundred port city bars that he had passed through in his life. He stepped out into the sunlit street, squinting and pulling his billed cap over his eyes for shade.

Joe Scott was only twenty-four years old, but even so, his leaving the orphanage in Havana as a boy seemed to him a distant memory, dreamlike in quality. Nonetheless, he remembered clearly all the words and the lessons learned from Sister Elena and Fr. Tomas, and from Capt. Juan Bautista y Silviera, and he had filed them all in his mental record of those things that are right and wrong, and those things that he should live his life by. To that extent, he would never lose them.

Joe had grown tall, 6' 2", with black hair cut short in military style. His piercing blue eyes had become a command tool aboard his ship, where his sincerity and the forcefulness of his orders could be read not only from the words that he said, but also from the look in his eyes. Those features, along with his years of maritime experience and training, had landed him a job as Master of a small coastal trading freighter at the age of twenty-three years. Now, a year later, he was a seasoned Master with high prospects of rising up through the merchant marine ranks and larger motorships with his employer, the Caribbean Fruit & Produce Company. Unfortunately, that would mean more trips to this hell hole, Lower Kingston, where the life-blood of Jamaica in the form of bananas and citrus crops flowed across the wharfs endlessly for delivery to the rest of the world.

On King Street the traffic of human and mechanized commerce was madness. The cries of street vendors selling their wares of every kind and description was muted only occasionally by the roaring passage of mostly rusty, beat up old produce trucks careening their loads of bananas crazily down from the mountains to the wharves, only to turn and grind back up the mountain for the next load. Joe walked casually past the gaudy one-storey shops and rickety bars lining King Street, taking in the sights and sounds of Lower Kingston. He had had his khaki uniform cleaned and pressed by a Chinese servant at the hotel. His white, black billed captain's cap was banded in gold braid, his shoes were polished and his brass belt buckle shone bright in the sun. He had made himself, and was every bit the bright young ship's Master that *El Capitan* had urged him to be.

Kingston's main wharf at the foot of King Street was built on crude, rusting iron piers overlaid with heavy, creosote soaked planking. Dilapidated sheds, most painted green or red, depending on purpose, lined the length of the wharf for storage of incoming and outgoing cargos. When he reached the head of the wharf, Joe Scott could see *Cimboco* moored almost at the end, only her gleaming white cabin and pilothouse visible above the pier. She was abuzz with the activities of embarking passengers and the movement of luggage and cargo. In 1926, the Cayman Islands Motor Boat Company had built the 120 ton motor ship at the George Town yard on North Church Street in Grand Cayman. *Cimboco* (an anagram of the company's name) was launched in 1927 and had become the only reliable freight, passenger and mail boat in Cayman history. She ran regular round trip service every three weeks between Grand Cayman, Little

Cayman, Cayman Brac and Kingston Jamaica. Since he was still quite unsure of his brother's intentions, Joe Scott had purchased only a one-way fare to George Town. In the worse case, he thought, he could catch a return ride back out of Cayman on the first east bound schooner.

Joe literally pushed his way down the wharf though the melee of men, women and children carrying dark green bunches of bananas to the counting gates. Joe skipped the line at the gate, where a giant sweating black man with a machete was easily lopping off the excess stalk ends from the banana bunches as they passed. Shortly thereafter, he arrived alongside *Cimboco* and dropped his seabag on the dock planks. Moving about the wheelhouse of the vessel, Joe could see his friend, Captain Ashlan Foster. Ashlan was from Cayman Brac and Joe had known him since he was a boy running his canoe or catboat back and forth between Cayman Brac and Little Cayman.

Capt. Foster had distinguished himself as a Cayman hero shortly after the great hurricane of 1932 when he immediately brought *Cimboco* from Kingston with food and provisions to rescue the starving and virtually homeless population of the devastated sister islands of Cayman Brac and Little Cayman. As brother seamen, Joe and Ashlan had run into each other frequently in later years as well, both having cargo trips running in and out of Kingston. Like most Caymanian seamen, they had spent time together among the seamy dives of Kingston, and had become fast friends in the process.

It was only a moment before Ashlan caught sight of Joe and leaned out the pilothouse window to yell down:

“Cap’n Joe! You scalawag! What the hell are you doin’ on the poor man’s wharf? I thought you were a big time sea captain now!”

Joe grinned broadly and tipped his cap with his right forefinger.

“Even us big time upscale boys have to visit our poor cousins now and again,” he responded. “Which reminds me, how about a little ride on this scow?”

“Are you kiddin’ me Joe? Come on aboard! But wipe your feet first. Even us poor boys have our pride!”

Joe retrieved his seabag and swung himself over the bulwark and onto the main deck. Then he jogged up the outside stairs to the upper deck and to the wheelhouse. There he and Ashlan grabbed right hands and embraced. Then Ashlan said:

“Alright, my friend, get one of my boys to find you the best first class cabin left while I get this ‘scow’ as you call her—the pride of Cayman—off the dock. Soon as I get her out of the harbour and around the point we can meet in the salon and catch up on old news.”

“Yes sir, Cap’n,” Joe replied. Then he saluted again with a grin, turned on his heel and headed below.

Schooner *Black Hawk* Under Sail
April 11, 1937

The *Black Hawk* had all sails out on a fair breeze. She was only hours out from Grand Cayman on a westerly tack but Allie knew they wouldn't make George Town until late that night—possibly in the early morning hours. All the crew was out of sight, probably below deck, except the ship's cook, Possum. Nobody except Allie knew Possum's real name—only that he was a displaced Cajun from the bayous of south Louisiana. Everybody thought he was probably an escaped convict, but that speculation only made Possum fit better with the *Black Hawk* crew.

Cap'n Allie was at the helm, where he almost always chose to be in the late quiet of each day when they were under sail. There was no sound except the slight whisper of passing sea and the low melodies Possum was playing on his harmonica. Some of his tunes carried a bright Cajun beat, but most were his favorite blues laments.

Allie's mood was somber. He could not get the *Juana Mercedes* out of his mind. Again and again he replayed his memories of *El Capitan* and the crew that was his only family from the day he set foot aboard the *Juana Mercedes* until he washed up virtually lifeless on the shore of Little Cayman. Inevitably, his thoughts turned dark with his memories of the Spaniard, whose face he could still see clearly in his mind's eye. But the stranger, Ebanks… He could only remember shadows of the face that had looked at him down the barrel of that deadly old pistol that last night on the *Juana Mercedes*. He could remember the blinding flashes of light, the thunderous noise of gunshots, and the dead, bloody stare of Cristobal Gual…

Of his own injuries Allie could remember almost nothing—only what Joe had told him—until he finally regained his health under the constant care and attention of Mama Lelia. Unconsciously, Allie reached up to his face with his left hand and slowly tracked the gnarled scar running down from his left ear to the corner of his mouth with his fingers. He gritted his teeth. *Now this man—Ebanks—is back...and he's still free.*

Cimboco

En Route to George Town
April 11, 1937

By 8:30 that evening Capt. Ashland Foster had secured his ship, set her course, and left the next watch to his First Mate. When he came out of the wheelhouse and down to the main deck, he found Joe Scott staring into the growing darkness, still in a deep reverie at the rail. The last bloody scarlet and deep orange hues of the past daylight were fast receding now in the west, casting the deck in ghostly shadows.

"Damn, Joe," Ash said, "things can't be that bad."

Joe was startled from his reflections, and turned quickly to greet his friend.

"I'm sorry Ash, it's just been so long since I've been back home. You know, Daddy Tenny and Mama Leila moved to Mobile after the great storm in '32. Hell, I haven't even seen Allie in over two years. It just seems a little strange goin' back. There just ain't anything left for me in the Caymans anymore."

"You've just been at sea too long, brother," Ash replied, slapping Joe on the back. "Come on and let me buy you a drink at my bar."

With that they moved into the main deck salon and took a table. Most everyone had retired to cabins already except the card players, who had filled the small room with a haze of smoke and small talk.

Capt. Foster got up and stepped over behind the corner whiskey bar, nudging thc ship's bartender/porter gently out of his way.

"What say Joe, how 'bout a drink? It's free! We'll put it on the Captain's ticket." He reached under the bar and fumbled around for his favourite.

"Thanks, Ash, really. Me and Daddy and Allie smuggled so much damned hooch in the prohibition days I just don't really have much of a taste for it anymore. But I'll tell you what. Do you have a really good cigar back there?"

"No sooner said than done, my friend." Ash Foster poured his own drink straight and brought it with one of his best Cuban cigars back to the table.

The Captain and Joe conversed for a while about family and friends, recounted and laughed again about youthful adventures, and finally fell into silence.

Then Ash Foster said to his friend, "Joe, what's troubling you? You're just not the Joe Scott I know. What's going on?"

Joe leaned back in his chair and finally smiled. "Come on, Ash, you know me—I just worry too much. I got a wire from Allie to come to George Town. I mean, that was it: Come to George Town. What the hell is goin' on in George Town anyway? It would be easier for him to come to Kingston."

"Damn, Joe, is that all? You know Grand Cayman—the only problem there is too many preachers and too few sinners—women anyway. Hell, they got some cars now and no decent roads to drive 'em on, got a telegraph office—even finally got a good bar. You remember ol' Cap'n Ben Grainger? He came back to George Town and by God built him a good whiskey bar. All the preachers hate him and all the men love him. That's it. That's the news. Except...wait, you're probably too young to remember this guy named Gideon Ebanks..."

Capt. Foster turned in his chair to the bartender and said, "Malcolm, you got a copy of the *Daily Gleaner* back there? Bring it over here."

Malcolm brought the newspaper over to their table and laid it out before them. The front page of the April 11, 1937, edition carried the following article:

GIDEON EBANKS BREAKS GAOL

Rewards Officially Offered for Capture of Colourful Caymanian Bad Man.

ISLAND'S HONOUR.

GRAND CAYMAN, April 11—'What are they going to do with the prisoner, Gideon Ebanks?' Wherever they met in Grand Cayman answers to that question were surmised.

No one thought of asking, What is Gideon doing with himself?' But this was the question dramatically answered on the morning of March 31st. Gideon Ebanks escaped.

A Public Notice gives the following information:

On the 31st of October 1922 one of the foulest and most atrocious crimes of recent years was committed in the Caribbean. A Schooner the Juana Mercedes was piratically seized and her and master, loyal crew and passengers brutally murdered. Among those last were two children whom it appears were thrown overboard alive.

It is alleged that two of the three assassins were, to the disgrace of the Cayman Islands, natives of this Dependency. One was arrested and escaped again on March 31, 1937.

It is the duty of all persons, of no matter what age or sex, to assist in the recapture of this man, for, apart from the duty of all civilized persons, it is only by his being brought to trial that the fair name of Cayman can be restored.

The following rewards are hereby offered:

(a) Twenty-five Pounds to the person or persons, not being members of the Constabulary Force, who effect his arrest.

(b) Ten Pounds to the person or persons, not being members of the Constabulary Force, who may give information leading directly to his arrest.

(c) Five Pounds to the person or persons, not being members of the Constabulary Force, who may give information which will lead directly to the conviction of any person or persons who may aid, assist, succour or abet the said Gideon Ebanks in his escape from the gaol at Georgetown, his maintenance or sustenance whilst at Georgetown, or his possible final attempt to leave Grand Cayman.

(Sgd.) A. W. CARDINALL
Commissioner
Cayman Islands, B.W.I.

Chapter 23

Aboard *Black Hawk*
Hog Stye Bay, George Town
April 12, 1937

The schooner *Black Hawk* was resting quietly at anchor only a hundred yards offshore from the barcadere in George Town.

The bright blue morning sky was spotless, and the little community of George Town looked as idyllic as a sprinkling of white doll houses scattered in a green profusion of shrubbery and flowering trees, all lined along neat, white lanes of crushed coral marl and shells.

Bertie Panton had completed his customs and quarantine inspection of the *Black Hawk* earlier that morning. He had a brief but cordial conversation with Capt. Allie Scott, who signed port of entry forms, paid the small customs tariff, and helped Panton back aboard the Government skiff for his return to shore.

Capt. Allie was now below deck in his cabin. He was seated behind his chart table carefully studying several charts and maps of Grand Cayman. A few minutes earlier, he had sent for the ship's cook—his friend Possum.

Hearing a light knock at the door of his cabin, Allie responded, "Enter."

Possum ambled in nonchalantly and stood briefly before his Captain before Allie motioned him to be seated. Bright daylight was streaming down through the cabin's portholes on the chart table, so Possum easily recognized the charts spread before them. Allie used his Zippo for a light and pulled several times to get a glow on the tobacco in his pipe. When he was sure it was lit, he looked across the table and said:

"Possum, you been sailin' with me for a long time and you always will be until one of us dies or you decide to quit. You know all that by now don't you?"

"Well Cap'n, I rekin' I know that by now. We already been mostly killed, captured, arrested, and chased bad wemmin' together. I figure we got a purty lucky deal goin'."

"O.K. Possum. We understand each other. I got a job to do and only a swamp rat like you can get it done quick. It's got to be done here…now…on this island. That's what I need. Can you do it?"

"You mean get down in the swamp on this island, Cap'n? This ain't nothin' compared to back home. What you want me to do?"

"Here's the deal, Possum: There's a fella here on this island that I want to meet real bad. Problem is, the Law wants him real bad too, and they been lookin' for him and can't find 'im. 'Course that's cause he's got local help and he's most likely up hidin' in the North Sound swamp 'til he can get back off the island. That's where you come in: I want you to find him first and let him know we can get him back off the island on the

Black Hawk. All you got to do is find him and make a time for me to meet him personally to cut the deal. An' don't forget to remind him that there's got to be some money in the mix if I'm goin' to get him off this island. You got it?"

"I got it Cap'n. Won't take me a day or two most to find this fella' on this 'lil island. Wha'd you say his name was?"

"It's Gideon Ebanks. His friends call him Giddy. But you know you ain't gonna talk about this, right?"

"Right, Cap'n. You know me—I ain't sayin' nuthin' to nobody."

"Good. Here's what we're gonna do, Possum… I got lots of maps and charts of the island right here in front of us. We're gonna look at 'em and study 'em 'til you know this place like the back of your hand. Then we're gonna' get you supplied and you're gonna go find Ebanks for me. Deal?"

"Deal, Cap'n! I ain't had a fun job like this in a long time."

Possum's real name in his former life in south Louisiana bayou country was Guidry Bujeau. He had left that name behind ten years ago when he escaped a Louisiana chain gang by throwing down his shovel and diving into an alligator infested bayou. He was only nineteen years old at the time. Although the prison guard fired off a couple of half-hearted shots at his escapee, Guidrey was already well into the swamp and there was no way the guard was going to follow him. So, as far as the guard was concerned, that was the end of Guidry Bujeau.

After a few months, Guidry Bujeau was assumed dead by Louisiana authorities—either drowned or eaten by alligators or both. In any event, Bujeau wasn't worth mounting a real search in the hostile environment of bayou swamplands. After all, this particular inmate—Bujeau—had only killed a man in a drunken knife fight. Worse things happened. So it was that Guidry Bujeau was written off and quickly forgotten by Louisiana law enforcement.

What the authorities didn't know was that when it came to bayou swamp, Guidry was like a rabbit in a briar patch. A week after his escape, Guidry was in Baton Rouge hoping to stowaway on the first outbound ship he could find. As it turned out, that ship was the schooner *Black Hawk.*

In those days, *Black Hawk* was crewed by Captain Tenny Scott and his sons, Allie and Joe, along with a couple more Caymanian deckhands. The moonless night before they cast off for a cargo run from Baton Rouge to Havana, Guidry managed to slip aboard and squeeze into a crawl space between some tarp covered crates on deck.

It wasn't until *Black Hawk* was well into the Gulf of Mexico en route to Havana that Allie pulled off the cargo tarp and found the stowaway, who met his eyes but didn't move. Allie motioned for Daddy Tenny to come over and take a look, which he did.

Tenny said, "I'll be damned, boys! We got us a stowaway!" He and Allie were both grinning now, but Guidry Bujeau still didn't move or speak. He was sure he'd be turned back over to the American authorities.

"What's your name, Lad?" Tenny said, smiling at Bujeau. Still he got no response from the cajun.

Then Tenny said, "O.K., boy. That's O.K. if you got no name, hidin' down in there like you're dead. We jus' gon' call you Possum. Now, Possum, let me tell you somethin'. *Everybody* on this boat got to work, so get yo' ass outta there so' I can figure out what you can do." By that time the whole crew was laughing.

Sure enough, in no time Tenny and the crew discovered that Possum could cook…*really cook!*

Now, ten years later, Possum was still the ship's cook. He'd stood side by side with Capt. Tenny and the boys through the best of the rumrunning years and—like the rest of them—Possum had amassed enough of a retirement that he could quit the sea if he wanted. But that wouldn't happen. Guidry Bujeau had found family with Capt. Tenny and the Scott boys. He had found a new life and a new world on the sea. He had found his place—no regrets.

After Allie and Possum had studied and discussed the Grand Cayman charts and inland maps, they gathered a rucksack full of supplies and water that Possum would need for the search. They anticipated that he would probably have to spend as many as several nights out in the North Sound mangrove swamp, because night was most likely the only time Ebanks would be out and moving around.

When Possum was satisfied that he had everything he needed, Allie rowed him to shore on the ship's skiff and put him ashore at the barcadere. There Possum hoisted his rucksack, strapped it over his shoulder, and set off along Church Street toward the two storey white frame Court House. There he turned on Shedden Road and started the trek for North Sound.

By that time it was early afternoon and the sun was out in full force. Possum pulled the brim of his floppy felt hat down low over his eyes to help protect against the blinding glare of the white, coral marl road. As many times as they had passed through George Town over the years, this was the first time Possum had made it further from the waterfront than Capt. Ben Grainger's Tavern. It really was a very beautiful little town, he thought, with its trim, whitewashed fences enclosing yards of white sand and mostly small, white frame cottages with brightly coloured shutters.

This day the shutters were all opened for the mild weather, and many of the Cayman women were outdoors busily using twig brooms to sweep all litter of coconut fronds, almonds and breadfruit leaves from their immaculate white sandy yards. Some of them were trimming back the tangles of flowering vines that draped their fences or tending the many-coloured azaleas, jasmine and bougainvillea that surrounded their little neat houses.

Occasionally one of the women would acknowledge Possum with a glance, to which he would respond by tipping his hat and making a pleasant comment. He felt quite sure that they were all wondering what a stranger like him was doing wandering through town. *More the reason*, he thought, *to keep my search quiet and low key.*

On the outskirts of town Shedden Road split into a fork at North Sound Road and Crewe Road. Possum took the left fork toward North Sound, a huge lagoon or shallow bay on the northwest end of the island. As he walked further toward North Sound the upland tree cover of palms, casuarinas, almond and breadfruit trees diminished completely until the road became nothing more than a double rutted track built through the middle of mangrove swamp. The roadway had been filled and compacted enough to accommodate wagons and the very few automobiles that were now on the island, but it was still primitive by modern standards.

At the end of his long walk through the swamp, Possum found North Sound—a huge open water embayment encircled on three sides by deep mangrove swamp. On this clear day he could see that the north quarter of the sound was protected by reef, and from Cap'n Allie's charts he knew that there was only one channel entrance through the reef that was broad enough and deep enough to accommodate the passage of Cayman's many turtling schooners.

Possum moved quickly away from the open road and settled back into some thick underbrush to survey the bay.

He could see that North Sound Road dead-ended at the foot of Government Pier—a broad, wood planked dock that ran another several hundred feet out into the bay. At the end of the pier was a tall pole, like a ship's mast, with a rope through a pulley suspended from the top like a flagpole. Clearly, that rig was used to pull up a lantern at night to serve as a lighthouse or marker for night traffic on the bay.

Off to the east of the pier were a series of several large open pens that were built out from the shore into the shallows of the sound. These were built of hundreds of posts driven into the sand and interwoven with branches, vines and rope to form corrals—turtle crawls. These were built to keep live turtles in while they awaited reshipment to foreign markets—mostly the United States. On the shoreward side of the crawls were several small, rough-cut wooden shacks for the men who served as the crawl tenders. At this moment, none of the men who served as crawl maintenance and watchmen could be seen moving about. Possum assumed they were in their shacks and only made periodic rounds to check the crawls.

No turtle schooners were presently in port, so other than a few unattended skiffs tied alongside the pier, all was quiet.

Guidry Bujeau scratched the stubble of whiskers on his chin and thought out what he might do in Gideon

Ebanks' situation: Ebanks knew he would be jailed again and then extradited to Cuba if he was caught. His only choice was to get off the island. His best bet was probably to stowaway on a Cayman turtle schooner right here at this pier, maybe with the help of friends or family. Ebanks was much more likely to be seen and apprehended if he tried to pass back over the island through George Town to catch a ship, so his best chance of escape was right here off Government Pier on a departing local turtler—the same way he had come back to Grand Cayman. But Ebanks had to have food and water—probably coming at night right to this spot to meet whoever was helping him to get resupplied. It was unlikely that Ebanks would be traveling along the northeast shore because he would have to come and go through the crawl tenders' camp. Possum concluded that Ebanks was hiding somewhere in the swamp surrounding the westerly rim of the sound, so that was where he would start his search.

Possum shouldered his rucksack and started moving to his left keeping in the cover of thick brush along the shoreline. There was a narrow white sand beach running from the pier several hundred yards before the shore diminished into mangrove swamp. At the last point of sandy ground, Possum put down his rucksack, took off his brogan shoes and put on a set of rubberized hip waders, held up by suspenders. Then he took out a sheathed machete on a belt and fixed it around his waist.

When he was set, Possum again closed and shouldered his ruck and set out into the black water and frenzy of mangrove roots and thick foliage of the swamp.

Back in George Town, Allie had decided to set out on a search of his own. He rowed the ship's skiff back to shore and secured her at the barcadere. Then he strolled through town on Church Street and continued along Seven Mile Beach toward the village of West Bay. If anyone knew where Gideon Ebanks was, Allie figured it would be someone from the west end of the island where Ebanks grew up. Although he didn't hold out much hope that anyone would talk to a stranger about Ebanks, he was restless and determined to give it a try. He knew he had to occupy himself until his brother Joe arrived, and he knew he couldn't make any progress sitting in Cap'n Ben Grainger's Tavern.

Chapter 24

Aboard *Cimboco*
Approaching George Town
April 13, 1937

Joe Scott stood at the rail on the bow of *Cimboco* and grinned. George Town had changed, indeed, but not much since his last visit... Even as a boy sailing with Daddy Tenny it had been one of his favourite places—the "big city" of the Cayman Islands.

Still, on their approach to Hog Stye Bay from the Caribbean Sea, George Town looked much the same. The scattering of white houses and cottages with a few frame business buildings and Court House at the foot of Shedden Road, all aligned amongst the greenery on bright white streets of ground coral with the occasional touch of pastels on the buildings to make them—at a distance—seem as if they were tiny models set in an arrangement of children's toys. The bay, crystal clear and flat as glass, only emphasized the impression of a still life painting of a village in paradise, even down to the pristine strand of Seven Mile Beach running all the way to West Bay.

But the approach of *Cimboco* set the community to life and changed her personality completely...

At the time, *Cimboco* was manned entirely by Caymanians. That fact, combined with the hope and expectation of the arrival of interesting strangers from the outside world, still brought George Town residents out in droves for the arrival of *Cimboco*.

Two huge almond trees had grown up close to the waterfront overlooking Hog Stye Bay. They were beautiful and bore the best almonds in town. But more importantly for the local community, they served as a lookout point for incoming ships. Schoolboys had nailed pieces of plank up one of the trees to serve as a ladder to the highest vantage. There they took turns spotting for maritime traffic. With a good eye and some attention, a Cayman boy on station could spot a vessel from the top branches as far to the East as Bodden Town or maybe even coming around Northwest point.

Today was no exception. *Cimboco* had been spotted early on and Joe could easily hear the tolling of church bells and even an occasional conch horn heralding their arrival.

The major difference from earlier days was that now all the community greeters were walking down and congregating behind Malley McTaggart's store on the bay. McTaggart and several other local businessmen had the foresight to build a pier on the bayfront to receive shipping and passengers, and obviously it had been a good idea.

There were at least fifty or sixty people milling around on the pier awaiting clearance for their friends, family and visitors when Capt. Ash Foster brought *Cimboco* alongside the pier. Her lines were made fast and the gangway was put out. But even with all the melee of excitement, Bertie Panton still strictly required an identification check at the foot of the gangway as passengers disembarked, so the excitement only intensified as the line formed for returning passengers.

But even with the focus on returning Caymanians, there was a throng of generally interested bystanders who made it a point to visit every arrival just to see what stranger might arrive to bring news and share stories of the outside world. Consequently, the crowd of spectators always far exceeded the friends and families of returning Caymanians. This day was no different.

Joe Scott immediately noticed that a whole group of young ladies, mostly formal and circumspect in ankle length dresses, were gathered around a short, austere looking preacher dressed totally in black with his white choker tight around his thick neck. He was cautiously keeping his flock away from the presumed influx of smokers and drinkers who may be invading their Christian domain. *No doubt*—Joe thought—*he's here to greet another missionary sent to save native souls.*. Then his eye caught, for a mere second, the intense glance and fleeting smile of the prettiest of the church girls. She averted her glance almost immediately, but Joe simply thought, not self-effacing but realistic—*you deserve better than me sweetheart.*

When the last of the passengers were disembarking from *Cimboco* it seemed as if the whole population of young men and sailors in George Town came streaming down toward the waterfront from Cap'n Ben Grainger's Tavern. They were laughing and joking as they walked alongside an old ramshackle Ford roadster. The car—popping and coughing loudly—was piloted loosely by a giant of a retired sea Captain known as Cap'n Ben Grainger.

Ben Grainger was a local seafaring legend in his own right. He was big, blonde and barrel-chested with huge hands and a perpetual grin. Even at his age (nobody knew exactly what that was) Ben was strong as an ox team and twice as stubborn. He had sailed everywhere, knew everybody who was anybody on the waterfront, and was the first man who had the *cojones* (as he put it) to build a real liquor bar in the Cayman Islands. He dared the preachers to disagree and he had a huge, tough following of young and old sailors alike who followed his religion (or politics, as the case may have been).

Joe Scott was the last passenger to come down the gangplank from *Cimboco.* He greeted Bertie Panton politely but briefly, showed his formal identification papers, and headed immediately to the Grainger congregation. An entourage of young men and boys were grouped around Cap'n Ben's old roadster, where he and Cap'n Allie Scott sat with their feet propped up on the dashboard. They were laughing mightily at some joke one or the other had told. Then Allie saw his brother approaching in the waning crowd and he raised his hand, waving crazily.

"Joe! Joe!! I see you boy! Get yo' ass over here and give me a hug!"

Joe threw his seabag in the rumble seat and literally fell across his brother, giving him a mighty hug while slapping Cap' Ben on his huge shoulder with his other hand.

"Well *Jesus* Joe, this don't mean we have to kiss does it?" Allie said, winking at Cap'n Ben.

Joe stepped back instantly and took a long look at his brother.

"Hell, I hope we don't have to kiss, brother," Joe responded, "I swear you get uglier every time I see you!"

Cap'n Ben Grainger laughed heartily with a twinkle in his mischievous blue eyes and said, "I don't give a damn what either of you say, I'm purtier than both of you put together an' I can't imagine nobody kissin' either one of you, even on a bad day!"

With that, Cap'n Ben cranked his old Ford with a bang and a sputter. After grinding it in gear, Ben popped the clutch and the old car lurched forward, leaving a rooster tail of shell fragments and white dust behind them. With that, Cap'n Ben's whole bar crowd turned laughing to follow him and the Scott brothers the two or three hundred yards back to Cap'n Ben's Tavern.

At that same moment Guidry Bujeau was moving slowly through knee deep water and a profusion of mangrove roots. He had his machete out of its sheath but used it mostly to push back limbs and branches. He was carefully picking his way through the swamp back toward the open water of North Sound. He had now spent two days and two nights methodically crisscrossing the swamp back and forth from North Sound to higher ground, searching for any sign of human movement. So far, his efforts had been unsuccessful.

Possum's plan was to cover as much ground as possible each day, but with each swamp crossing taking him further to the north and farther away from Government Pier. Each night he had ended in a position close enough to the open water of the bay to detect the movement of anyone passing along its edge. To say the environment was inhospitable for human traffic would be an understatement.

Even the higher salt marshes that Possum had covered were black and dry, sun-cracked expanses, or shallow ponds covered in water lilies or black sawgrass and prickly reeds. The deeper swamp was overgrown in tough, twisted stilts of mangrove with gnarled roots and ragged branches. The dry ponds and mudflats that he had crossed were covered by thousands of crabs of all colour, kind and size. They were startling to see if for no other reason than their immense numbers. It seemed to Possum as though they scurried in waves with each step he took, all baring their one large claw toward him in unison as if they were willing to fight this huge intruder among them.

Then there were the snakes everywhere... Possum knew from Allie that there were no poisonous snakes in the Caymans, but even so they were annoying. It was not uncommon that a footstep in the murky, shallow water would bring out a dark, slithering water snake to swim between his legs. Often there were camouflaged tree snakes coiled around or dangling from the mangrove limbs as he pushed his way through.

It was not that Guidry Bujeau was frightened or intimidated…hell, he had grown up in the swamps of south Louisiana. This swamp was nothing new…it was just *different*.

And so Possum pressed on, more determined than ever to find Ebanks for his Captain.

It was almost dark before Possum could hear the distant roar of breakers on the northern reef of Great Sound. In a few more minutes he had pushed forward enough to see the sun's orange reflection on the open water of the lagoon. As he continued his slow, deliberate course, Possum couldn't help but feel a pang of disappointment that he had found no trace of human activity or even a good hiding place, much less Ebanks himself. He was beginning to doubt his own judgment about Ebanks' general location.

But then his luck changed. Possum froze in place. Tied off among some mangrove roots near the open water of the bay he could see a canoe. As his eyes slowly scanned the tangle of mangrove forest inland of the canoe, Possum could make out what appeared to be a dense, small palm island. Although it was clearly surrounded by mangrove swamp, Possum could see that the palm canopy of the small island rose above the lower tangle of foliage surrounding it.

I should kick my own ass, Possum thought. *I should have known he was using a canoe to come and go.*

I'm the only one dumb enough to slog through this damned swamp.

Now he knew he had to think out how he would approach Ebanks…if it *was* Ebanks using that canoe. *Hell, for all I know he may have a gun or a knife or a couple of friends with him.*

Possum settled quietly back on a knot of mangrove roots and began to plan his strategy. But before he could form a thought, he stiffened to the sound of cracking foliage…

Back toward the palm island he had heard movement. He was sure of it…

Possum reached up carefully and quietly parted some brush that was obscuring his view. Sure enough, the sound of footsteps crackling in dried palm fronds echoed again across the shallow water to his position. Possum squinted his eyes and hardly breathed.

Now he could see a man moving about in the brushy foliage of the palm island. Then the man appeared full body, standing on the edge of the island bank. He was pulling at black rubber knee boots, apparently trying to get his feet adjusted in them. When he was done with the boots, the man picked up an unlit lantern and waded slowly into the shallow dark water. He was obviously heading for the canoe. *It's now or never*, Possum thought, *I'm gonna lose him if he gets to that canoe…*"

Possum yelled out:

"Ebanks! Gideon Ebanks! I'm here to help!"

Ebanks literally jumped and almost toppled backward over a mangrove root. It took him a moment of splashing around to regain his footing. Then he stared out in Possum's general direction.

"Who the hell are you?! What do you want?" Ebanks shouted.

Possum could see that Ebanks' hair and clothes were disheveled and his face was covered in dark stubble. His eyes looked sunken and tired. Possum concluded quickly that Ebanks wasn't faring well hidden in this swamp and needed to get out.

"Look, Ebanks, I told you I'm a friend. I can help you get off this island. Our schooner is anchored off George Town. Do you want to hear what I've got to say or not?"

Ebanks still couldn't discern exactly where Possum's voice was coming from. He scratched his chin for a few moments, furtively scanning the mangrove forest before him. Finally he said:

"All right Mister. I reckon if you was police you'd already showed yourself…so come on out an' let me see you. I ain't got a gun, so I might as well hear what you got to say."

With that, Possum slowly emerged from the brush and waded carefully toward Ebanks, his empty hands open and held out so Ebanks could see them.

Chapter 25

George Town
Wednesday
April 14, 1937

The arrival of *Cimboco* the preceding day had inevitably led to a rowdy homecoming party at Cap'n Ben's Tavern that night. Allie and Joe had stayed up to celebrate with Ben's local crowd. They were late returning to the *Black Hawk*, but still they were both excited and restless. They laid out on the stern deckhouse and looked up at the stars, quietly recounting the stories of their childhood and adventures together.

There had been much talking and storytelling at Cap'n Ben's earlier, of course; but never had the brothers revealed their beginnings on the *Juana Mercedes*—only to Daddy Tenny after he adopted them. Tenny had made up an elaborate story when they were boys about taking in two impoverished nephews from the Bay Islands off Honduras. He had told everyone that's how the boys knew Spanish. That was the story they had stuck by all these years.

So now—fifteen years later—the horror of the *Juana Mercedes* was but a distant memory for Joe Scott. His brother Allie was a different matter. Perhaps it was that Allie was a little older, or that he was so grievously injured, or that he was saved from certain death only by the efforts of a small child—now his adoptive brother. Whatever the reasons, Allie had carried within him a fire of hatred from the *Juana Mercedes* that would not be extinguished. So Joe had learned never to speak of the *Juana Mercedes* with Allie—he didn't like the dark side it brought out in his brother.

Joe knew, however, that this visit to Grand Cayman was somehow about the nightmare of the *Juana Mercedes* incident. He knew it could not be coincidental that Allie had insisted on coming back to Grand Cayman after the public revelation that Gideon Ebanks had returned and again escaped imprisonment.

But this night—only the second visiting his brother in several years—Joe didn't want to think about the *Juana Mercedes*. He put it out of his mind for the moment.

Joe and Allie and Cap'n Ben were sitting together this evening engaged in serious conversation at Ben's Tavern. They had elbows, drinks and an ashtray on the round, marble top table and Joe was occasionally puffing his perennial Cuban cigar.

"It's over, I tell you it's over!" Cap'n Ben stated emphatically, "How's anybody going to make a living on a sailing ship a few years from now? It's all gone to steam and oil. What's a real sailor going to do? Why'd you suppose I quit and got me this tavern?"

"You may be right, Ben," Allie replied, "but how do you think them big smoke bellies are goin' to get around to the folks scattered on islands all around this Caribbean? Hell, most places the water's too shallow for passage of those guys."

"Motor barge!" Ben responded, "You wait and see! It won't be long before somebody comes up with flat bottom, shallow draft motorized barges. Shoot, they already got 'em working inland on all the big ports and rivers in the U.S. You'll see Allie, I'm tellin' ya…you gonna end up bein' a dinosaur."

After a moment of silence Ben continued, "I mean look at your brother. Joe's already got his own steamship. Before you know it, he'll be runnin' international routes on one of them huge tankers or freighters."

"You're probably right about all that, Ben," Allie replied, "an' I know you're jus' tryin' to give me good advice, but my life is sailing. That's where it started, and that's where it'll end. Besides, we did pretty good in the prohibition. Heck, Ben, don't you think I know how you got the money to build this tavern and live the good life on land? Don't worry about me…I'm gonna be O.K."

Joe leaned silently back in his chair and took another pull on his cigar. He knew this conversation would go nowhere with Allie. He knew that in his mind and in his heart, Allie was still on the *Juana Mercedes*. He was First Mate to his first father figure—*El Capitan*—and he would live out his life under the command and expectations of his beloved first mentor. Joe knew that time would not change *El Tigre*. He decided to change the subject.

"Ben, where the hell did you get that damned monkey?" he said, motioning over to the gangly spider monkey crouched in the sill of the open front window of the tavern.

"You won't believe it Joe—Ol' Slick is the best pet I ever had. An old sailor came through here a couple years ago on a South American schooner. He had dysentery bad and ended up dyin' right here on this island. Nobody knew what to do with his monkey, so I took 'im. Turns out he's a smart little bugger. He loves the women and they love him. Hell, I couldn't get a woman to come in this tavern if it wasn't for Ol' Slick. They all make over him and he loves it. Even better yet, he don't like children. Any time a curious kid comes around, Ol' Slick screams and hollers and jumps around like he's crazy, an' that keeps the kids away. A lot of people like that…"

Now that the conversation had turned to bar talk, Allie sat back in his chair and let his mind wander. Evening had turned to dark and still he had not heard back from Possum. This was the third day since Guidry Bujeau had set out to find Gideon Ebanks and Allie was starting to be concerned. He knew the Cajun could take care of himself, but still his apprehension was beginning to show in his dark mood.

Allie's reverie was broken when a feminine voice said:

"May I get you another drink, Captain Allie?" A pretty negress was standing beside him with a small notepad. She was wearing a brightly coloured, knee length cotton dress with sandals. *Pretty scandalous if you ask the local preachers*, he mused.

"Thank you, Vanessa," Allie responded, "I'll have another please."

"Cap'n Allie, you should know by now you can call me 'Vannie.' Everybody else does." She left him with a smile and went back behind the long bar to mix his drink.

There's no way I could ever leave the Caribbean, he thought. *My ship and these islands and this sea are my soul.*

Allie smiled as he looked around Ben's Tavern and took it in again.

Ben's Tavern was much the same as innumerable other Caribbean bars he had been in. It was a big, wooden barn-like space with open rafters and a long, plank faced bar. Most of the building, if not all, was probably built from salvage timbers taken from a local shipwreck. The bar had a copper top, and the walls were hung everywhere with drawings, paintings, and a few photographs of mostly local sailing vessels and their captains and crews. The two attractive barmaids were moving among the noisy patrons scattered in a mix of mismatched tables and chairs. An old black man was sitting in a corner playing and singing tunes on his banjo. Occasionally a rowdy sailor would make a song request and he and his buddies would sing along with the old man.

Allie thought again with a smile, *there's no way I'm leaving the Caribbean.....*

At that moment, his thoughts were again interrupted by Vanessa's voice:

"Cap'n Allie, there's a gentleman here to see you. He didn't want to come in...he's on the front porch. I think he's one of your crewmen."

"Thanks, Vanessa, I'll be right back," Allie responded, "don't let my buddies' glasses get empty, love."

Then he rose quietly and left without interrupting the animated conversation between Joe and Cap'n Ben.

Possum was back in the shadows on a corner of Ben's front porch when Allie pushed out through the red swinging doors of the tavern. He glanced around to Possum and stepped over to meet him.

"Damn, boy!" Allie said, "You look like you been rasslin' a shark!"

Possum was disheveled and covered in splotches of mud. His hair was wild and his beard had grown out to a mat of black stubble. The exposed skin of his face and arms was covered in scratches, abrasions and reddened mosquito bites. But his eyes were sharp and focused, even in the shadows.

"No problem, Cap'n," Possum responded in a low voice, "just followin' orders."

Allie lowered his voice in turn, "So what's your report, Possum?"

"Ebanks is gonna meet you at nine o'clock tomorrow night at the foot of Government Pier. He claims he'll have plenty of money, but you'll have to bring *Black Hawk* around to North Sound to smuggle him on board 'cause he figures he'll be caught if he tries to come back down here through town."

The corners of Allie's mouth twisted up into a slight smile. Possum couldn't help but notice that his yellow-green eyes seemed to glow in the dark.

Chapter 26

Two Days Later
Great North Sound
Grand Cayman

Never had a more glorious, beautiful or exciting day presented itself in the young life of Vincent Prendergast. His father was at sea, as usual, but this day his strict, moral and demanding mother had been called upon to attend the funeral of a relative in Bodden Town—way over toward the east end of the island. Admittedly, roads were better than they used to be from West Bay to George Town, Commissioner Cardinall had seen to that, but it was still pretty much sand and marl and razor rock on a rutted track over to Bodden Town toward the East End. Mama would be gone for at least three days and Vincent had formulated a plan for her absence.

Vincent's Schoolmaster at the West End School was aware of his mother's family loss, and surely he would believe the forged note that Vincent contrived to excuse his absence to attend the funeral. So—there it was—Vincent's plan was pure and simple and worked like a charm. Mama was over in Bodden Town, which might as well have been the other end of the earth, and Vincent was in his small canoe fishing on the glimmering Great Sound in the bright sunlight of that Friday, April 16, 1937.

Like most Caymanian lads—black, white, or the racial mix of colours in between—Vincent was lithe, adventurous and strong for a boy of his age. The same as most of the other Caymanian boys of his generation, and all before them, he aspired to a life at sea. His youthful sense of adventure and bravado had inspired his flawless plan to forge an excuse and skip school, so this bright Friday morning he was full of himself and his heady, albeit fraudulent, absence from the endless boredom of listening to the schoolmaster for hours on end.

By ten o'clock that morning he had caught three sizeable angelfish—"Queens" they were called—an island favourite. But he really wanted to fill the canoe with his own personal choice: mangrove snapper from the shallows of the mangrove forest along the east side of the Great North Sound. So he had fished and paddled his way across from west to east, coming into the great mangrove swamp just past the huge turtle pens northeast of Government Pier

Vincent's canoe was perfect for the mangrove shallows. His father had personally carved it out of a huge mahogany log with just enough room for two or three men to work. It was short and double ended, so Vincent could negotiate the shallows and narrow brushy maze of the mangrove forest.

Smiling, Vincent paddled into the mangrove swamp, baited his hook and cast out his line. In devising his plans for this trip, he had also salted away a small pouch of his father's tobacco, so he laid back in the canoe and rolled a cigarette in store bought paper. He thought cheerily, as he lit up and took a deep drag, emulating his father: *This is the life for me. No more school—just freedom and adventure.*

He had not caught a single fish in the mangrove before he drifted off into a self-satisfied nap.

It may have been only minutes, or maybe hours—later he couldn't remember—but when Vincent awoke his bait was gone and the mangrove forest surrounding him was eerily devoid of all sound. The sky had clouded over and the brush and vines and water around him were all in shadow. Then started a misty rain.

For the first time in this glorious day of escape and freedom, Vincent felt a twinge of alarm. He could not get oriented in the overcast, and he had no idea how to get back out of the mangrove forest with no visible sun to follow. The ancient human reaction to his perceived predicament caused the hair and skin to prickle on his neck, and he was urged on to a fearful sensation of watery bowels and weak knees, and suddenly he wanted to throw up. The enormity of his personal sin this day and the specters of superstition he had grown up with simply overcame him. He jumped out of his canoe into the shallows and thrashed through the tangled black roots of the mangroves trying to find his way out to the clear open air of the Great North Sound.

He momentarily forgot his canoe and yelled out, hoping for some response from the turtle crawl tenders or nearby fishermen. Then he tripped on a mangrove root and crashed down in the black water with a cold thud. But his fall into the shallow water was broken by what he later recalled as being like falling on a huge, cold lump of clay. It seemed—he later told his friends and family—

that it tried to grasp him and entangle him with dangling arms and legs, and tried to pull him down, and he rolled over and fought and thrashed out and pushed the creature away. As Vincent struggled and pulled himself out of the muddy quagmire and groping arms of the creature—he glimpsed it as he ran, splashed and crashed away in his panic. As he retreated, he recognized the thing in his mind's eye as a human body.

Arlie (Arlington) Seymour and Ernest Ebanks were sitting with their legs dangled over the end of Government Pier on Great Sound when they first saw Vincent Prendergast paddling furiously in his canoe out of the mangrove swamp from the northeast. They were bottom fishing on the pilings and whiling away the afternoon with frivolous talk and great plans and schemes when Vincent first appeared. At first it was a source of great amusement for the boys to see that their young friend Vincent was also skipping school. Both the boys were pointing and chortling as they watched Vincent's frenzied paddling past the turtle crawls toward Government Dock. But it didn't take the boys long to realize that Vincent was in a real panic—in some kind of real trouble. His face was white and he was screaming for them to help from the time their eyes first met from afar. At first they thought that it might be a joke, but Vincent's pale countenance and frantic paddling convinced them otherwise. They both jumped up and ran back up the dock to shore to meet Vincent in the shallows at the beach where he landed the canoe.

"*Vince! Vincent! What's goin' on mon*?!" they urged in unison. Vincent grabbed Arlie around the shoulders and fell and pulled himself out of his canoe into the knee deep water where they were standing. Breathless, he said:

"There's a dead guy in the mangroves, mon! I swear! I saw him wi' my own eyes!" Vincent was so breathless and panicked that he could hardly get the words out, and the jaws of his two young friends dropped.

Then Arlie ventured, "What you mean mon, you trickin' us? It ain't funny."

"No Arlie, I swear. I was tryin' to pull my canoe back out of the mangroves and I tripped right on 'im! I'm tellin' ya, he was face down and cold as a stone!"

"Well, did ya try to see who it was?" Arlie Seymour queried. Still huffing, Vincent looked over at Arlie with surprise and some contempt.

"What you mean mon?! You think I'm waitin' roun' that swamp for somebody to kill me too? Why don't you go on in that swamp yo'self Arlie…jus' walk right up and shake his hand and say 'How do?' What's yo' name mon?' You ain't jus' dumb, Arlie, you're crazy to boot."

The three of them hurriedly pulled Vincent's canoe up on the sandy beach and Vincent plopped down to rest. He sat in the sand with his elbows on his knees and his chin cupped in his hands. The other two boys sat down on either side of him, all quietly contemplating the reality of their crisis. Vincent had found a dead body and they were all skipping school.

"Wha'd we gonna do mon?" Arlie said to no one in particular. Then he said, "Vincent, you found 'um, what you gonna do?" "Wha'd we gonna do mon?"

Again Vincent snapped his head around, this time toward Arlie. He sneered, "What you mean what ***you*** gon' do? You sittin' here with me, and you an' Ernest spose to be my friends? I'll tell you what ***we*** gonna do—***we*** gonna go back in there together and get him out an' pull 'im up here where the crawl tenders gonna find 'im. We ain't gon be nowhere 'round to be seen…"

"You crazy mon!" Arlie snapped back. "We can't drag no dead body out here in the clear daylight… we'd be caught for sure. An' I ain't speakin' for you, but I ain't goin' in that mangrove swamp to pull out no dead man. Next thing we all gon' be dead in that swamp. I know yo' mama and daddy's gone an' they won't know you ain't home, Vincent, but me an' Ernest can't stay here 'til after dark. My Daddy's gonna tear my ass up if I ain't home on time. Sides that, he'd check with the Schoolmaster to see where I went after school, then he'd find out we done skipped school today. Then wha'd we gon' do?"

The three hopeless young miscreants sat silently for another three or four minutes before Vincent finally spoke up:

"I'm gon' tell ya now boys, there ain't no way out of this 'cept to do the right thing. We can't leave no dead body in the swamp an' go home. That man's ghost gon' follow us around from here on out if we don' do 'im right. You know them duppies, what they get up to. Him and the rest of them dead duppies an' ghosts gon' follow us around from here to kingdom come!"

Arlie and Ernest sat quietly with no response. They knew that the simple logic and truth that Vincent told was unavoidable.

Hearing no protest after another couple of minutes of contemplation, Vincent said: "Ernest, you're the strongest and the fastest, you gotta run as hard as you can over to George Town and find Inspector Watler or one of the Constables. They need to get over here 'cause we ain't goin' back in that swamp. Me an' Arlie gon' find somebody 'round here, maybe a crawl tender or a fisherman to go back out there in the swamp and find that duppy man. We gon' get some help, but we ain't none of us goin' back in there! If we do what we spose to do we can maybe all be home before dark."

Again, there was no escaping Vincent's simple, clean logic.

Ernest jumped up and started to run before he yelled back over his shoulder, "I'm gone. I'll get the police back here in no time!" In truth, Ernest was relieved beyond any other words. Just the thought of hanging around to help find a cold dead duppy man in the swamp gave him chills, and he ran toward George Town with all the youthful strength and resolve the Lord had given him.

After Ernest left on the run, Vincent and Arlie walked close together, side by side, each looking warily from time to time over his shoulder. The silent thoughts of each mirrored the other: *This wouldn't be a good time to find a cold dead duppy man comin' up behind you.*

It happened that Bertie Panton was sitting as Justice of the Peace in the Court of Petty Sessions that same day when now *Inspector* Roddy Watler appeared unexpectedly in the rear doors of the second storey courtroom of the old George Town Courthouse. Justice Panton had been presiding over a seemingly endless Friday afternoon session of petty claims and misdemeanors, and he thought in desperation that he would quit if he had to hear another accusation of chicken stealing or witchcraft mojo. It was already late in the afternoon and when Justice Panton saw Inspector Watler discretely signal the necessity to come forward and approach him, Mr. Panton didn't hesitate a moment to slam his gavel down and announce in a loud voice:

"Ladies and Gentlemen, it is now getting late on in the afternoon and I have other pressing business to attend to. This case, and all others that have not been heard as scheduled today, will be continued to a future date to be set by the Court. This session of the Court is closed!" Then he slammed his gavel down again with such authority that even the timbers of the old wooden Courthouse seemed to tremble. Constable Verle Bush, who served as Bailiff of the Petty Sessions of the Court was caught off guard. He snapped back from his bored haze and jumped up, perhaps a few moments off his proper timing.

"All rise!" he intoned loudly, "God Bless the King and this Honourable Court!" There was already much movement and commotion in the Courtroom gallery, and considerable muted grumbling among those whose cases had been scheduled and remained to be heard, but such was the legal system from time immemorial. Mr. Panton shook his head. *At least we don't lop your heads off or throw you in prison without a right to be heard*, he thought to himself.

Mr. Panton had stood when closure of the session was announced, but as the last of the litigants and onlookers filed from the Courtroom, he sighed and sunk back down in the soft and padded leather chair behind the judicial bench. Mr. Panton was convinced that it was by far the most comfortable chair in the entire Cayman Dependency, except, of course, those provided to His Majesty's Commissioner of the Cayman Islands—now His Honour A.W. Cardinall—in the Comissioners' Mansion several blocks away from the old Courthouse.

Mr. Panton had no time to enjoy his brief respite, however, because before the Courtroom was entirely clear Inspector Watler was already standing stiffly at attention before him. Watler had his right hand raised to his white pith helmet, palm outward in a stiff formal salute before speaking:

"Permission to be heard, Mr. Justice!" Inspector Watler said in a loud, formal voice. Constable Bush, now the only other person remaining in the courtroom, moved from the back of the room to the front row of seats, his curiosity piqued with the unusual late Friday appearance in Justice Panton's Court. Bertie Panton sat up and rested his forearms on the judicial bench before him. He said calmly, "Inspector, what brings you here at this hour of the afternoon? Relax! Stand at ease! For Heaven's sake, you don't have to do this protocol with me. I've known you since you were on your Mama's breast. What's so important at this hour on a Friday afternoon?"

Inspector Watler snapped his right arm down to his side to close his salute and responded, "Your Honour…Mr. Panton, a dead body has been found in the North Sound. Some local boys found the body and there's already a rumour there may have been foul play."

Bertie Panton was startled with the news, but made a conscious effort not to let it show in his demeanor. Serious crime in the Caymans was rare, he knew, and murder was virtually unheard of—at least since the departure of the pirates several centuries ago. "Who is it Inspector, do you know?"

"No sir. It was reported by a young man, Ernest Ebanks of West End. He had run at least two miles from the Government Dock before he found me, and he had been telling others along the way. I believe he's telling the truth, Sir."

Besides his many other positions and responsibilities in Cayman Government, Bertie Panton was also the official Coroner and his duty was clear. Without further hesitation he said, "Constable Bush, you go out right now and find Dr. Overton and find some way to get him to Government Pier. You, Inspector, you go find us some way to get over there without walking. I've had about all I can stand today."

It was still daylight when Coroner Panton and his official entourage reached the Government Dock at the south end of the Great Sound. The entire area, which was normally quiet and mostly deserted when a turtle schooner or freight boat wasn't in at the Government Dock, was alive with activity this late afternoon. As it had turned out, the boys who found the body had apparently managed to find and alert everyone within miles of the scene. Then, to make it worse, those that heard the news had told friends and neighbors and now at least fifty people, mostly men and some boys, had gathered on the beach and the Government Dock, and some in small boats, had come to follow the action.

Inspector Watler, still in his white summer uniform—blue trousers with broad vertical crimson stripes and white formal tunic with bright brass buttons, led the way toward the end of Government Dock. His formal white British pith helmet bore the gleaming insignia and Coat of Arms of His Majesty the King and he carried his usual polished black baton, swinging it back and forth at his side in perfect pace with his stride. It was unnecessary to tell the onlookers to step back out of the way. The Inspector of Police for the Island, followed by the single most important Civil Servant and his official entourage told the story without words. This solemn occasion was serious business on this small, obsolete Dependency of Great Britain.

As a result of his powerful position and long tenure with the Government, Mr. Panton recognized and knew by name every single resident adult on Grand Cayman, and most of the older children as well. Bertie Panton smiled and acknowledged many, even tipping his brown fedora hat for the few local women who had made it to the alleged crime site. Already the assembled citizens were whispering among themselves that there had been a murder, and Mr. Panton knew that the rumour to that effect would have spread to most every household on the Island before the morning.

When he reached the end of Government Dock, Mr. Panton could see several small boats scattered in an area about 500 yards to the northeast past the huge turtle crawl fences in the shallows next to the fringe of the mangrove forest. Several of the men from the boats were wading in about waist deep water and seemed to be indicating and focused on something in the water close by.

Mr. Panton murmured something to Inspector Watler, and then turned to study the various male citizens on the dock. He knew, of course, those who were intelligent and responsible, and those who were less than reputable from his many years of service as Justice of the Peace, Magistrate and Clerk of Court. In a moment, he looked at one of the gentlemen in the crowd and said, "Elroy Bodden, could you step over here for a moment?" Constable Bush, who had remained in attendance to Mr. Panton, quickly separated the man from the crowd and escorted him to Mr. Panton, who shook the man's hand and indicated that he should take a position at Mr. Panton's side. Panton continued the exact same process ten more times, at which point he was satisfied. Then he instructed Constable Bush to clear the rest of the onlookers from Government Dock. Constable Bush jumped to his instructions immediately, herding the remaining onlookers to the foot of the dock, most of them muttering and grumbling, resentful that they would not be privy to the details of the drama playing out before them.

In the meantime, Inspector Watler, following Mr. Panton's orders, had commandeered two of the larger boats at Government Dock, holding them and their owners for further instructions from Mr. Panton.

After the Constable pushed the crowd back from within earshot, Mr. Panton turned to address his eleven inductees. "Gentlemen," he said in a low, but typically authoritative voice, "in my official capacity as Coroner of this Island, I have selected you to serve as the Coroner's Jury in this matter. In your capacity as a Juror, you are called upon to investigate this matter with me and, thereafter, to render a verdict as to the cause of death of the person we are about to view. It will be, and it is your duty to disregard from this moment any rumour or innuendo that you may have heard about this incident. Is there any of you who cannot meet such a burden, speak up now?"

Hearing no response, he continued, "Is there any of your number who cannot for reasons of health or otherwise attend a viewing of the body with me this afternoon, and be present for a Coroner's Inquest tomorrow afternoon?" Again, hearing no response, he said, "All raise your right hands please," to which command he received their immediate compliance.

Then Mr. Panton stepped back a couple of steps and raising his own right hand swore his jury: "Do you solemnly swear that you will faithfully and truly serve as a Coroner's Jury in this matter, so help you God?" The response was an immediate, and forceful unified voice, "I do!"

It took less than ten minutes to load up the commandeered boats and row out to the body, still floating face down. The two boatloads of inquest jurors lined up on each side of the body, where two men were still standing in the water beside it. Mr. Panton addressed one of the men immediately:

"Verneal, how long you been here?"

"It's probably been a couple hours now Bertie—I mean—Mr. Panton. Me and Dolen here was the first ones to the body after the boys found it." Verneal looked at his friend Dolen who was bobbing his head up and down vigourously as if the truth of his friend's answer might be in question.

"Well, simply tell us what happened the best you can Verneal," Mr. Panton requested politely.

Verneal glanced briefly around at the men in the two boats on either side of him. "You all know me," he said, "me an' Dolen here mind the turtle crawls day an' night to make sure they don't get no holes an' the turtles don't get out, or they don't get stole an' that sort of thing. Well, a couple hours ago, I guess, here come young Vincent Prendergast and his friend Arlie Seymour, all yellin' an' screamin' wavin' their arms. All the commotion got Dolen out of the tender shack and the boys start to tellin' us they done found a dead body an' such. Well, Vincent had his canoe right there at Government Dock, so we paddled out here with him to check it out, and sure enough, he showed us where this body was back in the mangroves."

"So this isn't where you found the body?" Mr. Panton interrupted.

"No, no...," Verneal responded, " we figured you'd have a hard time getting back up in them mangroves. It's real thick in there. Sides that, Vincent an' Arlie had to go home early so's they wouldn't get in trouble, so they had to take his canoe on out of here. So me an Dolen, we figured the best thing to do was to pull 'im out here and wait for the police to come. They told us Ernest Ebanks done run on to George Town to get the police, so we figured we'd stay right here and not let this body get away in the tide or somethin'..."

Again Verneal glanced over at his friend Dolen who had continued to bob his head periodically so as to affirm everything his friend was saying. Verneal looked around again at the boatloads of jurors, smiling and feeling quite smug and proud of himself for the help they had rendered. Bertie Panton realized, of course, that the area where the body had been found had been completed compromised—if it was a crime scene—by the activities of the boys and the turtle tenders. But he decided to ask anyway:

"Verneal, when you first saw this body, was there anything—anything at all—unusual about the spot you found him...I mean, were there any signs of a struggle or anything else in the water, like a gun or a knife or anything?"

"No, *Sir*!" Verneal responded with some emphasis, again quite pleased with himself. "Me an' Dolen done waded all 'roun an' couldn' find nothin', 'cept of course them damned mangrove roots snarled up everywhere and some snakes an' black crabs... Hell, Bertie, you know what inside them mangroves looks like around here as well as anybody!" By this time, Verneal had gotten his confidence up and didn't even glance at his friend for confirmation, but there it was anyway, Dolen's head still bobbing up and down.

"What about the body, Verneal, was it face down like this when you found it?" "Yes Sir, Mr. Panton, jus' like you see it. We jus' each of us grabbed a foot and dragged it out here to get clear of the mangroves.

Panton sat silent for a moment, studying the corpse floating between the jury boats. Then he looked around at his jurors and inquired whether any of them had any questions specifically about the matters he had already covered. No one spoke up, so Panton looked back to Verneal and said, "You boys afraid to turn this body over?" He knew that neither of the men wanted to do it, but that they would probably be too proud to protest.

After glancing furtively at Dolen to see if he was going to speak up, Verneal looked back up to the Coroner and said, "No sir, Mr. Panton, we'll do anything you say."

"Thank you Gentlemen," Panton said respectfully, "now here is what I want you to do… Both of you please stand at the feet of the body and each take hold of a foot." He watched quietly as they complied. "Now Gentlemen, each pass a foot to the other so that the legs are crossed… Good! Now twist the crossed legs around one another until the body rolls itself over…do you understand?" Neither of the men in the water spoke, but they faithfully followed the Coroner's instructions until the maneuver forced the corpse to slowly turn face up between the jury boats.

The silence was palpable for a moment, but then whispers and mutterings began to be heard among the jurors. The corpse was shocking to behold with the eyeballs and part of the lips gone to feed the voracious crabs in the mangrove community, but despite some bloating and the horror of the victim's mutilated visage, there was no doubt—it was the escaped prisoner, Gideon Ebanks

Chapter 27

George Town
Saturday
April 17, 1937

Bertie Panton hurried to his office early the morning after finding Ebanks' body. He had arranged for Inspector Watler to meet him there, and Watler was at his door when he arrived.

"Stand at ease Inspector," he said without greeting, "I'll get to you in a moment."

After hanging his coat and hat on the corner hat rack, Panton sat down, took out a clean piece of Government letterhead, and immediately started writing:

April 17, 1937

Honourable A.W. Cardinall
Commissioner, Cayman Islands
British West Indies

Sir, I beg respectfully to report to you the following re Gideon Ebanks, escaped prisoner.

I was informed last evening that he was found dead in the Great Sound & immediately repaired to the scene accompanied by the Inspector of Police, Collector of Customs & his Assistant. On arriving there I found several men on the Gov't pier & I summoned 11 of them to serve as Jurors; took them to the body in two boats. On arriving there we saw the body floating in the sea near to the mangroves by a turtle crawl on the N. side of the pier. The body was viewed by all present & a pair of handcuffs was found on one of his wrists. It was unanimously decided it was the body of Gideon Ebanks, the escaped prisoner.

I sent for the Gov't Med. Officer & on his arrival he examined the body in the presence of the Jurors.

I gave instructions to the Inspector of Police to have the body interred in a suitable place.

I propose by Your Honour's approval to hold an Inquest to-day.

A.E. Panton, Coroner

"Now, Inspector Watler," Panton said, "you will immediately deliver this message to Commissioner Cardinall and await his response. You will then return here where I will have a summons to appear prepared for service on Captain Allie Scott on the *Black Hawk*. This summons will be mandatory and you will accompany

Captain Scott back to the Courthouse for the Ebanks Inquest this afternoon. Understood?"

Inspector Watler saluted. "Yes, sir!" he said, taking the note from Panton's extended hand. Then he turned stiffly on his heel and left the room.

Joe and Allie were on deck when the Government Quarantine Boat came out from the barcadere. She bore an imperial crown plaque on her bow, while astern a blood red Union Jack blazed in the morning sun. The sputtering of her little motor broke the lazy, bright silence of Hog Stye Bay, immediately bringing the government launch to the attention of all at anchor in the harbour.

From the barcadere her path was set straight for thc *Black Hawk*, which brought Joe and Allie to the rail to watch her approach. Standing in the Quarantine Boat in spotless uniform and pith helmet was Inspector Watler, watching them intently as his two crewmen attended the boat.

"What the hell is *this*?" Joe said idly, not really asking a question he expected to be answered.

Allie stood silent for a long moment. Then he said, "You remember I asked you to come back to Cayman because I needed your help…this may be what I needed you for."

"What are you talking about?" Joe was now looking intently at Allie, trying to read his face.

"Listen, Brother," Allie replied, "if I need you, you'll know it. Until then, keep quiet and let me handle this."

Joe had taken off his cap and was scratching his tousled black hair when the Quarantine Boat bumped up against the side of the *Black Hawk.* Allie had moved down the deck to catch a line and greet her, and he called out, "Inspector Watler, welcome to my ship. How can I help you this fine morning?"

Watler remained expressionless when Allie reached out an arm to help him up the side of the ship and over her rail. When he was firmly on deck, Watler pulled down on his uniform tunic to straighten it and then handed a piece of paper to Allie.

"This is an official Summons to Appear in Court, Captain Scott. I am to escort you ashore to attend a Coroner's Inquest this afternoon."

Allie's lip curled slightly in an almost imperceptible smile. "Does this mean I'm under arrest, Inspector?"

"No, Sir, Captain. It simply means that I am to assure your appearance in Court as required by this summons."

By this time, several of Allie's crewmen had gathered on deck in a loose semi-circle around their Captain and Watler. Possum had taken out his knife and was idly cleaning and shaving his fingernails. Watler was suddenly sweating profusely from under his pith helmet. After several moments of silence, he was compelled to wipe the sweat from his eyes in order to see.

Allie finally broke out into his full, most charming smile. "Inspector Watler, it will be my pleasure to escort you to shore and to attend Court. In fact, I was looking forward to visiting Mr. Panton—excuse me, His Honour Magistrate Panton—one more time before we depart. May I ask what this proceeding is about, Inspector Watler?"

Watler was visibly relieved.

"I'm not sure why you will be attending, Sir, but the proceeding is an inquest into the death of the escaped prisoner, Gideon Ebanks."

Joe immediately focused his attention back on Allie. *What the hell was going on?* He was surprised, but not shocked, about the news of Ebanks' death. *The bastard deserved it no matter how it happened. But now, what has this got to do with Allie?* Allie's face was still fixed in a glowing smile.

"Inspector Watler," Allie said, "surely you will not protest my retrieving my formal coat and cap for these apparently important proceedings?"

"Of course not, Sir." Watler bowed slightly but did not salute.

Within a few minutes, Allie had changed into his most formal uniform and upon return told his crew to go on about their business. He stopped for a moment when he was passing Joe and whispered, "You might want to attend this proceeding Joe—it may be this is when I'll need your help." Then he followed Inspector Watler down into the Quarantine Boat. In no time they had cast off and were heading back to the barcadere.

Joe stood quiet at the rail of the *Black Hawk*, one hand scratching the stubble of a two day beard on his chin. Then he turned and went below to the Captain's cabin to retrieve his coat and cap. He quickly came back on deck and went to the stern, grabbed a line and pulled in the ship's skiff, got in and started rowing to shore.

When he reached the barcadere, Joe dropped a small anchor off the skiff to keep her off the jagged rocks and jumped into the shallow water with his shoes held over his head. After he waded to shore, he put his shoes on and bounded up the rock stairway to Church Street and crossed over to the George Town Courthouse. Fifteen stairs and a moment later he entered the second storey Courtroom. It was only a little after noon, but the courtroom was already filled with curious onlookers. The word had gone out overnight that Ebanks was dead and that fact in itself was enough to bring family, friends, acquaintances and just curious onlookers to the Courthouse to view the inquest.

Inside the rail at the front of the courtroom stood a judge's bench facing the gallery, and off to the right was an assembly of twelve wooden chairs for the jury box. In front of the bench was a railed podium for the standing testimony of witnesses. On either side of the witness stand, also facing the bench, were two tables to be occupied by the opposing parties or the accused and their counsel. At the table on the left, Allie sat silently with Inspector Watler awaiting the proceeding.

Even though all the windows were open, and a slight breeze was wafting through from the bay, the body heat from the packed courtroom was making it intolerable inside. Joe walked out on the second storey veranda and took a Cuban cigar out of his breast pocket. There was nothing to do but light up and wait it out.

The Official Inquest into the death of the alleged pirate and murderer Gideon Ebanks commenced at exactly 1 o'clock that afternoon. The eleven appointed coroner's jurors had been escorted in and seated in the jury box at least a half hour earlier. The big surprise of the day came, however, when Commissioner Cardinall personally made his entry and had a spacious area in the back of the little Courtroom cleared for his seating needs. As was usual in all formal governmental events, he was wearing his grand uniform of blue navy breeches and waistcoat with brass buttons, campaign medals and ribbons festooned over his chest with decorated epaulets on his shoulders. After he was comfortably seated, he removed his bright, white, plumed pith helmet and sat it on the bench seat beside himself. Clearly, he considered that this proceeding might be of some interest in this far corner of the world.

After a solemn entry by Justice Bertie Panton and a call to order and God Save the King by Inspector Watler, Magistrate Panton took his seat at the Bench and pounded the gavel before him.

"All will come to order! This is the Official Coroner's Inquest into the death of one Gideon Ebanks, a Caymanian citizen and former resident of West End Grand Cayman. Please let the record note that our Commissioner, Honourable A.W. Cardinall, is present for the review of these proceedings. Welcome, Sir!" Panton raised his hand slightly to recognize Cardinall, and then quickly proceeded.

"The record will also note that the decedent, Mr. Gideon Ebanks, was a fugitive—an escaped prisoner charged with the crimes of murder and piracy on the high seas. He was awaiting extradition to Cuba when he last escaped our custody on March 30."

Panton then addressed Inspector Watler: "Inspector! Call the roll of Jurors to assure that all are present!"

Watler saluted sharply and then turned on his heel to address the Jurors: "Gentlemen, harken to your names as called and respond please!"

One by one the names of the Coroner's Jurors were called and each responded affirmatively to his name. Then Panton had them all stand, right hands raised, and swear to render a true and fair verdict in the matter, which they did in unison, and were then seated.

"Now, Gentlemen of the Jury," Panton said, I shall read an account of the discovery of the decedent's body."

The courtroom was still as Panton read his lengthy report recounting the recovery and examination of Ebanks' corpse. When he finished reading, Panton looked at the jury and said, "Gentlemen of the jury, are there any additions, deletions or corrections to my report that you wish to offer?" Hearing no response from the jury, he said, "All members of the jury who accept my report as factual and accurate please raise your right hand." The jurors all raised their hands in unison for unanimous approval.

"Now, that having been done, it is incumbent upon me as Coroner to present the evidence and for you, Members of the Coroner's Jury, to render a True Verdict as to the cause of death. In most cases, this task might be considered inconsequential, but in the present case there are facts and circumstances that make further detailed inquiry appropriate. First, as you all know, Mr. Ebanks was at the time of his death an escaped prisoner charged with heinous crimes, including, among others, piracy, murder, theft, and jailbreaking on several occasions. These crimes run back over fifteen years, and justice has yet to be served. There is, in fact, an Extradition Warrant outstanding for the arrest of Mr. Ebanks for his return to Cuba to answer such charges. However, it is clear that this Cuban Warrant will not be executed under the circumstances. Only one of the original perpetrators, Evans Rivers of this Island, ever officially admitted his participation and suffered conviction and Cuban imprisonment for these crimes."

"Notwithstanding all of that, it has been common gossip that Mr. Ebanks remained free on this Island since his escape, possibly living with the help of local accomplices while avoiding the reach of law and justice the entire time."

"None of those circumstances, however, would justify his murder by one or more of those whom he may have aggrieved during his turbulent lifetime. It is our duty, therefore, to determine why and how he died and to render a verdict on the matter."

"Now, that being said, I will call the Coroner's first witness: Dr. George Overton, please come forward."

After Dr. Overton was sworn and took the witness podium, Panton said, "Good Day, Sir! How are you?"

"Fine Mr. Justice Panton, how may I help you?"

"Doctor, after the discovery of the body of the decedent, were you able to identify him to a certainty?"

"Yes, sir. The body was not so deteriorated that most of the jurors and many others standing by could not give definite confirmation of the identity. It was in fact the escaped prisoner, Gideon Ebanks. That was of course further confirmed by the handcuff still on one arm, clearly identifiable as one of the handcuff units that we use in our jail."

Panton paused a moment and asked, "Doctor, was the body in deep water when found?"

"No sir, actually very shallow. Of course that may have been the result of a wind or tidal action."

"Doctor, have you been made aware that Mr. Ebanks was reputed to be an excellent swimmer?"

"Well," Dr. Overton replied, "I inquired of many family members and friends and the response was always the same—Mr. Ebanks was an excellent swimmer, and even with that handcuff on one wrist, he shouldn't have been particularly impaired. There is some speculation, particularly among his family and friends, that Mr. Ebanks was murdered."

Panton paused again, this time to emphasize the gravity of his next question: "Well Doctor, those things known, were you able to determine the cause of death?"

Dr. Overton then paused a moment himself and said, "Frankly, there is no way to be certain. There was some water in his lungs, but it doesn't look like a typical drowning. There is some indication that he died from a lack of oxygen to breathe, but there was nothing notable to indicate whether strangulation or choking had been a factor. From what I could tell, there are no indications of a fight or bruising or abrasions, so I have no basis to conclude that he died except by lack of oxygen, most probably from drowning."

"Finally, Doctor, do you have an opinion as to when Mr. Ebanks died?" Panton looked right into the Doctor's eyes and did not waver.

"Mr. Justice," Dr. Overton said, "there was nothing that I could use as a basis for such a conclusion except what the crabs, fish and natural environment had done to deteriorate the corpse when I first saw it. It was certainly not so decomposed as to indicate a long period of submersion or exposure. I can only vaguely suppose that Mr. Ebanks died a day or two at the most before his body was found."

"In other words," Panton said, "on either the 14th or 15th of April."

"That is correct, Sir."

"Thank you Doctor," Panton said, looking around slowly at the jurors, studying their expressions, " Do any of the Jurors have questions?"

There was no response from the Jurors.

After excusing Dr. Overton, Mr. Panton took a brief break to review his notes and then retook his seat at the head bench. He waited quietly for the crowded Courtroom to come to order on its own. He did not resort to gavel, and shortly the courtroom silenced under his menacing glare.

"Coroner's Court is back in session. Inspector Watler," Panton said, "call our next witness, Captain Allie Scott."

Instantly the Courtroom was completely quiet. Nobody there had any idea why Justice Panton would call Capt. Allie Scott. Although most residents of George Town knew Allie at least by reputation, it was certainly not clear why he might be called to testify in this case.

When his name was called, Capt. Allie Scott rose and walked to the witness podium. He was garbed in his navy bluc uniform. Thc brass buttons on his double-breasted coat were polished and braided gold captain's stripes garnished his epaulets. Once he had taken his stance on the stand, Allie locked both hands on the polished wooden rail before him and looked straight at

Panton, his yellow-green cat eyes fixed on the Magistrate. If he was nervous, he didn't show it.

Panton had his witness sworn in and said simply: "State your full name and address, Sir."

"My name is Captain Allie Scott, Master of the sailing schooner *Black Hawk*, generally plying dry goods and other trade merchandise among the British and American Trade Routes and along Coastal Central America. I own and live aboard my ship, Sir."

"Captain Scott, may I ask why you happen to be here on Grand Cayman at the moment."

"Indeed you may inquire, Mr. Justice Panton, and I am most pleased to answer that I am enjoying a rare and restful opportunity to visit with my younger brother Captain Joe Scott and our old seafaring scalawag of a friend, Cap'n Ben Grainger, proud owner and proprietor of Ben's Tavern here in George Town."

"I see that your brother is here today as well, Captain Scott?" Panton's glance shifted over to one of the open plantation windows of the courtroom where Joe Scott stood leaning quietly against the window frame. "He sure is, Mr. Panton... my little brother Cap'n Joe is right there in the window watching, and he's a handsome devil isn't he! He came all the way over from Kingston on *Cimboco* just to visit me and Cap'n Ben and laugh about some of the old stories. Now what you want with him, Sir?"

The heat rose slightly in Panton's neck, and he was beginning to feel a bit unsure where he would go with this interrogation. He decided to cut to the chase: "Capt. Scott, when did you first meet the Decedent, Gideon Ebanks?"

"What makes you think I knew Mr. Ebanks, Sir?" Allie responded.

"Captain Scott, my Justice of the Peace in West Bay is a fine man and he doesn't lie. He reported to me that you walked all the way up Seven Mile Beach looking for Gideon Ebanks. Others who live in West Bay and West End have passed along the same information. It is reported that you were claiming to be an old friend and former shipmate of Gideon Ebanks. It is even said you might have gone all the way up to Northwest Point trying to find him. How do you explain that, Captain Scott?"

"The answer to that question is simple, Mr. Justice Panton." Allie paused a moment for effect. "Right downstairs in front of this Courthouse is a bulletin board. On that bulletin board is a notice issued by Commissioner Cardinall himself. It offers a reward for the capture of Gideon Ebanks. Did you think, Sir, that the Commissioner would post that reward and nobody would actually look for Ebanks?"

Again Panton felt the heat rising in his face and he said bruskly, "Then why, Captain Scott, did you tell everyone you were an old friend and shipmate of Ebanks'?"

Allie now had the slightest of smiles on his face. He appeared completely unruffled by Panton's questions and inferences.

"Mr. Justice Panton, do you really think I would go up to Mr. Ebanks' hangout on this island and tell everybody I was there to catch him so you could ship him off to prison in Cuba? That approach hasn't worked very well for you and your Police, has it Mr. Panton?"

Panton's face was now completely flushed and his discomfort showed.

Allie continued, "Anyway, I was only doing that 'cause I had nothing else to do before my brother arrived several days ago on *Cimboco*. Since then me and my brother Joe and sometimes Cap'n Ben have been together every minute. Why don't you ask them?"

Before Panton could form a response, Joe Scott interrupted loudly from his stance in the open Courtroom window:

"My Brother—Capt. Allie Scott—has been with me every minute since I got here on the 13th. We even sleep in the same cabin on the *Black Hawk*. Ask Cap'n Ben… Between Ben's bar and our bunks my brother has harmed nobody. It is time to move on and leave him alone. Most likely, this prisoner fella', Gideon Ebanks, finally jus' got what was comin' to him anyway."

Panton pounded his gavel. Joe Scott was speaking out of order and his courtroom had come alive with conversation. Everyone in the gallery was whispering or speaking openly among themselves.

Panton slammed his gavel again and virtually shouted, "Come to order! I will not have this conduct in my courtroom!"

Soon the courtroom was quiet again, but Panton hesitated. He knew he had come to a dead end. His own suspicions could not overcome an ironclad alibi.

Regaining his composure, he said: "All right, Captain Scott, your testimony is concluded. You may be seated now."

Panton called no further witnesses. He instructed the jury to retire to a separate room and render a verdict on the cause of death of Gideon Ebanks. The jury took no more than ten minutes.

When they returned to the courtroom, Panton called Court back to order and read the jury's verdict aloud to the gallery:

CORONER'S JURY VERDICT

We the Coroner's Jury find and conclude that Gideon Ebanks Died 16th April, 1937, Great Sound, George Town, Grand Cayman, male, bachelor, seaman, 43 years old, died by drowning, none being criminally responsible.

SO SAY WE ALL this 17th day of April, 1937.

The verdict bore the signature of all eleven jurors.

After reading it aloud, Magistrate Panton tapped his gavel and stated: "My thanks to Members of the Jury—you are now excused. This session of the Coroner's Court is now concluded." He tapped his gavel again and left the room with some measure of dissatisfaction—perhaps it was disappointment—in his demeanor.

The crowd in the courtroom dispersed quickly after the verdict was rendered. A few people stopped briefly to acknowledge Allie Scott and shake his hand, and Joe talked to several as they passed him on the covered porch.

When the courtroom was clear, Allie made his exit onto the porch and embraced Joe. He said simply, "You've always been there when I need you." Then Allie departed quickly down the stairs onto Church Street and left Joe with a perplexed look on his face.

Allie and Joe spent the afternoon and evening after Ebanks' inquest proceeding at Cap'n Ben Grainger's Tavern. It was a typical, boisterous Saturday night with not only the old banjo player, but also a local fiddler and Possum on harmonica cranking out the music. Before the evening was out, the whole rowdy crowd of sailors and fishermen were belting out sea shanties—arm in arm—with more rum-soaked camaraderie than music providing the entertainment.

Allie was in his natural element the entire evening, laughing and joking with Ben and his crew, and swapping sea stories with the other patrons. Joe, on the other hand, was quiet and pensive. He was troubled by a nagging dissatisfaction with the feeling that Allie knew much more than he was telling about Ebanks' death. Although he felt no remorse for Ebanks, Joe felt slighted by his brother. Allie had an apparently self-satisfied secret that he wasn't telling—even to his own brother.

Long before the tavern closed that evening Joe excused himself to have a cigar on the front porch, but then left quietly and returned to the *Black Hawk*. He was asleep when Allie arrived after midnight.

Chapter 28

George Town
Sunday
April 18, 1937

Joe and Allie awoke early the next morning to the sound of Possum clanging the ship's bell.

Allie immediately scrambled out of his bunk and pulled on his denim workshirt and trousers.

"Come on, Joe!" he said cheerily, "Let's get some breakfast while it's hot!" Before Joe sat up and rubbed his eyes, Allie was up the companionway steps and out of the cabin. Shortly after, Joe rose, dressed and followed him out on deck.

The *Black Hawk* crew and Allie were sitting around the stern cabin top on wooden crates eating breakfast. Possum was serving strong black coffee all around.

"C'mon, Cap'n Joe," Possum said, "sit down here and have some chow."

Joe sat down in a designated spot and Possum served him up coffee and a big plate of chopped sausage and scrambled eggs mixed in a dirty rice concoction with mushrooms and pepper sauce and biscuits and honey. The crew ate ravenously until the serving pot was empty.

When he was finished eating, Joe said:

"Damn, Possum, how do you manage to fix such good stuff on a raggedy old sailing ship?"

"Can't tell ya' Cap'n Joe," Possum replied, "if your brother knew how to do it he'd leave me off back in Baton Rouge."

Allie laughed. "You're right Possum, I couldn't have said it better myself…in fact, I'd leave the whole damned crew with you as well. It would've been easier raisin' a bunch of children all these years than it was raisin' you boys."

With that the rest of the crew chuckled and snickered and poked playfully at each other. Fifteen years ago this could have been the *Juana Mercedes*. Joe could see that Allie was the living embodiment of his first mentor and hero—*El Capitan*—and that the men in his crew *were* his children. To Allie, loyalty wasn't just something he expected of his crew—it was *everything*.

After the breakfast small talk was over Possum started gathering up the utensils and Allie said to his crew, "All right boys, I told you yesterday to get this ship ready to sail. Joe's leavin' on *Cimboco* today and we've got a load to fetch in Honduras. Move out!"

With that the crew scattered to their various chores.

Allie took his pipe and a tobacco pouch out of his breast pocket. After lighting it, he said quietly:

"Joe, do you trust me?"

Joe looked at him with surprise in his face.

"Of course I trust you, Allie, how can you even ask me that after all we've been through together?"

"You've got a lot of questions you want to ask me Joe. I know that. I can see it in your eyes. You've got questions about me, and about Ebanks, and about why we're really here. But if you trust me—and you say you do—you'll believe me when I tell you this: All your questions will be answered if you just do what I ask of you for the next couple of days. Can you do that?"

"Of course I can, Allie, and I will. But why not just tell me now?"

"Because I want what I have for you to be a gift that you will always remember me by. Like I'll always remember that you saved my life when you were just a little boy. I'll always be indebted to you for that, and it never leaves my mind even though we've hardly ever spoken of it since. Even as a man I can hardly bear to think about *El Capitan* and what happened on the *Juana Mercedes*, much less talk about it. So please, Brother, be patient with me. For now just trust in me and do as I ask… Swear it!"

"All right, Allie…I promise. I'll say no more. But I leave on *Cimboco* this afternoon. When will you tell me what you have in mind?"

Allie drew on his pipe and sat back against the polished stern rail. "Joe," he said, "do you remember the many times when we were still boys that we stayed over on Cayman Brac and explored the island together?"

"Of course, Allie, a hundred times over. We even skipped school sometimes to explore the caves on the bluff. Those were great days."

"Then you will remember the cave we discovered together—I called it 'the Cathedral'."

"Sure I remember. We even found a passage to a separate room off the main cave. You called that your special room—your secret place."

"You're exactly right, Joe. Do you think you could find it again?"

Joe hesitated for a moment. Then he said, "The '32 hurricane probably blew down some of the bigger trees and such, but I'm sure I can still find the entrance. All I've got to do is track the south face of the bluff and find the rockpile we built to mark the entrance. It'll still be there for sure... Is that what you want me to do—find the Cathedral?"

"Yes, Joe, that's what I'm asking you to do."

"So when I find the cave, what do I do then?"

"When you find it, you go in the Cathedral, find the passageway and go to my room. There you will find a gift that I left there for you some years ago. You were still too young to have it when I left it there."

"But Allie, how will I find this 'gift'?"

"Don't worry Brother, you'll know it when you see it. It will be in plain sight…but remember to take a lantern. Will you do this last thing for me? I promise I will ask no more favours of you. If you will accept this gift, I will consider the debt paid for saving my life and I'll never speak of it again. Will you do it?"

"Of course, Allie, but what is this all about? Why am I here? Why are we doing this?"

Allie was quiet for a few moments, still puffing slowly on his pipe. Then he reached into his back pocket and pulled out an envelope. It was sealed and had no writing on it. He handed the envelope to Joe and said:

"Joe, you must promise not to open this letter until you find the gift I left for you. It will explain everything, but only after you have found the gift. If you promise me that, I swear I will ask no more of you. If you wish, we will never have to speak of it again. Can I have your word on that?"

Joe could see the resolve in his brother's eyes, and he sensed the sincerity in his voice. He said:

"Allie, we have never lied to each other, and we have never let each other down. You can count on me to do exactly as you have requested and speak no more of it. You have my word on it."

At 3 o'clock that afternoon the usual crowd of George Town residents had gathered at the pier to bid farewell to friends and relatives departing the island on *Cimboco*. Captain Ashlan Foster was in the wheelhouse and his crew was on deck making ready for departure.

Most of the passengers, including Joe Scott, were already aboard.

Joe was standing at the rail on the upper deck by the wheelhouse, where he had greeted and been talking to his friend Ash. Capt. Foster was looking forward to this overnight trip to Cayman Brac, where he would disembark to be with his family for several weeks. A standby officer was to take *Cimboco* from Cayman Brac for this round trip to Kingston and back.

Since their conversation that morning, Joe and Allie had spoken no more of anything personal. They pitched in and helped the crew ready *Black Hawk* to sail, and then the two of them took her skiff to shore and went up to Cap'n Ben's Tavern to visit briefly and thank him for his hospitality. It was Sunday and the tavern was closed, but Ben insisted they have several drinks on the house. He toasted first their health, then their happiness, and finally their good fortune before he insisted on driving Joe the short distance to the pier in his old roadster. There they laughed at each other one last time, embraced and departed, each his own way.

Now Joe was standing at the upper rail on *Cimboco* watching Allie and his crew make ready to haul anchor. There was a light onshore breeze so when the anchor was up Allie raised the largest of his jibs to pull the bow of the *Black Hawk* downwind. Then he raised her main and mizzen and she started to reach offshore as her sails filled and she picked up speed. Joe raised his cap to wave farewell and Allie did the same. A few minutes later the *Black Hawk*, with all sails out, was running for the westerly horizon.

Aboard *Cimboco* the deck throbbed under Joe's feet with the vibration of her engine, and a roar of voices arose in goodbyes from deck and from shore as she departed Hog Stye Bay in route to Cayman Brac. The last thing to be heard from George Town was the tolling of Sunday church bells.

Chapter 29

Stake Bay
Cayman Brac
April 19, 1937

Although the weather wasn't unpleasant, Captain Joe Scott had not slept well with the cumbersome wallowing of *Cimboco* throughout the night. The rolling was just a necessary feature of the ride on a round-hulled wooden motorship, he figured.

Joe was on deck and ready to disembark well before daylight. The naked, cloudless Caribbean morning sun was already in her stride over the empty sea before Joe first saw the long, black line of Cayman Brac. It was much longer yet before he could see the sandy upper shore covered with tall palms and the green confusion of lower shrubs and underbrush already waving in the dance of rising heat. When *Cimboco* reached Cayman Brac that morning, her smaller sister island, Little Cayman, was glistening in the sunlight a short five miles distant. As was typical, *Cimboco* dropped her anchor briefly off Stake Bay at Cayman Brac while a couple of young, sun bronzed boys paddled a canoe out to receive the mail bag from George Town. Once they were alongside, they also delivered a mail packet from the Cayman Brac post office for delivery to Kingston.

After he had turned the ship over to his First Mate, Capt. Ashland Foster came down from the wheelhouse and he and Joe tossed their seabags down to the boys in the canoe. Then they climbed down the side of *Cimboco* into the little boat for a taxi to shore. Some of the other passengers had gathered on deck to bid them farewell with a wave of hands and a few kind words as the canoe departed for shore.

The '32 hurricane had done incredible damage to the small community of Stake Bay. The once beautiful and scenic beachfront community had been decimated, and the few original frame houses that still remained had mostly been carried by the sea to helter-skelter locations farther inland. The white sand beach itself was almost completely gone, and all that remained in its place was the base, ragged and razor sharp ironshore limestone crags that had once lain below the silken white sands of the beach. In all, the '32 hurricane had taken at least 109 souls and had left the island in shambles. Thank God, Ashland Foster's wife and children had survived. Ash and the remaining industrious survivors on Cayman Brac had already rebuilt much of the community and had a brand new Government Building to boot, but this time it was well up from the seashore and out of harm's way.

When he and Ash disembarked at the Stake Bay barcadere, Joe tossed his seabag over his shoulder and handed each of his young paddlers a generous shilling for their efforts. They gleefully took the coins and ran up toward the Government Building with the official mailbag to report their successful mission.

After a brief conversation, handshake and embrace, Ash Foster left Joe for his short walk home.

It had been a long time since Joe visited Cayman Brac. For years when they were younger, he and Allie had sailed their catboat there every day in decent weather to attend school. *No choice*, he thought, *it was Mama Lelia made us do it.* In any event, he wandered the shorefront for a while, smelling the sea-lavender and watching the scurry of yellow crabs under the clear lapping waves. Up in the sea grapes, the lion lizards and iguanas were still foraging, and an occasional red-breasted, lime green Cayman parrot squawked his gibberish. Joe looked for a moment across the glittering channel at the long, dark green profile of Little Cayman and smiled. Finally he was back home.

After some time in thought, Joe walked the quarter mile of white coral marl road up from the sea to the Stake Bay Government Building. There he left his seabag with the Clerk, borrowed a kerosene lantern and a water bladder, and set out on his quest to find the Cathedral.

In order to reach it, Joe had first to climb to the crest of the rocky spine of Cayman Brac known simply as "the Bluff" and cross over to its south side. There, as he recalled, the Cathedral was located in a remote, still completely primitive area at the crest of the Bluff. At that point it was overgrown with almost impenetrable vegetation, even for boys like Joe and Allie when they were still young. To make it worse, the Bluff was literally riddled with remote, ragged caves and caverns of different sizes, many of which had yet to be found or explored by human beings. As he started to climb the rough trail up the Bluff from Stake Bay, Joe muttered to himself: *pirate caves, my ass, they'd never work that hard to bury a treasure*. But, promise he had made to Allie, and promise he intended to keep.

Joe was already in a sweat when he reached the relatively flat crest of the Bluff, so at least the walk would be mostly level for a while. Many of the residents living along the lower shoreline of the island had built rough cattle pens, plantain and vegetable patches along the plateau of the Bluff, so the path from Stake Bay to the south side of the Bluff was relatively passable. It was only when he reached the upper crest on the south side of the Bluff that the real work began. At that point, Joe began to make his way in an easterly direction along the rugged, southern cliff of the Bluff. The rock surface was jagged and harder than flint to walk on, and any contact scratched unprotected hands and arms relentlessly. Below the rim of the Bluff was a sheer face of vertical rock, and any semblance of a path, had there ever been one, was non-existent. It seemed at least an hour of crossing razor-backs and dog-toothed hollows before Joe found the camouflaged entrance to The Cathedral.

When they were exploring as boys, Joe and Allie had followed the entire southerly crest of the Bluff to the summit of the rocky cliff at East End. By the time they returned, they were virtually cut to ribbons by jungle vegetation and razor rock. But on the way back they found a large overgrown hole in the rocky surface that dropped straight down about twenty feet to an open bottom. It had been easy at the time to climb down in the hole on the huge roots and vines that extended to the bottom and in some places sent gnarled stringers into the surrounding nooks and crannies of the cave.

Once inside, the boys discovered that the relatively small surface opening had dropped down into a large, open vault of mostly smooth and water worn limestone. The cavern had huge pillars of stone from floor to ceiling, and still wet and colored pointed cones of calcium carbonate rising indiscriminately from the floor and suspended from the ceilings. The colours of the stone faces and ceilings—mostly in damp oranges, tans, browns, greens and blues—decorated the chamber. Seeping water had formed a small central pool of clear water on the pebble strewn floor—and the silence of the cave was almost otherworldly. The two boys had sat for a long moment without speaking when Joe, still only 11 years old, had blurted out, "The Cathedral at the Orphanage!" And so it had been known for many an adventure thereafter: "The Cathedral."

But today was a different day and it was many years later, and Joe's instructions from Allie were clear: "Just go to my room in the Cathedral."

In actuality, Joe hated Allie's secret room in the Cathedral. It was only one of many side caves they had explored off of the main cavern, and Joe disliked the black dark, knee crawling and winding passage it took to get to its main chamber. Nonetheless, this day he lit the lantern he had borrowed in Stake Bay and resolved himself to press onward.

Joe searched out a dark corner of the main cavern and bent down to enter the mouth of a dark, ragged hole on the south end. The odour at the entrance was so musky and acrid that he hesitated and sat down for a moment, holding the lantern high enough to see a shallow distance into the crawl space. He actually momentarily cursed himself with the realization that the cave was still large enough to enter even in the fullness of his manhood. *Dammit!*, he said aloud to himself. He scrabbled around the cavern floor for a moment with his free hand and found a medium stone, which he threw as hard as he could into the depths of the dark opening.

The stone ricocheted and bounced a few times in the depths of the passage before all again became momentarily quiet. Then hearing the rise of an alarming sound from within, Joe said out loud to himself again, *Dammit!* In a rush of incomprehensible sound and motion, resident cave bats were swarming on, over and past him to the overhead mouth of the Cathedral. In an indescribable rush of noise and flapping bodies, a thousand bats swarmed almost immediately through the small passage, many of the soft bodies and weblike wings crashing into him and fluttering about, looking only for an escape from the crisis he had created. As always in the past, Joe crumpled into a fetal position, hands and arms about this face and head, and rolled to the floor until the noise and movement had subsided. Finally, when all the noise was gone, he said to himself again, *Dammit!* But this time he added, under his breath, *Damn you Allie, this better be worth it!*

It took him a long moment to regain his composure, but eventually Joe gathered up the tumbled kerosene lantern and crawled on his hands and knees through the stinking, bat guano coated passage that eventually led to "Allie's Place."

In actuality, Allie's Place was another cathedral-like cavern with only the one, bat-infested entrance for access. But this cavern was different. It had a high, dome-like ceiling, but its walls were mostly smooth and it had three narrow and jagged cracks in the outside wall of the south cliff on the Bluff that let some diffused sunlight into the chamber and thereby precluded residence by the bats. Unlike the main part of the Cathedral, it was dry and almost dusty.

Joe put the lantern down on the cavern floor and momentarily scratched his head. *Why the hell would Allie have me come here?* For a moment, his eyes had to readjust to the muted light.

In the center of the open space was a wooden crate that he and Allie had used to play cards on. It was covered in dust and the wax drippings of the many candles he and Allie had burned, but nothing else immediately came to his attention.

Joe picked up the lantern and walked to the center of the cave. Then he raised the lantern and slowly started to scan the back wall, now throwing light into the dark crevices along the back wall.

Suddenly he froze in place. His skin prickled and the hair on the back of his neck tingled. All he could hear was the sound of his own shallow breathing.

The light of the lantern held over Joe's head was flickering on a face in the shadows. It was a face that Joe could never forget, with the dark hollows of the eyes set over high cheekbones and a wicked toothy grin. A fleck of light reflected off a silver front tooth.

It was the Spaniard!

Joe had only seen him in occasional nightmares over the last fifteen years, and now he was here—the same evil grin on his skeletal visage. But this time was different…

In the moments—or minutes—it took for Joe's heart to stop racing, he realized that the phantasm before him was only the shell of the man in his nightmares…

Slowly, carefully, Joe approached the Spaniard and sat the lantern on the cavern floor in front of his remains. The flesh had long since rotted and fallen from the body and his clothing was in rags and tatters. But still there was no doubt—it was the Spaniard.

His skeletal remains were seated against the back wall of Allie's room. Resting atop the skull was a dusty, splotched white pith helmet. When Joe removed it to look into the face, ragged patches of dried skin and black hair still clung to the skull and inside the helmet.

Joe felt as if he was moving in slow motion as he tossed the pith helmet aside and studied the earthly remains of the Spaniard. Only the tatters of an open linen jacket and a collared shirt loosely covered the rib cage of the torso. What was left of the shirt was black and stained from the chest down into the empty belt and baggy lap of his trousers.

Joe reached over with his right hand and carefully peeled tatters of shirt away from the Spaniard's skeletal chest. There, buried to the hilt in the breast plate, was Allie's bone handled switchblade knife. Also there, suspended from a heavy silver chain just below the hilt of Allie's knife, was Joe's silver crucifix.

For a long moment Joe sat on the cave floor, transfixed in the memories of his youth and the man before him. Inexplicably, he thought about the many lessons that Fr. Tomas and Sister Elena had tried to teach him, and about the hard realities he had lived with *El Capitan* and the crew of the *Juana Mercedes*. Was there any real lesson to be learned from any of it, or was it simply senseless? He didn't know…

Finally, he reached across and wrenched Allie's knife from the breastbone of the remains. He folded the blade back into the handle casing and put it in his pocket. Then he reached back over and closed his hand around his crucifix. When he snatched it, the Spaniard's spine gave and his skull flew off and skittered across the floor of the cave. The hollow, lonely sound of it was still ringing in Joe's ears when he left the cave.

Joe was sweating profusely when he climbed out of the Cathedral and made his way back to the southern precipice of the Bluff. He found a passably smooth outcropping to sit down on. He dangled his legs over the cliff and—for a long time—looked out over the deep blue and purple hues of the sea. The air was fresh and pure and the sky was still cloudless. Everything was perfect, just as God had made it.

Finally, Joe reached into the breast pocket of his shirt and took out the envelope Allie had given him. He tore it open and took out the letter Allie had written for his eyes only. As he read the letter, Joe's mouth moved into a long, wry smile. When he was done reading, Joe put the letter back in the envelope and the envelope back in his pocket.

Then he rose and started the long trek back to Stake Bay.

Epilogue

Present Day

My father's name was Captain Joe Scott. He was licensed from a very young age as a Master of "All Ships-All Oceans."

As a boy I always knew my father was Caymanian. Even though he became a naturalized American because of his service in World War II, my father was proud to be Caymanian. But it was only after both my father and mother died that I set out to find my Caymanian roots. I'm sure that's why my father wanted me to have his old World War II sea chest. It was that old trunk and its contents that led me to write this book about an early episode in his life.

But the bits and pieces from Daddy's trunk didn't tell the whole story of the *Juana Mercedes*. Much of it I put together later from old newspaper archives and Caymanian Government records.

Most importantly, Daddy's trunk *did* yield the end of the story. That came in the form of a brief handwritten letter from my Uncle Allie Scott to my father. I found it in the same cigar box that I found the first 1922 newspaper article about the piracy of the *Juana Mercedes*. The letter was brown with age and moisture stained. It was also written in Spanish, and I had to have it translated. I only found out later that my Uncle Allie never learned to write in the English language even though he spoke it well. That letter, dated April 17, 1937, reads in translation as follows:

Dear Brother,

I think you already know that I killed Ebanks. If you don't, you must suspect it because you lied for me at the inquest. I knew you would.

As for Ebanks, I drowned him just as he would have drowned us when we were children. He was weak from a dissolute life and I had only to hold him under water by the chain of his handcuff.

By now you have also found the Spaniard. He made the deadly mistake of returning to Cayman and I happened upon him by chance. Daddy Tenny helped me take his body to the Cathedral. You were still young and Daddy didn't want you involved.

The gift that I left for you in the cave was not the Spaniard. The gift was on a chain around his neck and I trust you have found it by now. It is the only treasure the Juana Mercedes will ever yield.

By the way, if you found my knife, please keep it. I will have no further need of it.

Your Brother Always, Allie

Actually, this letter was not the last thing in the bottom of the cigar box. Under it I found a bone handled switchblade knife and a tarnished silver crucifix and chain—my father's Cayman Cross.

Historical Footnotes

Vincent Prendergast, the Caymanian boy who found the body of Gideon Ebanks, received a Ten Pound reward to be divided proportionately with his friends, Arlington Seymour and Ernest Ebanks.

On August 4, 1938, Magistrate A. E. ("Bertie") Panton suffered a stroke coming down the front stairs of the George Town Courthouse after a long day in Petty Sessions Court. Four days later he passed away at the age of 74. During his eulogy for Mr. Panton, Commissioner A.W. Cardinall said, in part: "We have lost a faithful friend, one whose career has been full of service, endearing himself with everyone who came into contact with him and many who knew him personally."

Evans Rivers was extradited to Cuba where he was tried and convicted for his complicity in the piracy and other crimes committed on the *Juana Mercedes*. After a lengthy term of imprisonment in Cuba, he eventually returned to Grand Cayman where he lived out the remainder of his life as a respectable citizen.

Gideon Ebanks earned historical recognition as the only Caymanian pirate to be identified in the comprehensive work, *Pirates! An A – Z Encyclopedia* (Jan Rogozinski, Ph.D., Da Capo Press, 1996).

So far as has been publicly reported, the remains of the Spaniard, Eulogio Paz a/k/a Pablo Konig, have not been found.

ACKNOWLEDGMENTS

My loyal critics and most persistent editors have been my wife JJ and my son, Tripp, both of whom I love dearly and sincerely thank for their patience and assistance.

To the many other friends, family members, literary professionals and others who gave me advice, assistance and encouragement, I thank you all as well. I do not begin to name you personally for fear I will fail to properly recognize your individual contributions.

The most important single source of information and documentation that I drew on for the historical foundation of this novel was the Cayman Islands National Archives (CINA). The professionalism and personal assistance of CINA staff has been invaluable to me.

Also, the outstanding public archives of the *Kingston Daily Gleaner* provided an amazing window into the history of the Caribbean and its people, and I certainly recognize and appreciate their contributions.

Finally, I thank the Cayman people themselves. You are my inspiration for this novel. Like you, I was raised up with stories of pirates and duppies, wreckers and may cows, and a heritage steeped in tales of adventure on the high seas. Notwithstanding all that, I now know the truth: Gideon Ebanks is the only real Caymanian "pirate" of record. In reality, the Cayman people are among the kindest, most gentle people on earth.

Made in the USA
Charleston, SC
01 November 2012